'Sapper': The Be

'SAPPER' is the pen-name of Herman Cyril McNeile, born in 1888 at the Naval Prison in Bodmin, Cornwall, where his father was Governor. Educated at Cheltenham College and the Royal Military Academy, Woolwich, he served in the Royal Engineers (popularly known as the 'sappers') from 1907 to 1919, being awarded the Military Cross during World War I and finishing as a Lieutenant-Colonel. He started writing in France, adopting a pen-name because serving officers were not allowed to write under their own names. His first stories on life in the trenches in France were published in 1915 and were an enormous success. But it was his first thriller, *Bulldog Drummond* (1920), that launched him as one of the most popular novelists of his generation. It had several immensely successful sequels, including *The Black Gang* (1922), *The Third Round* (1924) and *The Final Count* (1926), and McNeile's friend, the late Gerald Fairlie, wrote several Bulldog Drummond stories after his death. Bulldog Drummond also inspired a successful play, with Gerald du Maurier playing Drummond, and several films variously starring Ronald Colman, Ray Milland, Jack Buchanan, and Ralph Richardson. *Jim Maitland* (1923), a volume of short stories featuring a footloose English sahib in foreign lands, was another popular success. Altogether McNeile published nearly 30 books. A vast public mourned his death in 1937 at the early age of 48.

'Sapper'

THE BEST SHORT STORIES

J.M. Dent & Sons Ltd
London Melbourne

This selection first published in Great Britain by J.M. Dent & Sons Ltd
1984
This paperback edition first published by J. M. Dent & Sons Ltd 1986

Selection, Introduction and Select Bibliography © Jack Adrian 1984

Text © The Trustees of the Estate of the late Colonel H.C. McNeile 1920,
1923, 1924, 1925, 1927, 1928, 1937

Printed in Great Britain by
Richard Clay(The Chaucer Press)plc, Bungay, for
J.M. Dent & Sons Ltd
Aldine House, 33 Welbeck Street, London W1M 8LX

British Library Cataloguing in Publication Data

Sapper
   The best short stories.
   Rn: Herman Cyril McNeile I. Title
   823'.912[F] PR6025.A317

   ISBN 0-460-02456-6

CONTENTS

Introduction by Jack Adrian   *vii*

The Hidden Witness   1
Mrs Peter Skeffington's Revenge   17
The House by the Headland   32
Mark Danver's Sin   47
Out of the Blue   62
A Hopeless Case   74
The Man with his Hand in his Pocket   88
The Other Side of the Wall   104
The Old Dining-Room   119

The Exploits of Bulldog Drummond

Lonely Inn   134
The Mystery Tour   152
The Oriental Mind   169
Wheels Within Wheels   186
Thirteen Lead Soldiers   205

Select Bibliography/Acknowledgements   223

Introduction
JACK ADRIAN

For over a decade, from the 1920s through the early 1930s, Lieutenant-Colonel Herman Cyril McNeile—'Sapper' to his millions of readers—was the acknowledged master of the popular short story: a piece of fiction roughly four to seven thousand words in length, of no particular literary merit or significance (at least in academic terms), but told in a brisk and entertaining manner and containing a goodish helping of mystery, romance, adventure, horror or suspense (or a heady brew-up of all those ingredients) with a beginning, a middle and an ending with a sting in it—the sharper the better, and preferably in the last couple of lines.

Magazine editors competed vigorously for Sapper's stories and paid extravagant prices for them. Gerard Fairlie, his close friend and collaborator, has put it on record that Sapper was the highest-paid short story writer of his time. The name 'Sapper' in bold upper case on the cover of the *Strand* or *Hutchinson's Magazine* invariably caused a jump in circulation. His American publisher George Doran (later Doubleday Doran) took the extraordinary step of issuing his stories in 'Special Edition' booklet form, one or two tales per issue. Sapper's hardback collections such as *The Man in Ratcatcher*, *Out of the Blue*, *Word of Honour* and *The Saving Clause* sold in their tens of thousands at 7/6d a copy, and then in their hundreds of thousands at the reprint prices of 3/6d and 2/-.

Sapper had the good fortune to be alive to exercise his remarkable skills as a storyteller at a time when the written word was more important than the screened image and when books were published to be read, eagerly, rather than as fodder for the remainder shop. More to the point, it was a time when dull and dusty Victorian periodicals were being replaced by a new kind of monthly magazine whose sole object was to divert rather than to instruct or improve.

Introduction

These days the *Strand* is perhaps the only familiar name in the vast assortment of new-style monthlies published during the first forty or so years of this century. Not surprising, really. It carried the enormously popular Sherlock Holmes stories almost from its first issue, and most of P. G. Wodehouse's output from 1910 to 1940. It had quality, but it was by no means the best of the breed although it was certainly the first—the creation of arch-populariser George Newnes, who wanted an unstodgy monthly as a stable-mate for his bright and busy weekly *Tit-Bits*. It was also the last, for it survived all the rest (though in a somewhat shrivelled form) by nearly a decade.

But there are riches hidden under that throwaway phrase, for 'all the rest' included the *Grand Magazine*, the *Novel*, the *Royal*, the *Windsor* and *Woman's Journal* (both Dornford Yates territory), the *Storyteller*, *Hutchinson's*, *Cassell's* (not the drab 1880s' effort, but a sparkling monthly with a full-colour cover), the *Sovereign*, the *London*, *Nash's* and *Pall Mall* (later merged into one glorious large-size glossy), *Pearson's*, *Pan*, *Modern Woman*, the *20-Story*, *Lloyd's*, the *Ludgate*, *Britannia & Eve* —the list is not endless but it would take another dozen or so titles to reach the barrel-scrapings.

Each had its own particular character and distinctive style. To be sure, some were whales and some were minnows. Some used the finest artists of the day to cheer up their pages, while others looked as though the office-boy had been at work with a dip-and-scratch; some used no illustrations at all. Some were printed on glossy stock, some on cheap pulpwood that, after only a year stored in attic or garden shed, had all the brittleness of autumn leaves. Some featured articles (lively rather than instructional), others did not. But all had one thing in common, the essential ingredient that lured bookstall browsers as well as staunch newsagent regulars: fiction.

Fiction in large doses, fiction in small doses. Short stories, short-shorts; novelettes (up to 30,000 words), novellas (up to 50,000 words), serial-slices; even round-robins (in which several writers took a hand at stirring the pot, usually at Christmas): romance, drama, comedy, mystery. Unquestionably the thirty years from 1910 to 1940 were glorious ones for those who read to be entertained and stimulated rather than merely educated.

Even so, hardback collections of short fiction were viewed with despondency by publishers still influenced by the traditions of a previous generation, when fat three-decker novels, sometimes running to 150,000 words or more, had been the profitable norm. Received opinion was that short story volumes did not sell; that circulating libraries (who bought the bulk of a publisher's initial print-run, and who had only very recently, and very grumpily, given up the lucrative three-decker for the new-fangled, and cheaper, single-volume work) refused to take them; that there was a massive reader-rejection.

Thus on dust-jackets and in press publicity publishers would often equivocate, to say the least. 'The latest from So-and-so!' they would thunder, without mentioning that it wasn't the latest novel they were pushing but a volume of shorts. Sometimes they would simply lie in their teeth. 'So-and-so's great new novel!' would be bannered across the dust-jacket front, and readers who happened to like the author in question would not realise what they were buying until the end of the first 'chapter' had been reached.

With Sapper no such subterfuges were required. His short story collections sold as briskly as his Bulldog Drummond thrillers; and that was very brisk indeed. His publishers, Hodder & Stoughton, never made any bones about what was on offer; indeed, they seemed positively to revel in pouring new collections on to the market. Of the fifteen books published between 1920 and 1930, the period of Sapper's greatest popularity, no less than seven were collections of shorts. And this does not include three books—*Jim Brent* (1926), *Shorty Bill* (1926) and *John Walters* (1928)—which were revamped reissues of his tales of trench warfare; nor does it include the massive 1000-plus-page tome which Hodders then issued in 1930, cranking the reprint handle yet again on those same war stories.

It was these stories, originally published during the Great War, which had created the vogue for Sapper (the pseudonym was bestowed by Lord Northcliffe on McNeile when his stories began to appear in the *Daily Mail*). His first two collections — *The Lieutenant and Others* and *Sergeant Michael Cassidy, RE* — were both published in 1915, and both, together, over the following twelve months, achieved a sale of over 200,000 copies. This was phenomenal even then, when the war was still popular, paper was unrationed, and anything even mildly connected with 'our fighting forces' sold prodigiously.

Many of the early stories are little more than sketches or brief incidents, although most have that snap at the end, that twist in the tail, that became the Sapper trademark. It was what singled him out from the ruck of pseudonymous officers beavering away in dug-out, cramped cabin, or tin shack —'Peter', 'Taffrail', 'Bartimeus', 'Wings', and the rest of them— providing not very authentic life-at-the-Front fodder for the fiction factories back home.

The stark truth—the horrors of trench warfare, the appalling blunders of the General Staff, the reality of nickel-jacketed rounds smashing through flesh and bone—was never revealed to the magazine- and paper-buying public. It would not have been acceptable or politically expedient. The ersatz version, served up by writers who certainly had to suffer the reality at first hand, was largely a world of jolly japes and minor public school high-jinks, of leathery old world-weary Sergeants and comic Cockney privates, where the worst enemies were the rats. This fitted in neatly with the odious poster propaganda, then current, that played up the romantic nature of the war.

The Sapper method of bringing the 'truth' of the war to those far from it may be gauged from the introduction to his third book *Men, Women and Guns* (1916):

Two days ago a dear old aunt of mine asked me to describe to her what shrapnel was like . . .

Under the influence of my deceased uncle's most excellent port I did so. Soothed and in that expansive frame of mind induced by the old and bold, I drew her a picture — vivid, startling, wonderful. And when I had finished, the dear old lady looked at me.

'Dreadful!' she murmured. 'Did I ever tell you of the

terrible experience I had on the front at Eastbourne, when my bath-chair attendant became inebriated and upset me?'

Slowly and sorrowfully I finished the decanter—and went to bed.

But seriously, my masters, it is a hard thing that my aunt asked of me. There are many things worse than shelling—the tea-party you find in progress on your arrival on leave; the utterances of war experts; the non-arrival of the whisky from England . . .

And so on for another couple of thousand words. Nowhere does Sapper actually get to grips with an experience—that of being pounded incessantly by high explosive—that must have been terrifying. Indeed, his relentless facetiousness makes the experiences he is describing less and less believable, at least to the modern reader. And yet the response to this kind of fairy-tale stuff was more than merely enthusiastic. The critic James Douglas wrote:

I rate these stories . . . very high . . . They are something far more terrible than anything Kipling or Stephen Crane or Tolstoy or Zola ever imagined. There is a dreadful black passion in them—all the blacker and all the more dreadful, because it is illumined by flashes of humour . . .

Well, other times, other standards. It is reasonable to suppose that Douglas, along with the rest of the critical fraternity, had never been shelled or shrapnelled and thus took on trust what was presented to them by one who surely knew. Perhaps an anonymous critic on the *Daily Mail* supplies the true explanation of Sapper's immense popularity: 'He has a delicate vein of grim description which brings the reality of war home to the reader without a surplus of lurid and revolting details.'

Of course there is no reality to war other than that which encompasses 'a surplus of lurid and revolting details'. But that was not what fiction magazine editors wanted to buy, for the simple reason that it was not what their customers wanted to read. Drama, yes; tragedy, yes; pathos, yes; humour, yes; and perhaps a mild jolt of discomfort every now and again (rats, *uggh!*—but yes).

Sapper's genius lay in his ability to supply all of these elements in a more vigorous manner than any of his contemporaries, yet still without disturbing or offending the reader. His drama was melodrama; his tragedy was searing; his pathos heart-wringing; his humour rumbustious buffoonery. Too, he demonstrated in his stories a hatred for the enemy which was almost pathological, but which perfectly suited the prevailing mood. Without exception Germans are portrayed as monsters of depravity, bayoneters of babes and sucklings, defilers of pure and innocent womanhood. There are no compromises; all is in stark black or pristine white.

In everything but the real horrors of warfare Sapper went way over the top, and beyond. His rivals simply could not match the melodramatic overkill which so captivated the reading public, who desperately wanted the war to be as exciting, as tragic, as jolly and, above all, as simple as Sapper made it out to be. The odd disquieting hint (that 'delicate vein of grim description') at the more grisly aspects of the conflict, dropped judiciously into the narrative, merely served to give a story that extra flavour of authenticity.

After the Great War, and with the publication of *Bulldog Drummond* in 1920, Sapper became sensationally popular. But his fictional world did not alter, although his heroes now emanated that dark charisma of having fought in and survived a terrible and bloody war. Much could be made of that in the plotting of stories and novels, and much was.

Like all great popular writers Sapper was a merchant, and his wares were crafted to suit the paying customers. In his case these were the post-War middle classes who had just enough money and leisure to indulge in those glossy fiction magazines, but not enough to be able to transform drab reality into the stuff of dreams contained within their covers. No one had that kind of money, because Sapper's world — like the worlds of his co-fabulists E. Phillips Oppenheim (glittering Mayfair) and Dornford Yates (Arcadian England)—did not exist. But the customers demanded that it exist, and the customers must be satisfied.

Sapper's world was skilfully fashioned. It was a world of large and rambling country houses where the central heating worked and servants needed no prompting to enter the drawing-room of an evening to close the curtains. It was a world where straight-backed men rode hard to hounds, and topping girls whacked lustily at tennis balls and never even glowed. It was a world where evening dress was not an affectation, where children were sensible and babies did not bawl at three o'clock in the morning, and where long, low cars swept noiselessly through a countryside that was eternally green and pleasant.

But such a world must have its darker, more tragic aspect, and thus it was also a world where bleak-eyed, doom-pursued drunks lined up dead bottles in regimental order, where emotion-shattered youths used photographs of ex-fiancées clipped from *The Tatler* for revolver practice, where the vengeance of a good woman was more terrible by far than the black carnage wreaked by the Furies, and where a man was a swine not merely because he'd seduced another man's wife but because he'd eaten that man's salt *and then seduced his wife*.

In a world such as this the hero must of necessity be not merely good but extravagantly noble. It is sometimes the case in a Sapper story that a tragic and ghastly situation may be saved at the outset by the utterance of, say, one word, and yet because of the code, the rules of the game, the Sapper hero would rather go to the ends of the earth—and frequently does —before he will utter that word. But then a ghastly situation saved would have meant no story, and no story would have meant no villain.

It was important in the Sapper world to play the game, and what distinguishes the Sapper villain is not only that he doesn't, but that he doesn't in the most spectacular way. He is not just evil but grossly malevolent; he is not simply nasty but cruelly, monstrously vindictive. He kicks dogs, beats horses, bully-rags women. There is not a shred of decency in him.

That in real life evil men have their good points, and good men their darker side, was far too complex a proposition. Sapper's world, like its creator, was essentially uncomplicated by such fine shading. Good was good, evil was evil. That was half its attraction to the nine-to-fiver who inhabited a generally unfriendly and distinctly perplexing real world. Basically, Sapper was an action-man—which was the other half of his allure to those whose life was pretty well mapped out from the age of twenty-one onwards.

In the actual construction of a story Sapper is rarely to be faulted. In his autobiography* Gerard Fairlie recalls his friend's definition of the perfect short story, which Sapper, a fanatical golfer, likened to 'the perfect iron shot':

> Start with a bang . . . in your first sentence if possible, certainly within your first few paragraphs . . . just as the golf ball is crisply hit away by the club . . . The interest must continue in an ever-increasing trajectory until the climax is reached, just as the ball flies . . . rising all the while. Then finish as quickly as possible, with all the back-spin you can use . . . in one paragraph for perfection . . . which should contain an unexpected twist.

This was invariably his way. The very best of Sapper's short stories crack off, hurtle to a climax, and then suddenly plummet to an unforeseen hole-in-one.

His primary influences were de Maupassant, Ambrose Bierce, and particularly O. Henry, a writer he revered (the only editing task he ever undertook was of a bumper *Best of O. Henry* volume, which contained a hundred stories), although he had none of those writers' basic humanity, or their tolerance and instinctive sense of irony.

Sapper wrote of an impossible world inhabited by incredible people who did preposterous things. Other popular periodical writers of his generation—plucked out of the air and in no particular order of merit: Gilbert Frankau, F. Britten Austin, Stacy Aumonier, Denis Mackail, Valentine Williams, Edgar Jepson, Roland Pertwee, B. L. Jacot—all exhibited a more coherent grasp of the subtleties of characterisation, even within the natural limits imposed by the short story form, and displayed a talent for lively dialogue and often acute observation

---

* *With Prejudice*, Hodder & Stoughton, 1952

entirely lacking in Sapper. Even Edgar Wallace becomes a writer of profound depth and luminosity when placed beside him.

But of course one does not look to Sapper for any deep psychological insight, character-analysis, or witty conversation. All these may be had elsewhere. One looks to Sapper for action piled upon incident, a meaty plot (however far-fetched), and an ending that tips one's expectations neatly and ingeniously upside down.

In his short stories Sapper always had one strong central idea or surprise in mind and he worked towards it relentlessly. Character-development, scene descriptions, clever dialogue were all ruthlessly pitched aside; nothing must distract him from his goal. Inevitably the reader is swept along by this single-minded pursuit of the final jolting twist, and for all his faults Sapper at his best, with all cylinders firing, was without peer as a spinner of the kind of yarn that grips and enthralls and positively demands to be read to its explosive, shocking and sometimes bitter end.

The nine stories in the first part of this collection have all been gathered from previous Sapper collections, although none has been in print for over 40 years. They rank amongst Sapper's finest.

Here are to be found all the ingredients that helped to make him one of the best-known and most widely read short story writers of the inter-War years. Here, in 'The Other Side of the Wall', is stark drama; here, in 'A Hopeless Case', is even starker tragedy. Here is horror, not simply of the supernatural kind as in 'The Old Dining-Room', but in the vivid description of the fierce, gloating pleasure on the face of the murderer in 'The House by the Headland'. Here, in 'The Man with his Hand in his Pocket'—which begins with a desperate gambler with only £1000 to his name losing £5000 at poker—is the perfect narrative hook. And here is not only 'Out of the Blue', one of the most sublime twist-ending tales in popular fiction, but also 'The Hidden Witness', in which Sapper brilliantly achieves that notable rarity, the double-twist.

The Hidden Witness

I don't know exactly when it was that I first realized that Miles Blandish was in love with Mary Somerville. As a general rule men are very unobservant in such matters, and I suppose I was no exception. All I know is that when I mentioned the matter guardedly to Phyllis Dankerton she observed, brightly, that the next great discovery I should make was that the earth was round. So I suppose it must have been fairly obvious.

Anyway, it doesn't much matter, except that I'd like to get it accurate. The house party was all there when I arrived. To take them in order there were, first of all, our host and hostess — John Somerville and his wife. He was a wealthy man—something in cotton—who had reached such a position of affluence at a comparatively early age that he could, had he wanted to, have given up business altogether. But he preferred to have something to do, and now, at the age of forty-five, he still went up to London five days a week. A smallish man, thin and spare, with shrewd, thoughtful eyes that missed very little that went on around him.

It was through Mary, his wife, that I had got to know him. She was fifteen years his junior, and if ever there was a case of wondering why two people had got married, this was it. She was one of the most lovely creatures I have ever seen—the sort of girl who could have married literally anyone she chose. And then quite suddenly five years ago she had married John.

Personally, I have always thought that money had a good deal to do with it. Not that John wasn't quite a decent fellow, but having said that you'd said all. By no possible stretch of imagination could he be regarded as the sort of man to inspire romance in a girl's heart. He was far too self-centred, far too much the business man to the exclusion of everything else. And yet Mary, with numerous men at her feet, had selected him.

My own impression was that she had begun to regret it. They got on very well together, but it was a very restrained relationship. She liked him, and he was inordinately proud of her—and that was the end of it. So much for our host and hostess.

There was a married couple—Peter Dankerton and his wife. She was a bridge fiend, with the tongue of an adder, but distinctly good-looking and very amusing company.

The younger element consisted of Tony Merrick, a sub-altern in the Gunners, and a jolly little kid called Marjorie Stanway, who spent most of their time practising new steps in the hall to a gramophone.

And finally, there was a man called Miles Blandish, who was the only one I had never met before. He was a planter of sorts out in the FMS. About thirty years old, he seemed to have been everywhere and done everything. He had rather a lazy, pleasant voice, and a trick of raising his eyebrows when he spoke that made the most ordinary remark seem amusing; and little Marjorie, to the fury of young Merrick, adored him openly. In fact, he was the outstanding personality of the party, Mary always excepted.

She introduced me to him as soon as I arrived.

'The only one you don't know, Bill,' she said. 'Miles—this is Bill Canford, who is almost a fixture about the house.'

'A very pleasant occupation,' he remarked, lightly, and I got the impression that his eyes were very observant. 'If I could afford to become a fixture, I should choose an English country house to do it in.'

We talked on casually for a while, and he was certainly a most interesting man. And an efficient one. His knowledge, obviously acquired on the spot, of rubber and its future showed him as a man who could observe and think for himself.

'And where,' I said, after a while, 'is our worthy host?'

'My dear Bill,' laughed Mary, looking up from the tea table, 'John has got a new toy. His present secretary's face is so frightful that he can't bear her in the same room with him. So he has got a sort of phonograph machine—a super-dictaphone, I think he calls it—and he dictates his letters into it. You don't have to talk into a trumpet like you do with most of them. It stands in a corner, and looks just like an ordinary box. Then she comes and takes off the records and writes down what he has said.'

'It might almost have been worth while to change his secretary,' said Blandish, lazily. 'Still, he is doubtless very happy.'

He leant over to light her cigarette, and I was struck by the atmosphere of physical fitness that seemed to radiate from the man: hard as nails; without an ounce of superfluous flesh on him. In fact, a pretty tough customer in a rough house.

I suppose a woman would have spotted the lie of the land that night after dinner. In the light of subsequent events I now realize that the tension was already there, though I didn't get it personally. It was just a little thing—a casual scrap of conversation between two rubbers. Blandish was shuffling the cards, and Phyllis Dankerton, who had been his partner, made some remark about the excellence of his bridge not having been impaired by his living in the back of beyond.

He grinned and said: 'We're not all savages, Mrs Dankerton. Even though there aren't any Ten Commandments, and a man can raise a thirst.'

'At the moment,' remarked John Somerville, quietly, 'we don't happen to be East of Suez.'

The faintest of smiles flickered for an instant round Phyllis Dankerton's lips. Then——

'How marvellously Kipling gets human nature, doesn't he?' she murmured. 'You and I, Bill—and an original no-trumper of mine is open to the gravest suspicion.'

Yes, the tension had begun. To what extent it had grown I don't know; but it was there. As I say, I realized that afterwards. John Somerville suspected his wife and Blandish. Not that he said anything, or even hinted at anything that night, with the exception of that one remark. As always, he was the courteous, perfect host—at least, so it seemed to me. Though when, a couple of days later, I was discussing things with Phyllis Dankerton, she regarded me pityingly when I said so.

'My dear man,' she said, 'you must be partially wanting. There is an atmosphere in this house you could cut with a knife. Our worthy John is watching those two as a cat watches a mouse. It's all excessively amusing.'

'Do you think Mary is in love with Blandish?' I said.

'Wasn't it Maugham who said in one of his plays that a lot of unnecessary fuss is made about the word "love"? Quite obviously she is immensely attracted by him—who wouldn't be? I'm crazy about him myself. And my dear Bill, I might be eighty-one with false teeth, for all the notice he takes of me. It's cruel hard on a deserving girl. There's poor old Peter, who wouldn't notice the Alps unless they were covered with Stock Exchange quotations, and yet I throw myself at that brute's head in vain.'

'I wonder how Mary met him,' I said.

'Really, Bill,' she cried, impatiently, 'you're intolerably dull today. She met him in the same way that everybody does meet people, presumably. Anyway, what does it matter? The beginning has nothing to do with it. It's the end that interests me.'

'You really think that it's serious?' I said.

She shrugged her shoulders.

'With a woman like Mary, you never know. I don't believe she would ever have a real affair with a man if she was still living in her husband's house. But she's quite capable of bolting for good and all if she loved the man sufficiently. Cheer up, Bill'—she laughed—'it's not your palaver. By the look on your face Mary might be *your* wife.'

'I'm very fond of Mary,' I said, stiffly. 'We've known one another since we were kids.'

And at that moment young Merrick came in and the conversation dropped. But I couldn't get it out of my mind. That there should be even the bare possibility of Mary running away with another man seemed to knock the bottom out of my universe. And soon I found myself watching them, too, and trying to gauge the state of the affair. Was Mary in love with him? That was the question I asked myself a dozen times a day. That he should be in love with her was only natural. But was the converse true? I studied her expression when she didn't know I

4

was looking at her, and I had to admit that there was a change. For a few moments, perhaps, she would sit sunk in her thoughts, and then she would make an effort to pull herself together and be laughing and bright as she always used to be. But it was forced, and I knew it; she couldn't deceive me. And sometimes when she came out of her reverie, if Blandish was in the room, her eyes would rest on him for a second, as if she was trying to find the answer to some unspoken question.

Then I started to watch him. But there wasn't much to be got from Miles Blandish's face. Years of poker playing had turned it into an expressionless mask when he wished to make it so. But I managed to catch him unawares once or twice. After lunch one day, for instance. He was holding a match for her cigarette, and over the flame their eyes had met. And in his was a look of such concentrated love and passion as I have never seen before. Then, in an instant it was gone, and he made some commonplace remark. But to me it seemed as if the truth had been proclaimed through a megaphone.

And another time it was even more obvious. Without thinking I went into the billiard-room, and they were alone there. They were standing very close together by the fireplace talking earnestly, and as I opened the door they moved apart quickly. In fact, it was so obvious that I almost committed the appalling solecism of apologizing for intruding. Blandish picked up a paper; Mary smiled and said, 'Why don't you two have a game?' But once again the truth had been shouted to high Heaven: these two were in love with one another. What was going to be the end of it? Was Mary going to bolt with him, or would the whole thing die a natural death when he went out East again?

I believe it might have been the latter, had John Somerville not brought matters to a head. It was after dinner, on the same day that I had surprised them in the billiard-room.

'By the way, Blandish,' he said, as we were beginning to form up for bridge, 'when are you going back again?'

'I haven't quite decided yet,' said Blandish, lighting a cigarette. 'Not for some little while, I think.'

'Want to pay a round of visits, I suppose, and see all your friends. I've just remembered, my dear'—he turned to his wife —'Henry Longstaffe is very anxious to come for a few days, as soon as we can put him up. He and I have a rather considerable business deal to discuss.'

I glanced at Phyllis Dankerton: a smile was hovering on her lips; I glanced at Miles Blandish: his face was expressionless; I glanced at Mary: she was staring at her husband. All three of them knew, as I knew, that there was no spare room in the house. If Henry Longstaffe came to stay, somebody had to go.

'I'm afraid I shall have to fold up my tent and fade away very soon,' said Blandish, easily. 'Would the day after tomorrow do for Mr Longstaffe, or would you sooner he came tomorrow?'

'The day after tomorrow will do perfectly,' said Somerville. 'Sorry you can't stay longer.'

And then we sat down to bridge in an atmosphere, as Phyllis Dankerton afterwards described it, which would have frozen a furnace. Nothing more, of course, was said—but words were unnecessary. The gloves were off, and everyone knew it. Miles Blandish had been kicked out of the house as blatantly as if he had been shown the door. Moreover, it had been done in the presence of all of us, which made the matter worse.

'I think John is a fool,' said Phyllis Dankerton to me, just before we went to bed. 'And a vulgar fool at that. One doesn't do that sort of thing in front of other people. If I were Mary I'd give him such a telling off as he would never forget.'

'He's an extremely angry man,' I remarked, 'and that accounts for it.'

'Then it oughtn't to,' she retorted. 'It simply isn't done. To have said it to him privately would have been a very different matter. And you mark my words, Bill, unless I'm much mistaken, friend John will have achieved the exact opposite to what he intended. He has simply forced their hands.'

'You think she'll run away with him?' I said.

'I think she is far more likely to now than she was before. And if she does John will be very largely to blame. Tomorrow is going to be the crucial day, while he is in London. The great decision will be made then.'

She gave a little bitter laugh and her eyes were very sad.

'God! what fools women are,' she said, under her breath. 'What damned fools!'

Then she went to bed, leaving me to a final night-cap. And when I had followed her example, and lay tossing and turning, unable to sleep, there was one picture I couldn't get out of my mind. It was the picture of Mary and Miles Blandish together, leaning over the stern of an eastbound liner. And at last they turned and looked at one another, as man and woman look at one another when they love. Then they went below.

I must get the events of the next day straight in my mind. Phyllis Dankerton was right: it was the crucial day. But somehow or other things seem a little blurred in my head. I'm not quite certain of the order in which they happened.

First of all there came the interview between Mary and Miles Blandish. I overheard part of it—deliberately. They were in the billiard-room once more, and I happened to stroll past the little window at one end of the room, which is high up in the wall. It was open, and I could hear what they said distinctly, though they couldn't see me.

'My dear,' Blandish was saying, 'it's a big decision that will alter your life completely and irrevocably. It's a decision that cannot be come to lightly. Divorce and that sort of thing seem a comparatively small matter when applied to other people. But when it's applied to oneself it doesn't seem quite so small. Wait, my darling, wait. Let me have my say first. You are going to be the one who has to make the big sacrifice. It's not going to affect me; it never does affect the man. And in my case even less so than usual. My home is out East. It doesn't matter the snap of a finger what I do. But with you it's different. You're giving up all this; you're running away with a man who is considerably poorer than your husband. You are coming to a strange life, amid strange surroundings—a life you may not

7

like. But a life which, if you do leave your husband, you will have to stick to.'

Yes; he put it very fairly, did Miles Blandish. There was no trace of pleading or emotion in his voice; he seemed to be at pains to keep everything matter of fact. And because of that the force of the appeal was doubled.

'We are neither of us children, Mary.' The quiet, measured words went on. 'We know enough to disregard catch phrases like the world being well lost for love. It isn't, and nobody but a fool would think it was. And if you come with me it won't be—it will be changed, that's all. But it's going to be a big change: that's what I want you to get into your head.'

And then, at last, Mary spoke.

'I realize that it's going to be a big change, Miles. Do you really think that matters? I realize that life out there will be different from this. Do you really think I care? My dear, it's not any material alteration in surroundings that has made me hesitate—it's been something far more important and fundamental. I'm not going to mince words; you attracted me from the first time we met. But my great problem was—was it only attraction? If so, I'd have been a fool to go. It is a big decision, as you say—an irrevocable one, and to take it because of a passing whim would be folly. Last night—when John said what he did to you—I knew with absolute certainty. Every single instinct and thought of mine ranged themselves on your side. I've never loved John; now I positively dislike him.'

'That's not quite enough, Mary,' said Blandish, gravely. 'I don't want you to come with me because you dislike John. I want you to come with me because you love me.'

'Miles—my darling.'

I scarcely heard the words, so softly were they spoken. And then came silence. In my mind I could see them there staring into one another's eyes, staring down the unknown path that they were to take together. A little blindly I turned and walked away. The matter was decided, the choice had been made. For good or ill, Mary was going with Miles Blandish.

'Bill, what is the matter with you? Are you ill?'

With an effort I pulled myself together; Phyllis Dankerton was looking at me with amazement on her face.

'Not a bit,' I answered. 'Why should I be?'

'My dear man,' she said, brightly, 'I am partially responsible for Peter's tummy, but I hold no brief for yours. I don't know why you should be ill, but you certainly look it. By the way, I saw our two turtle-doves making tracks for the billiard-room. I wonder if the momentous decision has yet been reached.'

I said nothing. I felt I couldn't stand the worry any more. Phyllis Dankerton is all right in small doses, but there are times when she drives one positively insane. So I made some fatuous remark and left her, vaguely conscious that the surprised look had returned to her face. What the devil did it matter? What did anything matter except that Mary was going with Miles Blandish?

Nothing could alter that fact now; they were neither of them the type of people who change their mind once it is made up. And at dinner that night I found myself watching them curiously. They were both more silent than usual, which was hardly to be wondered at. And John Somerville, who obviously had not yet been told, kept glancing from one to the other.

That he would be told, I felt sure. The idea of bolting on the sly would not appeal to either Mary or Blandish: they weren't that sort. But would it be done after dinner, or postponed to the following day? Or would Blandish go in the ordinary course of events, leaving Mary to break the news to John?

The point was settled after dinner. John Somerville had gone to his room to write some letters, and suddenly I saw Blandish glance at Mary significantly. Then, with a quick little nod, he left the room.

'What about a stroll, Canford?' said young Merrick, and automatically I got up. 'Why not?'

'It strikes me,' he remarked, confidentially, when we were out of earshot, 'that there's a bit of an air of gloom and despondency brooding over the old ancestral hall. Somerville's face at dinner was enough to turn the butter rancid. And Blandish seems quite different these last few days.'

9

'When a man,' I remarked, 'is in love with another man's wife and the other man finds it out, it doesn't make for conviviality in the house.'

He stopped dead and stared at me.

'Good Lord!' he muttered, 'that's the worry is it? Well, I'm damned. I never spotted it. But I jolly well know which of the two I'd choose. Mine host, even though I'm eating his salt, is not much to my liking.'

'Perhaps not,' I said curtly. 'But he happens to be your hostess's husband.'

'You mean to say,' he began, and then suddenly he gripped my arm. 'My God! Canford—look there.'

We were about a hundred yards from the house. From one of the downstair rooms the light was streaming out through the open french windows. And the room was John Somerville's study. He was standing up with his back to the desk, facing Miles Blandish, and it was evident that a bitter quarrel was in progress. We could hear no actual words, but the attitude of the two men told its own tale.

'Damn it—let's clear out,' muttered Merrick. 'Rather rotten, don't you think? Seems like spying on them. I'm going back to the house, anyway.'

He strolled off, and then once again I riveted my eyes on the study window, on that grim, fierce, age-old struggle of two males for a female, the struggle that brings murder into the air.

And when ten minutes later I went into the drawing-room the atmosphere was not much better. Mary glanced up quickly as I came through the window, and her face fell when she saw who it was. Merrick made a grimace at me, And Phyllis Dankerton went on playing patience religiously. Even little Marjorie Stanway seemed to feel there was something the matter, and was fidgeting about the room.

Then suddenly, it happened. The door was flung open and Somerville's secretary dashed into the room. Her face was ashen white, and she was gasping for breath.

'Mrs Somerville,' she almost screamed, 'he's dead. There's a knife in his back. He's been stabbed.'

10

For a moment no one spoke. Then Dankerton said a little dazedly,'Who is dead?'

'Mr Somerville,' sobbed the woman. 'At his desk.'

And again, for what seemed an eternity, there was silence. Mary, her face as white as a sheet, was staring at the secretary, as if she couldn't grasp what had happened. Young Merrick was saying, 'Good God!' under his breath over and over again and watching me. And at last I heard a voice say, 'We must get the police.' It was my own.

'Don't you think that we ought to go and make certain?' muttered Dankerton. 'He may not be dead. Not the women, of course.'

And then,at last, Mary spoke.

'Where is Miles?'

It was hardly more than a whisper, but it sounded as if it had been shouted through a megaphone in the deathly silence. And at that moment he appeared in the window. For a second or two he stood there looking from one to the other of us: then he spoke.

'What on earth is the matter?'

It was Dankerton who answered him.

'Somerville has been stabbed in the back,' he said, gravely. 'His secretary says he is dead. We were just going along to see.'

'Stabbed in the back!' cried Blandish, in amazement. 'But by whom?'

'We don't know,' I said, and once again Merrick's eye met mine. 'Let's go and see if there is anything to be done.'

But there wasn't: that was obvious at the first glance. He lay there, huddled over his desk, his eyes glazed and staring. And thrust into his back up to the hilt was a knife I had often seen lying on the mantelpiece. For a long while no one spoke. Then Dankerton pulled himself together.

'Look here, you fellows, this is a pretty ghastly business. We must get the police at once. I'll tell the butler to ring up.'

'Yes,' agreed Blandish, quietly. 'We must get the police.'

His eyes were riveted on the knife. Then, with an effort, he turned and looked at us each in turn.

'He and I had a frightful row tonight.' He spoke with intense deliberation, and once again Merrick looked at me. 'A frightful row.'

'My dear fellow,' muttered Dankerton, awkwardly. 'Look here, I'll see about the police.'

He bustled out of the room, and suddenly Merrick took the bull by the horns.

'This is a pretty grim affair, Blandish. You see, Canford and I were outside there, and we saw you having words with—with him.'

'Then you must have seen who did this,' said Blandish, eagerly.

'Unfortunately, I didn't,' said Merrick. 'It seemed to me to be a private affair, and I went back to the drawing-room.'

'And I followed shortly after,' I remarked.

Once more silence fell, while Blandish stared at the dead man.

'I had a frightful row,' he repeated, mechanically, 'and then I went out into the garden through the window. Damn it,' he exploded, suddenly, 'you don't think I did it, do you?'

'Of course not, my dear chap,' I cried. 'Of course not.'

He walked a little stiffly out of the room, and I turned to Merrick.

'What's your opinion?' I said at length.

'What's yours?' he answered. 'Damn it, Canford—if he didn't do it, somebody else did. And if it was anybody in the garden we'd have seen him.'

'We might not,' I said. 'If he was hiding.'

'In the back, too,' he muttered. 'A dirty business. God! I wish the police would come.'

And in about half an hour they did. An inspector and a sergeant arrived, and with them the doctor. The cause of death was clear: the knife had penetrated the heart. Somerville had died instantaneously. Then came the turn of the police, and it soon became evident in what direction their suspicions lay. Blandish made no attempt to hide the fact of his quarrel with the dead man. It would have been futile in view of the fact that Merrick and I had seen it. But he flatly refused to say what it was about, and he denied absolutely that he was the man who had done it.

'Nobody said you were, sir,' said the Inspector, sternly. 'You go too fast.'

'Rot,' said Blandish, curtly. 'I'm not a damned fool. If I have a violent row with a man, and a few minutes later he is found dead, there's no good telling me that suspicion doesn't fall on me. Of course it does.'

And the next day suspicion became certainty. A fingerprint expert arrived from Scotland Yard, and the marks of Blandish's fingers were found on the hilt of the knife. It was proof irrefutable, and the only explanation he could give was that in the heat of the argument he had snatched up the knife from the mantelpiece. But he still denied that it was he who had struck the blow.

'Then how comes it that yours are the *only* prints on the knife?' said the Inspector quietly.

I think the only person who believed in his innocence through the days that followed was Mary. To us it was painfully, terribly clear. As I said to Merrick the night before the trial, it was the most obvious case, short of having an eyewitness, that could be put before a jury. And he agreed. He and I, of course, were two of the principal witnesses for the prosecution, but our evidence was really unnecessary. Blandish had never denied the fact that he and the murdered man had had a bitter quarrel. And that and the finger-prints on the knife formed the evidence against him.

He still refused to say what the quarrel was about, though we all of us knew it concerned Mary. And from the point of view of his innocence or guilt it didn't really matter. He and the murdered man had quarrelled over something, and in a fit of ungovernable rage Blandish had picked up the knife and stabbed him.

That was all there was to it when counsel for the Crown had finished his final speech. The members of the jury had obviously made up their minds already. It was difficult to see how they could have done otherwise. And Sir John Gordon—Blandish's counsel—was just rising to commence his hopeless task, when there occurred an amazing interruption. A

13

strange, distraught-looking woman, carrying a brown box, forced her way into court and shouted out: 'Wait! Wait! Don't go on!' Her face seemed vaguely familiar to me, and suddenly I placed her. She was John Somerville's secretary.

Everybody was so astounded that she had reached Sir John before anyone could stop her. And by the time ushers and attendants had rushed up to her, she had said enough to Sir John to cause him to wave them away.

'My Lord,' he said, 'this woman has just made a most important statement to me. In spite of the irregularity of the proceedings I propose to put her in the witness-box.'

And so Emily Turner was duly sworn, and made her statement. And when she had finished you could have heard a pin drop in the court.

'I understand,' said the Judge, 'that the position is as follows. The box in front of Sir John is the instrument which the murdered man used for dictating his letters into. This morning, not having thought of it since the night of the tragedy, you opened the box. And you found that a record had been made. You thereupon played that record, if that is the correct phrase, and you discovered that the conversation between prisoner at the bar and the murdered man was what was recorded. Is that correct?'

'Yes, my Lord.'

And then came a harsh voice from the dock: 'Smash the thing, I tell you. Smash it.'

'Silence,' said the Judge, sternly and Miles Blandish faced him steadily.

'My Lord,' he remarked, 'I give you my solemn word of honour that my conversation with Somerville that night had nothing to do with it. Moreover, it affects a third person. Therefore need that record be given?'

'It must certainly be given,' said the Judge. 'If what this witness says is correct, a vital piece of evidence has just come to light. Turn on the machine.'

I can still see that scene. Miles Blandish, impassive and erect; the jury tense and expectant; the public craning forward in their seats. And the centre of everything—that plain little woman bending over the box.

There came a faint scraping like a gramophone. Then it started.

'Sir, with reference to your last quotation, I beg to state——'

John Somerville's voice: God! it was uncanny. Things began to blur a bit before my eyes. John Somerville dictating a letter.

'May I have a few words with you, Somerville?'

A gasp ran through the court—instantly quelled. Miles Blandish had spoken. The living and the dead reproduced before us.

'Certainly, Blandish.'

'There is not much good beating about the bush, Somerville. Your wife and I are in love with one another.'

'How excessively interesting.'

How well I knew that cold, sneering tone of Somerville's. I could see now the slight rise of his upper lip. I could see the man himself again, as I hadn't seen him since that night—as I'd never expected to see him. He was dead, damn it, dead! And that cursed instrument had brought him to life again. What was he saying now?

'I certainly can't prevent my wife going away with you, Blandish. But it's going to be a little awkward for you both. Divorce proceedings bore me, and I hate being bored.'

'You mean you won't divorce her, Somerville?'

'You damned swine. You utterly damned swine.'

There came a pause, then Somerville's voice with fear in it.

'Put down that knife, you fool. Put down that knife.'

I hadn't told them that: I'd kept that dark. I'd seen Blandish pick up the knife—seen it myself. Just as he said.

'And now clear out, blast you.'

Somerville's voice again—icy, contemptuous. How I'd hated his voice, the thin-lipped swine. And it was then I remembered.

'Stop it!' I screamed. 'Stop it!'

People stared at me in amazement, and suddenly I felt icy calm. The machine scraped on, then—'Hullo, Canford! What do you want? I'm busy.'

Somerville's voice: he'd said it to me as I entered the room.

'What the devil—Oh, my God!'

Followed a little sobbing grunt: then silence. The record was over.

Yes! I did it. I'd always loathed him, and I loathed Blandish worse. Because Mary loved Blandish, and I loved Mary. And when Blandish rushed out past me into the night I saw my chance to get them both. I wrapped a handkerchief round the hilt of the knife to prevent fingerprints: I'd thought of everything.

Everything except that cursed machine.

Mrs Peter Skeffington's Revenge

This is the story of Mrs Peter Skeffington. She was a little fair haired thing, with a pair of the most pathetic looking blue eyes which deluded men into thinking she was helpless. Also into desiring strongly to kiss her. As far as I know Mrs Peter Skeffington did not kiss men.

The scene of the story is South Africa. The exact locality in which it took place is neither here nor there, and is immaterial, because South Africa is a crude country—though an almighty pleasant one—whether you regard her from the top of the Corner House at Johannesburg or from the stoep of a back veldt farm. And the last thing little Mrs Peter liked was crudeness.

She had another peculiarity—she adored her husband. Now far be it from me to say anything against Peter Skeffington. In his way he was a very good fellow; in his correct setting he might have done admirably. But South Africa was not that setting.

She is a crude country, but she is also a strong country, and she demands of those who seek to live on her that they fight and fight, and go on fighting. Skeffington gave up before the first 'i' in the first fight was dotted. In fact the only thing that happened before he gave up fighting was that South Africa discovered his weakness. She always does discover a man's weakness sooner or later; she found Peter Skeffington's before he'd used his first ten shilling book of chits at the Rand Club, of which he'd been made an honorary member for the duration of his stay in Johannesburg. Of that, however, more a little later.

What exactly brought the Peter Skeffingtons to the country is one of those little conundrums which no logic or argument can solve. At Surbiton—let us say—they could have lived, and moved, and had their being without any harm to Surbiton or themselves. In South Africa something had to happen. As food Peter and his wife were thoroughly indigestible to the land of their choice, and that entails a pain somewhere.

17

Why it was the land of their choice is, as I have said, insoluble logically. Any man who knew the conditions of living would have told them that they were totally unsuited for those conditions. He would also have told them that out of the many land advertisements appearing so bravely in the columns of leading London newspapers ninety per cent are cold blooded, dastardly swindles. Some day, incidentally, if I sit next to the editor of one of these papers at dinner I must ask him why he allows these advertisements, but prohibits moneylenders? You do get something out of a moneylender anyway; it would save trouble to drop your money in the sea in the case of the others.

To return, however, to the Peter Skeffingtons. Why they came matters not—they came. By a great stroke of fortune they missed the ninety per cent already alluded to, and stumbled into one of the seven per cent class, which are fair to good without being very good. The three per cent of very good are shy, retiring birds; they can afford to be.

They found themselves, did the Peter Skeffingtons, in a proposition which *in time*, when God and the Government decreed (principally the Government, in this case; it was the usual question of irrigation) would turn out thundering well and give them a very ample and pleasant return for their money. In the meantime there was nothing to do but to sit down and wait — which is a dangerous proceeding for some people in South Africa; especially for people with the weakness of Peter Skeffington.

To those who know, the fact that Peter's weakness was made manifest at the Rand Club is all that is necessary. There are others, however, who are not so well informed.

Of all the magnificent buildings in that marvellous mushroom city Johannesburg, the Rand Club is one of the most symbolical. In it you may obtain the comforts, cellar, and table of the most exclusive London club; in it you may see—the world. Every sort and condition of man who has been, is, or will be anything in South Africa at some time or another has stood at the great three-sided bar. There was one man whose boast it was that he hadn't, and he died of drinking poisoned water.

You will see a man there who yesterday made a hundred thousand on a rumour concerning asbestos; beside him is the man who lost a good part of it. You will see a cheerful, friendly soul surrounded by pals. The calling is on him, and why not? He only owes them half a million, and his present assets he would sell willingly for a hundred. Moreover, they know it. But in addition you will also see all the men who really count.

But one great rule is necessary for the stranger within the gates—learn to drink slowly. And since Peter Skeffington did not know this rule—though seeing that his weakness was what it was it wouldn't have much mattered if he had—South Africa had brutally probed the joint in his armour exactly one hour after he entered the bar of the Rand Club.

The trouble was threefold: first, he couldn't say 'no'; second, he had no head for drink; third, and worse of all, he thought he had. Which is just about as hopeless a combination as can be gathered together in a man. But had they remained in England there is no doubt in my mind that the Peter Skeffingtons would have carried on quite happily, and lived to a ripe old age. In the year 1960 he would have alluded to the days when he was young, and boys were boys, and whisky was whisky. Because, and this is the point, Peter Skeffington was not a drunkard. He was a weak young ass who periodically drank far too much when opportunity offered. But it was the opportunity that was required—not the drink. You could have locked him up in a cellar of wine with safety for a week; you couldn't trust him in a third-rate bar for half an hour with a couple of pals. And if only someone who understood could have explained that simple fact to his wife this story would never have been written.

In the particular portion of South Africa where the Peter Skeffingtons had settled opportunities were as blackberries on an autumn hedge. The type of opportunities, too, were of exactly the sort to prove most dangerous. In the first place he had nothing to do, in the second most of the days in which he had to do it were hot, dusty, arid, and shadeless; in the third there were exactly twenty-seven other men in a similar position to himself; in the fourth there was a club placed centrally in the community, where the twenty-eight met each evening for their sundowner and discussed what particular brand of nothingness they had done during the day. And discussion is dry work, especially when it concerns that ever prevalent subject—lack of water.

The net result was obvious. Peter Skeffington returned home in varying degrees of insobriety exactly six days of the week out of seven. That was due to the fact that the club was shut on Sundays. I was one of the twenty-eight, so I know. We didn't notice it particularly at first, because he never got offensively tight, but after a while its monotony made it obvious, and several of us refused to drink with him. But it didn't do any good; there was always someone who would. Particularly Jack Dernan.

Dernan was the typical product of a young country. Tall, broad-shouldered, powerful as a horse, tanned mahogany, he was a fighter from the beginning of the chapter. And if there was one thing for which he had profound contempt, it was weakness in any form. Now I don't think he realized for a moment what he was doing with Peter Skeffington. Certainly not at first. He regarded him with a kind of good-natured toleration, mingled with slight wonder. He was so completely the type of man that Dernan had no use for, that he was a source of amusement. Possessed of a head that no amount of liquor ever had the slightest effect on, it was with genuine feelings of amazement that he regarded the amount necessary to render Peter Skeffington drunk.

'No well-conditioned fly could drown in it,' he once remarked wonderingly. 'The fellow's a damn freak.'

But he didn't seem to be able to let him alone. Peter Skeffington's complete inability to absorb liquor seemed to fascinate him. He used to take mental notes of the amounts each night, and the condition arrived at. And after a time he and two or three others started private side-bets on the result.

'Rather on the principle of the daily run on board ship,' he explained. 'Numbers from six to twelve, nine or ten are good favourites, but the high field hasn't an earthly. He'd be dead if he took more than a dozen, I should think.'

'Go easy, Jack,' said someone. 'It can't go on like this.'

20

'Great Scott!' cried Dernan, 'I don't want to make the fellow tight. He rushes at it with his mouth open himself.'

And so another of the tragedies—the square peg and round hole tragedies—began to gather form and shape; a tragedy which, as one traces it backwards, could have been so easily averted. If only someone could have explained things to Mrs Peter—the real truth, instead of what she thought was the truth. If only someone could have said: 'Take him away back to England, out of this country, and never let him return here save on a Cook's personally-conducted tour'—all would have been well. But no one did say it, and so she took him to Durban instead, to fight this insidious devil that had crept into her Peter's life—the devil of drunkenness.

She took him to Durban, where they could get sea bathing, and golf and tennis, and I saw them off at the station. And there was a look in Mrs Peter's pathetic blue eyes that I had never seen there before. It was not one of helplessness.

They stayed away three months, and the devil was conquered with surprising ease. But it was the wrong devil; the real one wasn't there to fight. There was lots to do in Durban; there was no small dusty club in Durban; and Peter, who was thoroughly ashamed of himself behaved adorably to her in Durban. He made her all sorts of promises and vows about the future, which he honestly intended to keep. And as proof of his assertions he pointed out to her the complete ease with which he had given up the stuff. Which would have meant a great deal more if they hadn't been chasing the wrong hare.

And so, the cure over, they returned triumphantly to begin all over again. For a fortnight the club never saw him, though he drove past once or twice behind a new horse he had bought —an ugly looking black brute with a vicious eye that no one but a Peter Skeffington would have touched with the end of a barge pole.

And then one evening, like a bolt from the blue, came the tragedy. Peter Skeffington came into the club, and found Jack Dernan and four or five others. That was at six. At six-thirty he was drunk, and our secretary was tearing his hair with irritation and anger.

21

'It's incredible,' he fumed. 'It's outrageous. It's indecent. Five—five drinks has that fellow had, and look at him. He's a menace to humanity. Why, damn it—a baby in arms would drink him under the table.'

'But look here,' I began angrily.

'*Mea culpa,* my boy,' he answered. 'I admit it. I said to the blighter when I saw him "Hullo, little stranger—have a drink?" I give you my word at the moment I'd completely forgotten all about the show. "I will," he answered, and then the matter passed completely out of my hands. I left him for about twenty minutes, while I talked to Jackson about that mealie crop, and when I got back I found he had had four more with Jack Dernan and some others, and was tight.'

He shrugged his shoulders helplessly.

'Man, you *can't* legislate for a bloke that gets tight on five whiskies and sodas.'

'It's Mrs Peter I'm thinking of,' I said. 'The poor little woman thinks she's saved Skeffington's soul from the curse of drink, and the first time he comes into the club he goes and does it again.'

A burst of laughter came from the bar, and I went in. There were about ten of them in there, and Peter Skeffington was holding forth very solemnly on the political situation in the Union. So I got Jack Dernan on one side, and put things in front of him.

'Look here, Jack,' I said, 'it's not playing the game to make that silly ass tight again.'

'Give you my word, old man,' he answered, 'no one was more surprised than I was. We were playing poker dice, and we'd only had four rounds when blowed if I didn't notice he was up the pole. Somebody had got the sweepstake going, and I found I'd drawn low field. Well, seeing that the first number is six I reckoned the pool was mine.'

He glanced at Skeffington, who was swaying gravely by the bar.

'I really am deuced sorry, but what can you do with a fellow like that?'

'Well, for Heaven's sake stop him drinking any more,' I said. 'We'll lay him out to cool for a bit, and then I'll drive him home.'

But Peter Skeffington had no intention whatever of being laid out to cool. He had got into the condition when he was very much on his dignity. Really, by the way we were talking, if it wasn't so perfectly ridiculous, anyone who didn't know any better might imagine that we thought he had had too much to drink. He was perfectly capable, thank you, of looking after himself, and he knew the time quite well, and also that his horse and trap were waiting outside, a fact to which he trusted no one took any exception.

Jack Dernan shrugged his shoulders.

'Hopeless,' he said to me. 'He's worse than I've seen him. And if we go on he'll get offensive, and someone will hurt him.'

It was half an hour later that Peter Skeffington descended the steps leading into the road. His eyes were slightly glazed; his speech was very precise; his legs moved stiffly. And suddenly—I know not why—an impulse came to me as I sat on the stoep watching him.

'I wish you'd let me drive you back, Skeffington. I'd rather like to feel the paces of that mare.'

He regarded me solemnly.

'Another time, Tredgett, I shall be delighted,' he said. 'At the moment, however, the other seat is occupied with two large bags of chicken food.'

'Well, for God's sake be careful with that brute tonight,' said the secretary uneasily, as he saw her ears go back and the whites of her eyes show up.

'I am perfectly capable of handling her,' replied Skeffington coldly, and even as he spoke he lurched against the mare, who lashed out viciously.

'Dash it,' cried the secretary, half rising to his feet. 'Ought we to let him go? He's not in a condition to drive.'

But Skeffington was already in his seat gathering up the reins with clumsy fingers.

'Go easy, man,' cried someone, and for answer the fool slashed the animal across the quarters.

For the fraction of a second she stood stock still at the suddenness of it: then it happened. With a spring like a thing demented the mare shot forward: there was a jerk and a crash, and the next moment she had bolted down the road with the trap swaying and bounding behind her.

'God! She's away with him.'

I turned to find Jack Dernan beside me, and his face was white. We were all out in the road watching and no one else spoke. For the chicken food had been hurled out, and the reins were trailing low, and Peter Skeffington was half-standing, half-sitting in that crazy, tearing buggy. Once we thought it was over, but it righted itself again somehow, and then came the end. One lurch into a rut, more crazy than the others, and Skeffington was flung out. And the next moment we were all of us rushing madly down the road towards him, for it seemed to us that he had hit a tree.

It was Jack Dernan who got there first, and when we got up there he was standing by the thing that lay on the ground, and his hat was off. Peter Skeffington *had* hit a tree—with his head.

In the distance a cloud of dust was disappearing, as the maddened mare, now completely out of control, galloped on, whilst here at our feet was sudden, stark tragedy.

'No good doing that,' said Dernan gruffly, as somebody put his hand on Peter Skeffington's heart. 'Look at his head.'

I did—and shuddered. Hid hands had hardly broken the impact at all. So we got the body back to the club, and there we had a council of war. And by common consent I was deputed to break the news to Mrs Peter.

'Of course,' said the secretary, 'you'll not mention the fact that he was drunk.'

'Of course not,' I answered, as I went out to start my Ford.

But I wondered as I drove there whether she wouldn't guess.

I found her waiting for me wild-eyed with fear. The mare had come back twenty minutes previously.

'What's happened?' she gasped. 'What's happened to Peter?'

'Mrs Peter,' I said miserably, 'you must prepare for a shock.'

'He's dead,' she said quietly, and I nodded.

'How did it happen,' she said after a while. 'Don't be afraid,' she added as I glanced at her. 'I shan't break down—yet. I want to hear everything.'

So I told her, and when I'd finished she only asked one question.

'Was Mr Dernan in the club?'

I stared at her in surprise: it was so completely unexpected.

'Why, yes,' I said. 'Jack Dernan was there.'

And into her eyes there came a look to which I had no clue. It seemed to show a sort of savage determination, but to what end or on what account I could not guess.

She seemed strangely docile during the next few days. For instance, I had anticipated that she would insist on seeing her husband's body, and there were reasons why she shouldn't. The poor devil had hit that tree hard. However, when I explained things to her she made no trouble, but seemed to understand perfectly. And another thing that surprised us all was the way she bore up. Even at the graveside she retained her perfect composure, and I heard Mrs Drage whisper to a woman standing next to her: 'She's like a woman in a dream: she'll wake up soon.'

But she didn't: that was the amazing part of it. What happened during the long nights when she was alone only she and God knew: certain it was that during the days that followed her husband's death I never saw a trace of grief on Mrs Peter's face. And I was up there, off and on, a good deal: she seemed to like having me about the place. Only that strange look—that look of set purpose—was stamped on her features, and it seemed to grow more quietly determined as time went by. She wasn't going to get rid of her farm, at any rate, not yet; and I used to give her advice about it.

And then, about two months after Peter's death, business called me up to Rhodesia. I should be away for six months, and I went up the afternoon before I left to say goodbye. She gave me tea, and afterwards I sat on talking about the farm and various things, though I could see she was paying no attention.

And then suddenly she shot the question at me out of the blue; at least it wasn't a question so much as a statement.

'Of course Peter was drunk that night.' She looked at me with a faint smile. 'There's no good denying it, Joe; your face has already given you away. Besides—I knew.'

'He undoubtedly,' I began feebly, 'had had something to drink.'

She stopped me with a weary little gesture.

'Oh, call it that if you like,' she said. 'I prefer not to mince words. He was drunk, and you know it. You remember I took him to Durban, don't you?'

'Of course, I remember,' I answered.

'And you know why I took him,' she went on. 'He was drinking too much at that—that damnable club. Every night, Joe; practically every night; I cured him at Durban; never once the whole time he was there did my Peter get into that foul condition. He was cured when he got back here.'

I said nothing; I didn't see that there was anything to say. Of what use to tell her that he wasn't cured at all, because there was nothing to cure. Such refinements were beyond her; to her a man who got drunk was a drunkard.

'He talked to me while he was in Durban,' she went on quietly, 'when he was fighting against the craving.'

'He told you he had a craving for it?' I asked curiously.

'But, of course, he must have had a craving for it,' she said, staring at me as if I was a fool. 'Why else should he have drunk? But he fought against it, and I helped him—and my Peter won. He was fine about it—fine.'

'Quite,' I agreed. 'It was fine.'

Once again there didn't seem anything else to say. I suppose it is finer to fight and conquer a terrible craving than to admit that one is so atrociously weak that you can't say no, even when you don't want the stuff.

'Yes, he talked a lot to me during those months,' went on Mrs Peter quietly. 'Particularly about Mr Dernan.'

'The devil he did,' I said, sitting up. 'What had he got to say about him?'

She had turned away and I couldn't see her face.

'A great deal about his character,' she answered almost carelessly. And then suddenly she swung round, and I gasped at the look in her eyes. 'To my mind,' she said tensely, 'there is no hell deep enough, no punishment sufficiently vile for a man of that type.'

'But, good God!' I stammered feebly. 'I assure you, Mrs Peter, that Jack Dernan isn't at all a bad fellow.'

And the look she gave me flattened me out.

'To get hold of a man who had been fighting to conquer a craving, and who has succeeded, and tempt him, and tempt him, and tempt him until he falls again is your idea of a good fellow, is it? It isn't mine.'

My mind went back to the night of the tragedy, and I realized the futility of any argument. To Mrs Peter, her husband was a man who had fought and won, only to yield at last to the devilish temptation cast in his way by Jack Dernan. And was any good to be obtained by telling her the truth—telling her that, as a matter of fact, the first drink he had had that night had not been with Dernan at all? Telling her, moreover, that it would have made no odds if no such person existed in the world as Jack Dernan, that Peter Skeffington had been of the clay which, in certain conditions, was unsavable?

So I let it go, and even now, looking back with the light of what was to come behind me, I should do the same thing again under similar circumstances. For who could possibly have told that a woman of the type of Mrs Peter could have done the thing she did?

I got back from Rhodesia eight months later, and one of the first men I ran into was Jack Dernan. He was in the club as I came in, and I stopped short and stared at him in amazement.

'Good Lord, old man!' I cried. 'What's the matter with you? Malaria?'

He looked ghastly: grey, with lack-lustre eyes, and a loose mouth. He stared at me vacantly for a while, then he spoke.

'Go to hell,' he snarled, and shambled out of the club.

'What do you think of him?' came the secretary's voice from behind me.

'What on earth is the matter with him?' I said as I swung round to greet him. 'The man looks dreadful.'

'Come and have a drink, Tredgett,' he answered gravely. 'I want to talk to you.'

I followed him into the bar and we sat down in a corner. Luckily we had it to ourselves.

'You know, I suppose, that he's never out of Mrs Skeffington's pocket?'

'What!' I almost shouted, my drink half-way to my lips.

'Never out of her pocket,' he repeated quietly. 'I'm pretty lax myself, as you know; anybody can do anything with reason as far as I'm concerned; but this has been a bit over the odds. None of the women here will have anything to do with her, but she doesn't seem to care. She's infatuated with the fellow, and he with her. But she's thrown the most rudimentary social laws to the winds. There's no reason presumably why they shouldn't get married; I've never heard of Dernan being entangled in any way. Instead of that he's up at her bungalow —alone with her until all hours of the night. And I'm really not surprised that everyone has put the worst construction on it.'

And in my mind was ringing a certain sentence:

'To my mind there is no hell deep enough, no punishment sufficiently vile for a man of that type.'

'But it's the change in the man himself that is so amazing,' went on the secretary. 'You remember what he was like; you saw him a few moments ago. And he's worse than that sometimes. His temper has become unbearable—positively unbearable. In fact, at times he's positively dangerous.'

But I was hardly listening; into my mind had come a sudden, ghastly suspicion.

'Has he seen a doctor?' I asked, striving to make my voice sound natural.

The secretary smiled grimly. 'Tim Murphy suggested that very thing to him,' he said. 'But he only did so once. Dernan flew into the most ungovernable rage, and went for him. Here in this actual bar. We had the devil of a job pulling him off, and Murphy was nearly throttled before we did. I tell you, Tredgett, the man's dangerous.'

'And has no one any idea what is the matter?' I said.

The secretary shrugged his shoulders.

'He's knocking off drink considerably,' he answered. 'Why, I don't know. Possibly the lady has a lot to do with it. And whether it's finding him out—rawing up his nerves, or something of that sort—I don't know. Anyhow, you've seen him for yourself, and can form as good an opinion as I can.'

I escaped as soon as I could, and went back to my bungalow. Suspicion was hammering at my brain, and I wanted to think. Could it be possible that Mrs Peter was poisoning him? That was the ghastly thought that would not be shaken off. Of what use to tell myself that the idea was incredible; that such things don't happen outside the covers of sensational fiction? Such things *do* happen, and though Mrs Peter was the last woman in the world one would have deemed capable of such a thing, I couldn't forget the look on her face the last time I had seen her. And if my suspicion was right, what was going to be the upshot? Sooner or later a man in Jack Dernan's condition of health would have to see a doctor—and what then?

I tried to concentrate on arrears of work, but the figures danced before my eyes. The short dusk had gone, and outside the African night had come down, bringing no relief from the heat of the day. But I felt I could stand it no longer; I must find out for myself. Nothing would be more natural, I reflected, than that I should go and see Mrs Peter on my return after such a long absence. And if Dernan was there I might be able to come to some conclusion.

I pulled out the Ford and started off. And it was only as I approached Mrs Peter's bungalow that I suddenly decided to leave the car in the road and walk up the last few hundred yards. My feet made no sound on the earth track, and I was within twenty yards of the house when I saw a sight which stopped me dead in my tracks.

The light was shining out from the drawing-room windows, and I could see every detail of the room through the mosquito netting. Jack Dernan was there, sitting on the sofa, and his arms were round Mrs Peter. His face seemed more ghastly than ever, though she was looking up into it lovingly. And suddenly he bent and kissed her.

'Isn't it time yet, my dearest?'

His voice, harsh and discordant, came to me through the still night.

She reached for a little box at her side, and drew out something that gleamed. And in my excitement I crept closer. He was holding out his arm with the sleeve rolled up, and I saw her taking the shining thing in one hand, whilst with the other she caught up a little roll of his skin. And then I knew: knew that what I'd suspected was true. She was giving him an injection from a hypodermic syringe.

For perhaps five minutes after she had done it he lay still, and you could almost watch his face change. The grey tinge disappeared: the shifty mouth grew firm: the eyes became clear. It was the old Jack Dernan who rose to his feet—more, it was a super Jack Dernan. He stood there, a magnificent figure of a man, with a look on his face of absolute triumph.

'My darling,' he cried, 'how long are you going to keep me waiting?'

His arms were stretched to her: even I could feel the commanding presence of the man.

And Mrs Peter lay in the corner of the sofa and laughed. 'You fool,' she answered very clearly. 'You damned fool.'

His arms dropped to his side and he stared at her.

'What do you mean?' he stammered.

'Only that I've been playing a game with you, Mr Jack Dernan—and I've won.' She rose and crossed to the other side of the room so that the table was between them. 'A game—you beast, you cur, and you never knew. You thought I was in love with you, when I hate you, loathe you, execrate you. If it hadn't been for you, my Peter would have been alive tonight, you — you murderer. Listen, Jack Dernan, listen now, while the dope is in you, and your brain is working clearly. I've led you on from the very beginning, even though the touch of your hands nauseated me, and there were times when I didn't think I could go through with it. It doesn't matter how I got hold of the stuff: it was during that time I went up to Johannesburg. I went up there to get it, and I got it. That's all that counts. Then I came back here, and I made you fall in love with me. And after that I tempted you—even as you tempted Peter. Do you remember that first night, Jack Dernan? It was a bit of a job, but I did it. You were frightened at first—frightened of drugs. Even as my Peter was frightened of drink. Then you saw me use the syringe on my own arm, and that persuaded you. But there was just plain water in mine, you fool, whereas yours had the drug in it.

30

And so it has been all the time: I've been injecting myself with water, and you with the drug. And I've acted, God, how I've acted! You've seen me, as you thought, run down, panting for it. Acting, you devil, acting.'

She paused, and the man still stared at her speechless.

'It's over now. Joe Tredgett has come back from Rhodesia and he would suspect. Tonight is the last night I shall ever see you: tonight finished my stock. But when the craving is on you, Jack Dernan, and every fibre of your body is shrieking for the drug it wants, think of the man you killed as surely as if you'd shot him. I've turned you into a drug maniac, and that is my revenge. Go, you brute, go.'

She stood there pointing to the window, and for a space there was silence. Then, with a strange, gasping cry, Jack Dernan turned, and, blundering through the mosquito netting as if it wasn't there, disappeared into the darkness.

Two months later Mrs Peter Skeffington sold her land and returned to England. And I don't know if she ever saw a paragraph in the Johannesburg 'Star.' It ran as follows:

'A dreadful tragedy took place last night in the Germiston district, resulting in the death of four men. Two of them were well known as being engaged in the traffic of cocaine and other drugs. The third was a native, and the fourth has been identified as a man called Jack Dernan. It is thought some quarrel arose over the disposal of the stuff, and revolvers were drawn. Three of the chambers of Dernan's revolver had been discharged.'

At any rate, that is the story of Mrs Peter Skeffington. It is not a pleasant one, but it happens to be true.

The House by the Headland

'You'll no get there, zurr. There'll be a rare storm this night. Best bide here, and be going tomorrow morning after 'tis over.'

The warning of my late host, weather-wise through years of experience, rang through my brain as I reached the top of the headland, and, too late, I cursed myself for not having heeded his words. With a gasp I flung my pack down on the ground, and loosened my collar. Seven miles behind me lay the comfortable inn where I had lunched; eight miles in front the one where I proposed to dine. And midway between them was I, dripping with perspiration and panting for breath.

Not a puff of air was stirring; not a sound broke the death-like stillness, save the sullen, lazy beat of the sea against the rocks below. Across the horizon, as far as the eye could see, stretched a mighty bank of black cloud, which was spreading slowly and relentlessly over the whole heaven. Already its edge was almost overhead, and as I felt the first big drop of rain on my forehead, I cursed myself freely once again. If only I had listened to mine host: if only I was still in his comfortable oak-beamed coffee-room, drinking his most excellent ale . . . I felt convinced he was the type of man who would treat such trifles as regulation hours with the contempt they deserved. And, even as I tasted in imagination the bite of the grandest of all drinks on my parched tongue, and looked through the glass bottom of the tankard at the sanded floor, the second great drop of rain splashed on my face. For a moment or two I wavered. Should I go back that seven miles, and confess myself a fool, or should I go on the further eight and hope that the next cellar would be as good as the last? In either case I was bound to get drenched to the skin, and at length I made up my mind. I would not turn back for any storm, and the matter of the quality of the ale must remain on the laps of the gods. And at that moment, like a solid wall of water, the rain came.

I have travelled into most corners of the world, in the course of forty years' wandering; I have been through the monsoon going south to Singapore from Japan, I have been caught on the edge of a water-spout in the South Sea Islands; but I have never known anything like the rain which came down that June evening on the south-west coast of England. In half a minute every garment I wore was soaked; the hills and the sea were blotted out, and I stumbled forward blindly, unable to see more than a yard in front of me. Then, almost as abruptly as it had started, the rain ceased. I could feel the water squelching in my boots, and trickling down my back, as I kept steadily descending into the valley beyond the headland. There was nothing for it now but to go through with it. I couldn't get any wetter than I was; so that, when I suddenly rounded a little knoll and saw in front a low-lying, rambling house, the idea of sheltering there did not at once occur to me. I glanced at it casually in the semi-darkness, and was trudging past the gate, my mind busy with other things, when a voice close behind me made me stop with a sudden start. A man was speaking, and a second before I could have sworn I was alone.

'A bad night, sir,' he remarked, in a curiously deep voice, 'and it will be worse soon. The thunder and lightning is nearly over. Will you not come in and shelter? I can supply you with a change of clothes if you are wet.'

'You are very good, sir,' I answered slowly, peering at the tall, gaunt figure beside me. 'But I think I will be getting on, thank you all the same.'

'As you like,' he answered indifferently, and even as he spoke a vivid flash of lightning quivered and died in the thick blackness of the sky, and almost instantaneously a deafening crash of thunder seemed to come from just over our heads. 'As you like,' he repeated, 'but I shall be glad of your company if you cared to stay the night.'

It was a kind offer, though in a way the least one would expect in similar circumstances, and I hesitated. Undoubtedly there was little pleasure to be anticipated in an eight-mile tramp under such conditions, and yet there was something—something indefinable, incoherent—which said to me insistently, 'Go on; don't stop. Go on.'

I shook myself in annoyance, and my wet clothes clung to me clammily. Was I, at any time of life, nervous, because a man had spoken to me unexpectedly?

'I think if I may,' I said, 'I will change my mind and avail myself of your kind offer. It is no evening for walking for pleasure.'

Without a word he led the way into the house, and I followed. Even in the poor light I could see that the garden was badly kept, and that the path leading to the front door was covered with weeds. Bushes, wet with the rain, hung in front of our faces, dripping dismally on to the ground; and green moss filled the cracks of the two steps leading up to the door, giving the impression almost of a mosaic.

Inside, the hall was in darkness, and I waited while he opened the door into one of the rooms. I heard him fumbling for a match, and at that moment another blinding flash lit up the house as if it had been day. I had a fleeting vision of the stairs—a short, broad flight—with a window at the top; of two doors, one apparently leading to the servants' quarters, the other opposite the one my host had already opened. But most vivid of all in that quick photograph was the condition of the hall itself. Three or four feet above my head a lamp hung from the ceiling, and from it, in every direction, there seemed to be spiders' webs coated with dust and filth. They stretched to every picture; they stretched to the top of all the doors. One long festoon was almost brushing against my face, and for a moment a wave of unreasoning panic filled me. Almost did I turn and run, so powerful was it; then, with an effort, I pulled myself together. For a grown man to become nervous of a spider's web is rather too much of a good thing, and after all it was none of my business. In all probability the man was a recluse, who was absorbed in more important matters than the cleanliness of his house. Though how he could stand the smell—dank and rotten —defeated me. It came to my nostrils as I stood there, waiting for him to strike a match, and the scent of my own wet Harris tweed failed to conceal it. It was the smell of an unlived-in house, grown damp and mildewed with years of neglect, and once again I shuddered. Confound the fellow! Would he never get the lamp lit? I didn't mind his spiders' webs and the general filth of his hall, provided I could get some dry clothes on.

'Come in.' I looked up to see him standing in the door. 'I regret that there seems to be no oil in the lamp, but there are candles on the mantelpiece, should you care to light them.'

Somewhat surprised I stepped into the room, and then his next remark made me halt in amazement.

'When my wife comes down, I must ask her about the oil. Strange of her to have forgotten.'

Wife! What manner of woman could this be who allowed her house to get into such a condition of dirt and neglect? And were there no servants? However, again, it was none of my business, and I felt in my pocket for matches. Luckily they were in a water-tight box, and with a laugh I struck one and lit the candles.

'It's so infernally dark,' I remarked, 'that the stranger within the gates requires a little light, to get his bearings.'

In some curiosity I glanced at my host's face in the flickering light. As yet I had had no opportunity of observing him properly, but now as unostentatiously as possible I commenced to study it. Cadaverous, almost to the point of emaciation, he had a ragged, bristly moustache, while his hair, plentifully flecked with grey, was brushed untidily back from his forehead. But dominating everything were his eyes, which glowed and smouldered from under his bushy eyebrows, till they seemed to burn into me.

More and more I found myself regretting the fact that I had accepted his offer. His whole manner was so strange that for the first time doubts as to his sanity began to creep into my mind. And to be alone with a madman in a deserted house, miles from any other habitation, with a terrific thunderstorm raging, was not a prospect which appealed to me greatly. Then I remembered his reference to his wife, and felt more reassured. . . .

'You and your wife must find it lonely here,' I hazarded, when the silence had lasted some time.

'Why should my wife feel the loneliness?' he answered, harshly. 'She has me—her husband. . . . What more does a woman require?'

35

'Oh, nothing, nothing!' I replied, hastily, deeming discretion the better part of veracity. 'Wonderful air; beautiful view. I wonder if I could have a dry coat as you so kindly suggested?'

I took off my own wet one as I spoke, and threw it over the back of a chair. Then, receiving no answer to my request, I looked at my host. His back was half towards me, and he was staring into the hall outside. He stood quite motionless, and as apparently he had failed to hear me, I was on the point of repeating my remark when he turned and spoke to me again.

'A pleasant surprise for my wife, sir, don't you think? She was not expecting me home until tomorrow morning.'

'Very,' I assented. . . .

'Eight miles have I walked, in order to prevent her being alone. That should answer your remark about her feeling the loneliness.'

He peered at me fixedly, and I again assented.

'Most considerate of you,' I murmured, 'most considerate.'

But the man only chuckled by way of answer, and, swinging round, continued to stare into the gloomy, filthy hall.

Outside the storm was increasing in fury. Flash followed flash with such rapidity that the whole sky westwards formed into a dancing sheet of flame, while the roll of the thunder seemed like the continuous roar of a bombardment with heavy guns. But I was aware of it only subconsciously; my attention was concentrated on the gaunt man standing so motionless in the centre of the room. So occupied was I with him that I never heard his wife's approach until suddenly, looking up, I saw that by the door there stood a woman—a woman who paid no attention to me, but only stared fearfully at her husband, with a look of dreadful terror in her eyes. She was young, far younger than the man — and pretty in a homely, countrified way. And as she stared at the gaunt, cadaverous husband she seemed to be trying to speak, while ceaselessly she twisted a wisp of a pocket handkerchief in her hands.

'I didn't expect you home so soon, Rupert,' she stammered at length. 'Have you had a good day?'

'Excellent,' he answered, and his eyes seemed to glow more fiendishly than ever. 'And now I have come home to my little wife, and her loving welcome.'

She laughed a forced, unnatural laugh, and came a few steps
into the room.

'There is no oil in the lamp, my dear,' he continued, suavely.
'Have you been too busy to remember to fill it?'

'I will go and get some,' she said, quickly turning towards the
door.

But the man's hand shot out and caught her arm, and at his
touch she shrank away, cowering.

'I think not,' he cried, harshly. 'We will sit in the darkness,
my dear, and—wait.'

'How mysterious you are, Rupert!' She forced herself to
speak lightly. 'What are we going to wait for?'

But the man only laughed—a low, mocking chuckle—and
pulled the girl nearer to him.

'Aren't you going to kiss me, Mary? It's such a long time
since you kissed me—a whole twelve hours.'

The girl's free hand clenched tight, but she made no other protest
as her husband took her in his arms and kissed her. Only it seemed
to me that her whole body was strained and rigid, as if to brace
herself to meet a caress she loathed. . . . In fact the whole situation
was becoming distinctly embarrassing. The man seemed to have
completely forgotten my existence, and the girl so far had not even
looked at me. Undoubtedly a peculiar couple, and a peculiar
house. Those cobwebs: I couldn't get them out of my mind.

'Hadn't I better go and fill the lamp now?' she asked after a
time. 'Those candles give a very poor light, don't they?'

'Quite enough for my purpose, my dear wife,' replied the
man. 'Come and sit down and talk to me.'

With his hand still holding her arm he drew her to a sofa, and
side by side they sat down. I noticed that all the time he was
watching her covertly out of the corner of his eye, while she
stared straight in front of her as if she was waiting for something
to happen. . . . And at that moment a door banged, upstairs.

'What's that?' The girl half rose, but the man pulled her back.

'The wind, my dear,' he chuckled. 'What else could it be?
The house is empty save for us.'

'Hadn't I better go up and see that all the windows are shut?'
she said, nervously. 'This storm makes me feel frightened.'

'That's why I hurried back to you, my love. I couldn't bear to think of you spending tonight alone.' Again he chuckled horribly, and peered at the girl beside him. 'I said to myself, "She doesn't expect me back till tomorrow morning. I will surprise my darling wife, and go back home tonight." Wasn't it kind of me, Mary?'

'Of course it was, Rupert,' she stammered. 'Very kind of you. I think I'll just go up and put on a jersey. I'm feeling a little cold.'

She tried to rise, but her husband still held her; and then suddenly there came on her face such a look of pitiable terror that involuntarily I took a step forward. She was staring at the door, and her lips were parted as if to cry out, when the man covered her mouth with his free hand and dragged her brutally to her feet.

'Alone, my wife—all alone,' he snarled. 'My dutiful, loving wife all alone. What a good thing I returned to keep her company!'

For a moment or two she struggled feebly; then he half carried, half forced her close by me to a position behind the open door. I could have touched them as they passed; but I seemed powerless to move. Instinctively I knew what was going to happen; but I could do nothing save stand and stare at the door, while the girl, half fainting, crouched against the wall, and her husband stood over her motionless and terrible. And thus we waited, while the candles guttered in their sockets, listening to the footsteps which were coming down the stairs. . . .

Twice I strove to call out; twice the sound died away in my throat. I felt as one does in some awful nightmare, when a man cries aloud and no sound comes, or runs his fastest and yet does not move. In it, I was yet not of it; it was as if I was the spectator of some inexorable tragedy with no power to intervene.

The steps came nearer. They were crossing the hall now — the cobwebby hall—and the next moment I saw a young man standing in the open door.

'Mary, where are you, my darling?' He came into the room and glanced around. And, as he stood there, one hand in his pocket, smiling cheerily, the man behind the door put out his arm and gripped him by the shoulder. In an instant the smile vanished, and the youngster spun round, his face set and hard.

'Here is your darling, John Trelawnay,' said the husband quietly. 'What do you want with her?'

'Ah!' The youngster's breath came a little faster, as he stared at the older man. 'You've come back unexpectedly, have you? It's the sort of damned dirty trick you would play.'

I smiled involuntarily: this was carrying the war into the enemy's camp with a vengeance.

'What are you doing in this house alone with my wife, John Trelawney?' Into the quiet voice had crept a note of menace, and, as I glanced at the speaker and noticed the close clenching and unclenching of his powerful hands, I realized that there was going to be trouble. The old, old story again, but, rightly or wrongly, with every sympathy of mine on the side of the sinners.

'Your wife by a trick only, Rupert Carlingham,' returned the other hotly. 'You know she's never loved you; you know she has always loved me.'

'Nevertheless—my wife. But I ask you again, what are you doing in this house while I am away?'

'Did you expect us to stand outside in the storm?' muttered the other.

For a moment the elder man's eyes blazed, and I thought he was going to strike the youngster. Then, with an effort, he controlled himself, and his voice was ominously quiet as he spoke again.

'You lie, John Trelawney.' His brooding eyes never left the other's face. 'It was no storm that drove you here today; no thunder that made you call my wife your darling. You came because you knew I was away; because you thought—you and your mistress—that I should not return till tomorrow.'

For a while he was silent, while the girl still crouched against the wall staring at him fearfully, and the youngster, realizing the hopelessness of further denial, faced him with folded arms. In silence I watched them from the shadow beyond the fireplace, wondering what I ought to do. There is no place for any outsider in such a situation, much less a complete stranger; and had I consulted my own inclinations I would have left the house there and then and chanced the storm still raging outside. I got as far as putting on my coat again, and making a movement towards the door, when the girl looked at me with such an agony of entreaty in her eyes that I paused. Perhaps it was better that I should stop; perhaps if things got to a head, and the men started fighting, I might be of some use.

And at that moment Rupert Carlingham threw back his head and laughed. It echoed and re-echoed through the room, peal after peal of maniacal laughter, while the girl covered her face with her hands and shrank away, and the youngster, for all his pluck, retreated a few steps. The man was mad, there was no doubt about it: and the laughter of a madman is perhaps the most awful thing a human being may hear.

Quickly I stepped forward; it seemed to me that if I was to do anything at all the time had now come.

'I think, Mr Carlingham,' I said, firmly, 'that a little quiet discussion would be of advantage to everyone.'

He ceased laughing, and stared at me in silence. Then his eyes left my face and fixed themselves again on the youngster. It was useless; he was blind to everything except his own insensate rage. And, before I could realize his intention, he sprang.

'You'd like me to divorce her, wouldn't you?' he snarled, as his hand sought John Trelawnay's throat. 'So that you could marry her. . . . But I'm not going to—no. I know a better thing than divorce.'

The words were choked on his lips by the youngster's fist, which crashed again and again into his face; but the man seemed insensible to pain. They swayed backwards and forwards, while the lightning, growing fainter and fainter in the distance, quivered through the room from time to time, and the two candles supplied the rest of the illumination. Never for an instant did the madman relax his grip on the youngster's throat: never for an instant did the boy cease his sledge-hammer blows on the other's face. But he was tiring, it was obvious; no normal flesh and blood could stand the frenzied strength against him. And, suddenly, it struck me that murder was being done, in front of my eyes.

With a shout, I started forward—somehow they must be separated. And then I stopped motionless again: the girl had slipped past me with her face set and hard. With a strength for which I would not have given her credit she seized both her husband's legs about the knees, and lifted his feet off the ground, so that his only support was the grip of his left hand on the youngster's throat, and the girl's arms about his knees. He threw her backwards and forwards as if she had been a child, but still she clung on, and then, in an instant, it was all over. His free right hand had been forgotten. . . .

I saw the boy sway nearer in his weakness, and the sudden flash of a knife. There was a little choking gurgle, and they all crashed down together, with the youngster underneath. And when the madman rose the boy lay still, with the shaft of the knife sticking out from his coat above his heart.

It was then that Rupert Carlingham laughed again, while his wife, mad with grief, knelt beside the dead boy, pillowing his head on her lap. For what seemed like an eternity I stood watching, unable to move or speak; then the murderer bent down and swung his wife over his shoulder. And, before I realized what he was going to do, he had left the room, and I saw him passing the window outside.

The sight galvanized me into action; there was just a possibility I might avert a double tragedy. With a loud shout I dashed out of the front door, and down the ill-kept drive; but when I got to the open ground he seemed to have covered an incredible distance, considering his burden. I could see him shambling over the turf, up the side of the valley which led to the headland where the rain had caught me; and, as fast as I could, I followed him, shouting as I ran. But it was no use—gain on him I could not. Steadily, with apparent ease, he carried the girl up the hill, taking no more notice of my cries than he had of my presence earlier in the evening. And, with the water squelching from my boots, I ran after him—no longer wasting

41

my breath on shouting, but saving it all in my frenzied endeavour to catch him before it was too late. For once again I knew what was going to happen, even as I had known when I heard the footsteps coming down the stairs.

I was still fifty yards from him when he reached the top of the cliff; and for a while he paused there silhouetted against the angry sky. He seemed to be staring out to sea, and the light from the flaming red sunset, under the black of the storm, shone on his great, gaunt figure, bathing it in a wonderful splendour. The next moment he was gone. . . . I heard him give one loud cry; then he sprang into space with the girl still clasped in his arms.

And when I reached the spot and peered over, only the low booming of the sullen Atlantic three hundred feet below came to my ears. . . . That, and the mocking shrieks of a thousand gulls. Of the madman and his wife there was no sign.

At last I got up and started to walk away mechanically. I felt that somehow I was to blame for the tragedy, that I should have done something, taken a hand in that grim fight. And yet I knew that if I was called upon to witness it again, I should act in the same way. I should feel as powerless to move as I had felt in that ill-omened house, with the candles guttering on the mantelpiece, and the lightning flashing through the dirty window. Even now I seemed to be moving in a dream, and after a while I stopped and made a determined effort to pull myself together.

'You will go back,' I said out loud, 'to that house. And you will make sure that that boy is dead. You are a grown man, and not an hysterical woman. You will go back.'

And as if in answer a seagull screamed discordantly above my head. Not for five thousand pounds would I have gone back to that house alone, and when I argued with myself and said, 'You are a fool, and a coward,' the gull shrieked mockingly again.

'What is there to be afraid of?' I cried. 'A dead body; and you have seen many hundreds.'

It was as I asked the question out loud that I came to a road and sat down beside it. It was little more than a track, but it seemed to speak of other human beings, and I wanted human companionship at the moment—wanted it more than I had ever wanted anything in my life. At any other time I would have resented sharing with strangers the glorious beauty of the moors as they stretched back to a rugged tor a mile or two away, with their wonderful colouring of violet and black, and the scent of the wet earth rising all around. But now. . . .

With a shudder I rose, conscious for the first time that I was feeling chilled. I must get somewhere—talk to someone; and, as if in answer to my thoughts, a car came suddenly in sight, bumping over the track.

There was an elderly man inside, and two girls, and he pulled up at once on seeing me.

'By Jove!' he cried, cheerily, 'you're very wet. Can I give you a lift anywhere?'

'It is very good of you,' I said. 'I want to get to the police as quickly as possible.'

'The police?' He stared at me surprised. 'What's wrong?'

'There's been a most ghastly tragedy,' I said. 'A man has been murdered and the murderer has jumped over that headland, with his wife in his arms. The murderer's name was Rupert Carlingham.'

I was prepared for my announcement startling them; I was not prepared for the exraordinary effect it produced. With a shriek of terror the two girls clung together, and the man's ruddy face went white.

'What name did you say?' he said at length, in a shaking voice.

'Rupert Carlingham,' I answered, curtly. 'And the boy he murdered was called John Trelawnay. Incidentally I want to get a doctor to look at the youngster. It's possible the knife might have just missed his heart.'

'Oh, daddy, drive on, drive on quick!' implored the girls, and I glanced at them in slight surprise. After all a murder is a very terrible thing, but it stuck me they were becoming hysterical over it.

'It was just such an evening,' said the man, slowly: 'just such a storm as we've had this afternoon, that it happened.'

'That what happened?' I cried, a trifle irritably; but he made no answer, and only stared at me curiously.

'Do you know these parts, sir?' he said at length.

'It's the first time I've ever been here,' I answered. 'I'm on a walking tour.'

'Ah, a walking tour! Well, I'm a doctor myself, and unless you get your clothes changed pretty quickly, I predict that your walking tour will come to an abrupt conclusion—even if it's only a temporary one. Now, put on this coat, and we'll get off to a good inn.'

But, anxious as I was to fall in with his suggestion myself, I felt that that was more than I could do.

'It's very good of you, doctor,' I said; 'but, seeing that you are a medical man, I really must ask you to come and look at this youngster first. I'd never forgive myself if by any chance he wasn't dead. As a matter of fact, I've seen death too often not to recognize it, and the boy was stabbed clean through the heart right in front of my eyes—but . . .'

I broke off, as one of the girls leaned forward and whispered to her father. But he only shook his head, and stared at me curiously.

'Did you make no effort to stop the murder?' he asked at length.

It was the question I had been dreading, the question I knew must come sooner or later. But, now that I was actually confronted with it, I had no answer ready. I could only shake my head and stammer out confusedly:

'It seems incredible for a man of my age and experience to confess it, doctor—but I didn't. I couldn't. . . . I was just going to try and separate them, when the girl rushed in . . . and . . .'

'What did she do?' It was one of the daughters who fired the question at me so suddenly that I looked at her in amazement. 'What did Mary do?'

'She got her husband by the knees,' I said, 'and hung on like a bull-dog. But he'd got a grip on the boy's throat and then — suddenly—it was all over. They came crashing down as he stabbed young Trewlanay.' Once again the girls clung together shuddering, and I turned to the doctor. 'I wish you'd come, doctor: it's only just a step. I can show you the house.'

'I know the house, sir, very well,' he answered, gravely. Then he put his arms on the steering-wheel and for a long time sat motionless staring into the gathering dusk, while I fidgeted restlessly, and the girls whispered together. What on earth was the man waiting for? I wondered: after all, it wasn't a very big thing to ask of a doctor. . . . At last he got down from the car and stood beside me on the grass.

'You've never been here before, sir?' he asked again, looking at me fixedly.

'Never,' I answered, a shade brusquely. 'And I'm not altogether bursting with a desire to return.'

'Strange,' he muttered. 'Very, very strange. I will come with you.'

For a moment he spoke to his daughters as if to reassure them; then, together we walked over the springy turf towards the house by the headland. He seemed in no mood for conversation, and my own mind was far too busy with the tragedy for idle talk.

But he asked me one question when we were about fifty yards from the house.

'Rupert Carlingham carried his wife up to the headland, you say?'

'Slung over his shoulder,' I answered, 'and then . . .'

But the doctor had stopped short, and was staring at the house, while, once again, every vestige of colour had left his face.

'My God!' he muttered, 'there's a light in the room. . . . A light, man; don't you see it?'

'I left the candles burning,' I said, impatiently. 'Really, doctor, I suppose murder doesn't often come your way, but . . .'

I walked on quickly and he followed. Really the fuss was getting on my nerves, already distinctly ragged. The front door was open as I had left it, and I paused for a moment in the cobwebby hall. Then, pulling myself together, I stepped into the room where the body lay, to halt and stare open-mouthed at the floor. . . .

The candles still flickered on the mantelpiece; the furniture was as I had left it; but of the body of John Trelawnay there was not a trace. It had vanished utterly and completely.

'I don't understand, doctor,' I muttered foolishly. 'I left the body lying there.'

The doctor stood at the door beside me, and suddenly I realized that his eyes were fixed on me.

'I know,' he said, and his voice was grave and solemn. 'With the head near that chair.'

'Why, how do you know?' I cried, amazed. 'Have you taken the body away?'

But he answered my question by another.

'Do you notice anything strange in this room, sir?' he asked. 'On the floor?'

'Only a lot of dust,' I remarked.

'Precisely,' he said. 'And one would expect footprints in dust. I see yours going to the mantelpiece; I see no others.'

I clutched his arm, as his meaning came to me.

'My God!' I whispered. 'What do you mean?'

'I mean,' he said, 'that Rupert Carlingham murdered John Trelawnay, and then killed himself and his wife, five years ago . . . during just such another storm as we have had this evening.'

Mark Danver's Sin

The letter came to me at breakfast—a bulky one, addressed in an unknown hand. The eagle eye of my hostess's small son had at once spotted the stamp, and an instant demand had gone forth that it should be presented to him in due course. It was a Tonga Island—one of those nice stamps which portray strange birds and animals in beautiful colours—and even as I promised he should have it, I was trying to think who on earth could be writing to me from such an outlandish spot. The letter had been readdressed on to me from my club, and after a while, in deference to young Jack's continued demands for the stamp, I gave up the delightful pastime of guessing and opened it. There were two enclosures inside: one a heavily-sealed envelope addressed to me in a well-known hand, but one that I had not seen for many long years; the other just a covering letter.

It was the envelope I studied first. What could have induced dear old Mark Danver to break the silence of years, and then label his letter 'strictly private'? And what a strange coincidence that it should have reached me in this of all houses!

Then I glanced at the covering letter, and for a moment I felt as if someone had given me a blow in the face. It was from a firm of lawyers, and was brief and to the point.

'Dear Sir,' it ran, 'The enclosed was amongst the effects of the late Mr Mark Danver. We should be glad if you would acknowledge the receipt in due course.'

I laid down the letter by my untouched breakfast, and stared out of the window. Poor old Mark dead—that priceless, cheery soul who had so strangely dropped out of our lives. In Tonga Island of all places. For he had known my host and hostess too, known them before I did. And now, seated at their table, I had got the news of his death.

I don't know why I said nothing at the time; I think perhaps that it was because Mark had been my particular pal, and now from the grave he was speaking to me. And I wanted to hear

47

what the old chap had to say first. So I put his letter unopened in my pocket, and I gave young Jack his stamp. And half an hour later I carried a deck chair into the shade of the chestnut tree and carefully slit the envelope. Inside were several sheets of foolscap covered with Mark's writing, and for a moment my eyes grew a little blurred. Then I began to read.

They tell me, old man, that I haven't very long to go. The doctor here, who diagnoses quite well when he's sober and operates quite well when he's drunk, broke it to me this morning. Incidentally I'd guessed it already, and I can't pretend that I mind very much. But since the end is coming fairly soon, I want to write to you, my oldest pal, and explain why I have cut myself adrift from you all these last few years. And also I want to put on record a confession which will come as a big surprise to you. In case anything should happen in the future you will have it by you, and will know what use to make of it. And apart from that, it's going to be a bit of a comfort to me to put it down on paper, and know that someone I trust will see it. One gets a bit cowardly towards the end—sometimes. Depends, I suppose, on the race you've run. And if there's been a bad foul it gibbers at you and mocks you. Especially at night, when you can't sleep. I've been sleeping damnably just lately.

There will be parts of this confession of mine that you know already; but I'm going to put it down in full in case it should ever be needed. I'll tell it to you, Dick, in the form of a story— my first attempt at literary work. But they say that everyone could write at least one yarn—the yarn of their own life, so perhaps the fact that it is true will atone for lack of style. Anyway—here goes.

It's just eight years ago this month that I was up on a shooting trip in Uganda. And on the way back through British East Africa I went down with a bad dose of fever. Luckily for me, there was a farm close by, and my boys carried me there. That farm belonged to a youngster whom you got to know afterwards—Jack Onslow. And since you know him I won't waste time describing him for you. Just sufficient to say that he was one of the straightest, cleanest boys that I have ever met; a

white man through and through. He was there by himself growing coffee, and he wouldn't hear of my going on until I was
absolutely fit. As a matter of fact I think he was glad of the
companionship; it's lonely work, that sort of life, as you know.

So I stopped on with him after I was fit, and day by day I got
to know him and like him better. And then there came an
evening when I asked him why he didn't get married.

'It's not good, Jack,' I said, 'for a man to live in the wilds
alone.' He turned a bit red, and fumbled in his pocket. Of
course, I guessed at once what he was looking for, but I tried to
look suitably surprised when he handed me a battered leather
case.

'I'm engaged, old man,' he said, a bit awkwardly. 'There's
her photograph. And I'm just trying to get the place into a real
going concern before she comes out to join me.'

I took the case and I opened it, and I tell you, Dick, I was
staggered. It was just a coloured photograph of a girl, and for
sheer flawless beauty I had never seen her equal. She was more
than beautiful—she was lovely, with the sweetest expression in
her eyes. And I just sat there holding the portrait in the circle of
the lamplight, drinking her in.

I hardly heard what Jack was saying, so absorbed was I in that
perfect face. He was rambling on, talking a little disjointedly, a
little shyly. His face was in the shadow, and for a while he
talked of the things that lie deep down in a man—the things
which it is not given often for another man to hear. I don't
suppose he evolved a single original idea, but who wants
original ideas? He just told me in a queer, half-jerky voice of
his hopes and plans; of what life was going to bring him; of what
he was going to do. But always he came back to his girl; it was
'we'—never 'I.'

'She's wonderful, Mark,' he said, and he took the frame out
of my hand. 'She's such a marvellous pal.'

'Well, frankly, Jack,' I answered, 'I felt nervous when I saw
you producing that frame. I have suffered before from lovers'
rhapsodies, and my sole coherent thought was that it's lucky we
don't all think alike. But this girl of yours strikes me as being
the loveliest thing I've ever seen. You're a lucky devil.'

He looked at me quietly.

'Wait till you see her yourself, Mark. She's a thousand times more lovely than this photograph.'

I smiled, and reached for the whisky bottle.

'I'll take your word for it, old man,' I said. 'In the meantime, a final night-cap, and I'm turning in.'

And I remember that night, as I was going to my room, I looked back at the wrong moment. He had his lips pressed to the picture, and I could almost feel the savage intensity of his longing. It is not good for a man to be alone in the Tropics.

I suppose it was a week later that it happened. I was returning from shooting when the native houseboy met me gibbering like a monkey. He was in the last extremity of terror, but I caught enough to make me start running like a hare towards the bungalow. Outside, the other servants were cowering together like frightened sheep, and I dashed past them up the steps and into the living-room. Seated at the table, quite motionless, with a revolver in his hand and an empty bottle of whisky beside him, was Jack Onslow. In the other hand he clutched a letter, and in front of him was a copy of the *Times*.

He paid not the slightest attention to me, though once his eyes, with a dreadful glitter in them, stared at me and through me. Then he began to laugh, hardly and discordantly, and my first thought was that he'd gone mad. Such things have happened before in the back of beyond. Then he stopped laughing, and stared at me again.

'Mark Danver, isn't it?' he croaked. 'Well, sit down, Mr Mark Danver, and don't dare to move, or I'll plug you as full of lead as a mine. Because I've been telling you lies—packs and packs of rotten damned lies—and you've got to hear the truth. I've told you, haven't I, that there was a girl in England of surpassing beauty? I was engaged to her, Danver, that wonderful girl. I was going to marry her, Danver, and she was going to come out here and live with me. I've shown you her photograph, haven't I?' He stared at me, and his head nodded a little. 'Speak, damn you, speak!'

'Yes, Jack, you've shown me her photograph,' I said, quietly.

'Well, if you look behind you on the wall you can see it a second time.'

I looked over my shoulder and saw the frame nailed to the wall. He'd been shooting at it with his revolver, and more than one bullet had gone clean through the picture.

'That's what it's worth, Mr Danver. That's all that rotten girl is worth. I've put five shots through her, and there's one left here for me.' He laughed again discordantly, and began muttering to himself ' "A fool there was, and he made his prayer." '

'You haven't told me yet, Jack, what's happened,' I said, steadily. At all costs I had to calm him sufficiently to get his revolver away from him, and to do that I wanted to get close to him without making him suspicious. Jack Onslow was mad right enough, but only with drink, for he was usually an abstemious boy.

'Haven't I told you?' he snarled. 'What a regrettable oversight! Well, I'll tell you now. This wonderful girl of mine has married another man. It's all quite in order; they've put it in the *Times*, and if you come round here you can see the announcement.'

It was what I was waiting for, and I crossed the room to his side. I didn't look at the *Times*—that could wait; but I caught his right wrist. He wasn't expecting it, and anyway I was a stronger man than he. And the next instant I'd slipped his revolver into my pocket.

He sprang to his feet, and for a moment or two I thought he was going to strike me. And then, quite suddenly, came the change. After all he was but a boy. He just crumpled up in his chair and, putting his arms on the table, he laid his head on them and sobbed like a little child. No—that is not right, for a child's tears are as a passing shower. And Jack Onslow sobbed as a man sobs, and there is no more dreadful sound in all this world. But I knew the danger was over.

After a while he grew silent. Only a deep shuddering breath every now and then told me was conscious: except for that he was motionless in his exhaustion. And my heart bled for the boy.

I had seen the announcement in the *Times*—scored and scored again by Jack with a thick blue pencil:—

Dryden: Carstairs.—On the 5th May, at the old Parish Church, Okehampton, Herbert Dryden to Joan Carstairs, only daughter of Captain Carstairs, late of Royal Navy.

And I marvelled in my mind that such a girl as she had seemed to me from her picture could do such a thing.

At length his breathing grew quieter, and he slept. I didn't touch him or disturb him; it was better to let Nature have her way. Through all the dreary months ahead he'd have to suffer; let him sleep now and forget. So I left him there with the letter still clutched in his hand. And when he woke the African night had come down and the lamps were lit.

He sat up and stared at me dazedly across the table. Memory hadn't come back; he didn't realize what had happened. And then he saw the letter in his hand, and his face went haggard.

'I've been asleep, Mark?' he asked.

'Yes, old chap,' I said, 'you've been asleep. I want you to eat some dinner now.'

He shook his head.

'It was that whisky,' he said, slowly. 'I've been mad. Did I say some terrible things, Mark, about Joan?'

He steadied his voice well—remarkably well—as he said her name.

'Whatever you may have said, Jack,' I said, putting my hand on his shoulder, 'it was only I who heard you. And when a man's lowered a bottle of whisky neat, only a fool pays any attention to what he says.'

He looked at me, and his eyes were tired.

'Dear old Mark,' he said, 'I think you saved my life. It's in here'—he touched his forehead—'like a bad dream—all that happened after you came in. But what I want you to understand, old man, is that it's not her fault. It's not one little bit Joan's fault. It's all in her letter here. You see, this man Dryden had her father in his power. Something about money it was; dear old Carstairs is the biggest fool in the world over money. And he threatened to ruin him and her mother unless she married him.' He shook his fists suddenly in the air, and the sweat glistened on his forehead. 'Great God!' he shouted, 'what a swine that man must be!' Then he pulled himself together again and went on quietly: 'So, you see, she couldn't help it— my little girl. She couldn't see her father and mother made penniless beggars, could she? So she sacrificed herself for them. It's all down here in the letter.'

'Confound it all,' I snapped, 'it seems to me she sacrificed you as well.'

For a moment his shoulder shook and he turned away. Then he steadied himself, and I went out on to the veranda. I wasn't in the mood to hear any more excuses about the girl; to me the big tragedy was the one at hand—that priceless boy. And then I heard his voice again, and looked back into the room.

He was standing by the photograph and I think he'd forgotten my existence for the moment, or else he thought I'd gone into the compound. But as he took it down from the wall he spoke.

'Forgive me, my darling. I couldn't help it. I was mad. But I understand. Joan; I understand now.'

And, damn it, Dick, I couldn't have spoken at that moment if my life had depended on it.

That's the first part of my confession, old man. You will probably say to yourself that up to now there's been nothing to confess. Quite right; but I had to put it down in detail so that you should know the terms I was on with Jack Onslow. He was a pal of mine—almost as great a pal as you yourself, save that he was a younger man. I want to make that clear; I want to emphasize it, for it has a big bearing on what is to come.

I suppose it was a month later that I left Jack. He was still carrying on, but all the spring had gone out of his work. Only once did he allude to the girl, and that was the night before I left.

'What's the use, Mark?' he said, with an odd twisted smile. 'I was doing it for her, and now, what's the use?'

The next day I left him. I was going back to England, and I remember looking back as the road turned for a last view of the farm. Jack was standing on the veranda and he waved his hand once. Then he went inside, and I pictured him sitting at the table staring in front of him with hopeless eyes.

'What's the use, Mark; what's the use?'

His words were echoing in my brain, and as I rode on I made up my mind that when opportunity offered I would seek out Mrs Dryden and I would paint a picture for her which she would not forget in a hurry. I would tell this girl exactly what the salvation of her father had meant to Jack Onslow. And it was three months later that I arrived in Okehampton with the intention of looking for her.

Of course, I had no idea where she was living, but since the wedding had taken place there I thought I should be able to get the information I wanted. And I was right; the first person I asked at one of the hotels told me where they lived. Then he looked at me a bit curiously.

'Do you know him—Herbert Dryden?'

'No,' I said, briefly, 'I don't. What sort of a man is he?'

'You'll see for yourself,' he answered, and I couldn't get any more out of him. But his tone of voice spoke volumes.

And as I ate my lunch I reflected that she deserved all she got; my mind was still sore over Jack.

I'm not going to weary you with a long account of how I got to know Dryden. It was through Brayfield, a major in the Gunners who was in camp there, as a matter of fact. I'd known him in the past, and he asked me up to dine one guest-night. And Dryden was there—a thin lipped, austere looking man of about fifty. His face seemed to be set in a continual sneer, and his eyes were cold and fishy. I remember I asked Brayfield about him, and he shrugged his shoulders.

'He's exactly what he looks like,' he remarked. 'Personally, I think he's one of the most horrible swine I've ever met in my life, and how he ever induced his wife to marry him is one of those things which are beyond human comprehension.'

'What sort of a girl is she?' I asked, carelessly.

'Well, I don't think I'm exaggerating,' he answered, quietly, 'when I say that she is the sweetest and most lovely woman I've ever seen in my life. And,' he finished up savagely, 'he treats her like a dog. By the way, you paint, don't you?'

'I dabble in it,' I said, rather surprised at the question.

'So does he,' answered Brayfield. 'I'll introduce you to him after dinner, and he's sure to ask you up to his house. And then you can see his wife for yourself.'

It fell out as he said. Dryden, it appeared, was inordinately proud of his water-colours, and liked nothing better than to show them to an appreciative audience. And since I wanted to get to the house I exaggerated my ability somewhat.

I went up the next day to lunch. It was a big house, standing in rather a lonely position. The grounds were well kept and extensive, and it was evident that Dryden had money. And a woman who could chuck Jack and marry Dryden for money must be pretty rotten. I'm afraid I didn't pay too much attention to the ruined father stunt; in fact, I had almost forgotten it. All I could think of was Jack sobbing his soul out as the night came down on his farm in Uganda.

And then I saw the girl. You know her, Dick, so I won't bore you with trying to describe her. But all I could realize at the moment when I saw her picking some flowers in the garden was that Brayfield had understated the case. She had on a cotton frock—I can remember it as if it were yesterday—and when she saw me she put down her basket and came towards me.

'How do you do?' she said, holding out her hand. 'My husband will be here in a moment.'

I stood there, Dick, like a callow schoolboy gaping at her, and then, moved by some uncontrollable impulse, I blurted out what was in my mind.

'Why, in Heaven's name, have you smashed Jack Onslow's life?'

For a moment I thought she was going to fall. Every vestige of colour left her face and she swayed dizzily. Then she pulled herself together, and I heard her agonized whisper:—

'Don't mention it before my husband, for God's sake!'

I heard a step behind me on the gravel, and turned round to find Dryden approaching. By day he looked even more unpleasant than at night, and it was with a feeling almost of repugnance that I took his hand.

'I see you have introduced each other,' he remarked, suavely. 'Mr Danver is interested in painting, Joan; and —what should appeal to you more—he has been in Uganda.'

Every word came out like a drop of iced water, and he was watching her as a cat watches a mouse.

She was superb.

'Indeed!' she said. 'How interesting! It must be a most fascinating country.'

She led the way towards the house, and we followed. Every hard thought I'd had about her had vanished—just been blotted out. I knew that it wasn't her fault—that Jack had been right. Knowing her as you do you'll understand my sudden conversion. All I knew and felt for certain was that some damnable tragedy had taken place, and that this fish-eyed brute was at the bottom of it.

I wish I could give you some idea of the devilish way he treated that wonderful, glorious girl. At lunch that day, for instance, he wouldn't keep off the subject of Uganda; asked me if by any chance I knew a man called Jack Onslow; hoped that he was in the best of health and spirits; trusted that he would marry some nice girl soon. And all the time his eyes were fixed on his wife—searching her face to see if his shots had got home. And I, fool that I was, had added to her burden by telling her that she'd smashed Jack's life.

Not by a quiver of an eyelid did she let her husband see that he'd scored. She sat there calm-eyed and disdainful, and I was torn between a desire to cry: 'Well played, you topping girl,' and a positive craving to hit the swine in the face.

She disappeared after lunch, and Dryden bored me with his rotten paintings. I escaped as soon as I could; I felt I couldn't bear the man any longer. And I wanted to see the girl again, and tell her that Jack was all right and that he understood. But there was no sign of her about the garden, and with a sick feeling of impotence I walked out over the moors. I felt I wanted to get away into the open, and try to get the taste of Dryden out of my mouth.

And then quite suddenly and unexpectedly I came on her. She was sitting down in a little hollow, and a terrier was at her feet. She stared at me as I came up, and the hopeless misery in her eyes made me catch my breath.

'So I've smashed his life, have I?' she said at length.

I sat down beside her on the grass.

'He's better now, Mrs Dryden,' I answered, gently. 'But I was with him when the news came—and he took it hard. Tell me—why did you do it?'

And then little by little the whole story came out. She wasn't very clear on the business points involved, but I gathered that it was concerned with a mortgage. Her father had speculated—led on, as she found out later, by Dryden. Then he had mortgaged his house and Dryden had taken it up—only to threaten to foreclose a month or two later. It was utterly impossible to find the money, and Dryden's price for not foreclosing was—her.

She had told him everything—gone down on her knees to him, but it was useless. He had wanted her for years, and her love for Jack Onslow was nothing to him. He wanted her for his wife, and he was going to have her for his wife. Otherwise utter absolute ruin for her mother and father. That was the choice he gave her.

'You heard him at lunch today, Mr Danver,' she said, and her voice was trembling. 'It's always the same. I believe he hates me; hates me because I won't pretend what I can't feel. I know I hate him, and though he forced me to marry him, he can't force me to love him. There will never be anybody in my life but Jack. And if'—the tears were running down her cheeks—'if you see him again, will you tell him so? Tell him that Tim and I come out here and talk about him.' She laid her hand on the dog's head. 'Tim is his dog, you know.'

I bit at my pipe, Dick, and sat there like a tongue-tied fool.

'Don't tell him I'm miserable, because that would make him miserable too. But don't tell him I'm happy, Mr Danver, because I couldn't bear him to think I could be happy tied to Herbert.'

'But look here, Mrs Dryden,' I cried, 'why go on like this? A man who could drive such an abominable bargain as your husband has doesn't deserve the slightest consideration. Write to Jack, and tell him to come home and take you away with him back to Uganda. It would be less wrong than going on as you are.'

She gave a little pitiful smile.

'Three days after we were married,, Herbert informed me that he still held the mortgage, and that should I be foolish enough to contemplate leaving his roof the question of fore-closing would again arise. He also stated that he was un-alterably opposed to divorce.'

And then she fell to asking me about Jack: how he was looking; how the farm was doing; all the little intimate details a woman wants to know about her man. Who looked after his clothes—of all things—God bless her. As if I knew.

And at last, after about an hour, she rose.

'Good-bye, Mr Danver,' she said. 'I think if you don't mind I'd sooner not see you again.'

'I'm going tomorrow,' I answered. 'And if I see Jack I'll tell him.'

She gave a little choking cry and was gone, stumbling over the rough ground, with Tim scampering round her feet. And having watched her out of sight I turned and strode away over the moor. I felt I'd like to hit somebody or something; I felt that life could hold no more wonderful joy than ten minutes alone with Herbert Dryden and a rhinoceros-hide whip. And at that moment, Dick, I saw him.

Sometimes now I think it was Fate's inexorable decree; sometimes now I think it was intended from the beginning of things. And then, at others, I lie sweating in the night and wonder. You know that they brought it in as an accident. You know that he was found with his head crushed in at the bottom of Dead Man's Pool, with his easel and his camp-stool on the edge of the cliff two hundred feet above. You know that at the inquest I gave evidence to the effect that I had seen him stand up with his pencil in his hand as if to take some measurements, and suddenly stumble and disappear into the depths below. And they brought it in as a sudden attack of vertigo.

It was a lie, Dick; I murdered him. I killed Herbert Dryden that evening at Dead Man's Pool, and I leave the verdict in your hands.

He saw me coming towards him and he waved his hand.

'Having a look round for some local colour?' he cried. 'Well, you won't find a better place to start than this. I've done it half-a-dozen times and the light is never the same.'

I stood by his side in silence, watching him work. For an amateur he wasn't at all bad, and had he been anybody else I should have been interested. It was an ideal spot for a sketch, with some wonderful colour effects. Deep down below us lay the sheet of black water—sombre and sunless—with the sinister name earned from tragedies of the past. Once, presumably, an old quarry, now it was disused, and the local people avoided it.

There were stories told about it: one in particular of a hard-riding, hard-living squire of a bygone day, whose horse had bolted with him and gone over the edge. And it was said that the great shout of 'Gone away' which he gave as he realized that he'd come to the last fence, and was falling like a stone into the depths below, could sometimes now be heard echoing faintly over the moors.

The top of the quarry lay in a little depression, so that we were at the bottom of a saucer, so to speak. And for a while I watched him getting in the wonderful yellow of the broom on the opposite side of the pool. He worked in silence, his fishy eyes absorbed in their task, until suddenly he put down his brush and looked at me.

'So you know Jack Onslow,' he said, with an ugly smile. 'Tell me about the young swine.'

It was then that something snapped, Dick; up to that moment I swear I had no thought of what I was going to do. But in my brain I could see only two pictures—Jack sobbing his soul out across the table, and this fish-eyed brute gloating in front of me.

But I didn't do anything rashly; to this day I can remember how ice-cold and clear my mind felt.

'I think it should interest you, Mr Dryden,' I remarked, 'to know that one of the last times I saw Jack Onslow, he was mad drunk on a bottle of whisky. He had a photograph nailed to the wall of his bungalow, and he was firing at it with his revolver. And the photograph was of your wife.'

I took one quick look round: there was no soul in sight. And then I picked up a huge stone lying at my feet. There was just time to see the unholy joy on his face turn to a fearful terror —but no more. I brought the stone down on his head with all my force, and he fell over the edge like a log. I heard the crash as he hit the rock below, and then he toppled into the pool. Finally I threw the stone far out into the water, picked up his camp-stool, which had fallen over, and went straight back and gave the alarm.

The result you know; there was no known motive in my killing him; there was never even any suspicion of it. It was an accident —and as such it has remained to this day.

But now, old Dick, as my own last fence is looming in sight, it haunts me sometimes. Was I justified in doing such a thing? Can anyone ever be justified in doing such a thing? When I can't sleep o' nights, I see those eyes of his staring at me out of the darkness—and they mock me. They seem to say: 'You're coming too, Mark Danver; you, who dared to judge me.'

But it wasn't for myself, Dick, that I did it—that much I can say. It was for Jack and that wonderful girl. And when those eyes of his get very bad there's another picture comes to my mind, and the eyes fade away. I see again Jack's farm, with Jack standing on the veranda. On his face is a look of dawning wonder, as he stares at the girl standing beside him. Just once he passes his hand across his eyes, and I hear him whisper: 'Dear heavens! but I'm dreaming.'

And then she goes to him and her arms are round his neck.

'Not dreaming, my darling—it's truth. It's all come right at last.'

At that I leave it. They must never know, Dick; they must never have an inkling that it was not an accident. But now that I'm going I've written this to you in case anything ever happens. It's not likely to, so long after, but it might. And if it did—you know.

The final punishment will lie in other hands, though it's begun already. These last few years have been hell. That's why I've buried myself and cut adrift from you all. You see, I loved her too, as I never believed I could have loved a woman. That's another thing they must never know.

Goodbye, old chap.

For a while I sat staring across the sunlit garden. On the lawn young Jack was being instructed in the rudiments of cricket by his father, while his mother kept wicket. And even more did I marvel at the strangeness of the coincidence that had brought Mark's letter to me in this of all houses.

At last the game was over, and young Jack departed with his nurse. And as they watched him go I saw Jack Onslow turn to the girl at his side. For a moment he looked at her as a man may look at only one woman and she gave a little happy laugh. Yes—it's all come right at last, dear old Mark—it's all come right.

Out of the Blue

Basil Pender looked thoughtfully round his sitting-room. Everything was just as usual—the prints, the photographs in their silver frames on the piano, the books in the corner: they were all just as they had been for the last five years. Tomorrow night also there would be no change. The same prints, the same books, the same ceaseless rumble of London traffic coming through the open window.

Tomorrow night it was true he would not be there himself. It was unfortunate but unavoidable. He would have liked to have spent the first few hours after he had murdered Sinclair in the surroundings where he had so often murdered him in spirit. But it was impossible.

It was something at any rate to have been able to begin his scheme in this familiar atmosphere. It augured well for success. No undue hurry: nothing precipitate—just the quiet, orderly, working out of a carefully considered plan. And the first move in the game had already been taken.

Such a simple little move—and yet very important. It was in details of that sort where brain came in. Who could possibly attach any significance whatever to the fact that he had removed one of his two cars from the garage where he habitually kept them both, and placed it in another, where he was quite unknown? What had such a simple fact to do with murder?

He smiled gently, as he helped himself to a whisky and soda. He was thinking of the conversation he had been listening to at the club only that very evening. Cresswell, of the police, had been holding forth on crime; and an intolerable bore he was. And yet there had been a certain amount of truth in what he had said.

Undoubtedly the motive in a case of murder is the first thing for which the police look. No one but a madman commits a murder without a motive. Passion, hatred, money—once the motive is established, it generally points with an unerring finger at someone. That was why Pender had left the club arm in arm with Sinclair, and walked with him part of the way to his house in Brook Street. A very normal proceeding on the part of one of Sinclair's best friends.

He'd been devilish clever about it. No one knew, no one had even the ghost of a suspicion of the deadly, black hearted hatred he felt for the man he had just left. The world thought they were friends: even Sinclair himself thought so—damned fool that he was. It would come as a slight shock to him tomorrow when he realized the truth.

But no one else would ever know it. And in case his plan, thought out and perfected in every little detail since he had heard that Sinclair was going down alone to his empty house in Kent—just in case it miscarried, the question of motive would never indicate him with unerring finger. He was safe on that point.

Not that the matter was ever likely to arise in this case. Before people begin talking about motive it must look as if the cause of death was murder. And he had no intention of allowing Sinclair's death to look like murder. It was to be accidental: a shocking, ghastly accident. He pictured himself hurrying back from Scotland when he heard the terrible news: comforting Enid—Sinclair's wife.

Widow, rather—not wife: Sinclair's widow. Just his card to start with: his card and a little message of tender sympathy for her in her great sorrow. Perhaps some flowers. And then after a week or so he would see her for a few minutes, and let her realize how his heart bled for her. Nothing precipitate of course, he was far too old a stager with women for that. But in six months perhaps—or maybe a year—the time would be ripe.

Basil Pender's white teeth bared in a sudden ungovernable snarl. What a waste of time! Six weeks, six minutes were too long to wait. How dared that swine Sinclair come between him and Enid? How dared he make her his wife?

The sweat glistened on his forehead, and he shook his fists in the air. Then with a great effort he controlled himself: this was a frame of mind in which he had forbidden himself to indulge. It destroyed the power of clear thought, and clear thought was essential for success. After all the perpetration of a murder was very much like a game of chess. Move followed move, and provided no mistake was made the result was mate. And there would be no mistake in this case.

Nerve, brain, and money: given those three attributes and the thing was easy. But it was interesting—devilish interesting. The whole thing had a fascination about it which he would hardly have believed possible. Once again his thoughts drifted back to Cresswell: what was it he had been saying? He could see him now with a fat cigar between his lips, lying back in his chair and emphasizing his points with a podgy finger.

'It's those unexpected, unlooked for, unallowed for, isolated facts against which no criminal can guard, however skilfully he lays his plans. He may think that he has allowed for everything —taken into account every possible contingency, then suddenly—out of the blue—comes one disconnected event, and the whole carefully thought out scheme goes wrong.'

Well, of course, there was something in that. But the same might be said of anything in life: not only crime. And in this case he had reduced the risk of anything unexpected happening to a minimum. There was nothing difficult about his scheme; in fact, it was extraordinarily simple. It amused him now to recall the complicated plans he had evolved in the past for killing Sinclair. For years he had hated him: from the days they were at school together he had hated him. And then, to cap everything, he had married Enid. It was that which had definitely suggested murder to his mind.

At first he had hardly treated the matter seriously. Idly he had thought out different schemes—schemes of all sorts and descriptions which had, however, one common factor. Each one of them ended in the same way—with Sinclair's death. And gradually the matter had insisted upon being taken seriously. He found himself thinking of it at all hours of the day. If he woke in the night the picture of Sinclair with Enid by his side would come to him out of the darkness.

But it is one thing to think of murder: to do it is altogether different. Murderers who get caught suffer an unpleasant fate, and Pender had no intention whatever of being hanged. And since in all his schemes the risk of his suffering that fate had been pronounced, they had remained just schemes. And then suddenly three days ago had come the idea. He had been dining with the Sinclairs, and the conversation had turned on White Lodge, their house in Kent. It had been in the hands of the builders; new bathrooms put in, fresh papers, all sorts of improvements. And now it was empty; the workmen had gone; the keys had been returned to Sinclair.

'A darned good job they have made of it, too,' his host had said. 'I've got to go down there on Thursday to get a gun of mine which I forgot to bring up with me. Why don't you come down with me Basil? I know Enid can't: she's got some show on that day. We could take down some sandwiches, and feed in the hall; and we'll test the new broadcasting set.'

It had been some power outside his own that had made him answer as he did. At that moment the devilish idea had not come to him; he was only conscious of a strong desire to make some excuse to avoid spending a day alone with Sinclair. If Enid had been going it would have been different.

'Thanks very much,' he had remarked, 'but I shall probably be starting for Scotland on Thursday.'

No more had been said: he usually did go to Scotland about that time: there was nothing strange or unusual in the fact. But when he returned to his rooms the idea had been born. He had not been going to Scotland on Thursday, but he had said so — said so in front of Enid. And Sinclair was going to White Lodge on Thursday—an empty house. He knew White Lodge well, he had stayed there in the past. It was a desolate sort of place, half a mile from the road and surrounded by trees. Enid had wanted her husband to sell it, but it had a sentimental attraction for him, and he had compromised by having it completely done up. And suddenly there had recurred to his mind a remark he had heard her make when she first saw the house.

'It looks the sort of place where anything might happen — murder or ghosts.'

Murder! Strange that she should have said that. Almost prophetic. Murder! For a moment or two he had recoiled from the thought: this was different to the fantastic schemes he had so often planned out in the past. This was the real thing: he knew that with a sort of blinding certainty even before he began to think out details. Well—what if it was? Step by step he had worked it out—discarding here, building up there. And after a while he became almost staggered with the simplicity of the thing. Surely murder must be a more complicated matter than this?

Coolly and logically he had examined every move, and could find no fault. And now once more on Wednesday night he strove to discover a flaw. It was not too late yet: he had done nothing incriminating so far. He had merely removed one of his two cars to a strange garage, and mentioned at the club that he was off to Scotland next morning. It was perfectly easy to return the car to its usual home and change his mind about Scotland.

And the other two things—the tiny phial filled with a colourless liquid, and the four short straps now reposing in the locked drawer of his desk. There was nothing suspicious about them. No question of poison—nothing so crude as that. Poison lingers in the system, and chemists ask questions if you ask them for poison. But a strong sleeping draught is quite a normal affair; and straps of all sorts and conditions are useful for motoring.

No, there was no flaw. And with a smile of satisfaction Pender turned out the light in his sitting-room and went to bed.

It was to his permanent garage that he repaired in the morning, and five minutes later he drove away in his touring Sunbeam. He left it in Waterloo Place, and getting into a taxi he gave the address of the second garage.

'Just starting for Scotland,' he informed the manager, and having settled his bill he drove round to his rooms for luggage. It was early yet for much traffic, and half an hour saw him not far from his destination—Hitchin. And in Hitchin, strange and peculiar magneto trouble occured—due doubtless to the use of a screwdriver in skilful hands on that delicate piece of mechanism. So pronounced was the trouble, however, that it became necessary to invoke the assistance of a local garage. And with becoming gravity Pender listened to the diagnosis.

'I see,' he said, when the mechanic had finished. 'Possibly some hours, you say. Then I think that I will go out and call on friends and return later. I might even stay the night with them. That will give you plenty of time to make a good job of it.'

With which remark he left the garage, and made his way to the station where he took a first class return ticket to London. The excellent train service was one of the reasons which had made him decide on Hitchin. It was not too close into London, but the journey did not take long. And it was essential that he should be at the White House before lunch time.

He ran over the car time table as he sat in his corner seat. He would take the Sunbeam from Waterloo Place, and motor down to White Lodge in it. He knew the exact spot where he would leave it—not too near the house, not too far away. A deserted spot where the chances of the car being seen were remote. And even if it was seen who would pay any attention?

Then after it was over he would return to London, and leave it in St. James's Square. Not Waterloo Place again; the man in charge there might recognize him. And then back to Hitchin by train. It would depend on the time whether he telephoned to his usual garage from there, or from some place farther north.

'Completely forgot the Sunbeam; send a man round to St James's Square for it.'

That would be the message; further proof that he was on his way to Scotland. But he couldn't have done it if both cars had been at the same place. It looks silly to get one car to start with and then go back a few minutes later to get the other.

Brain—that was it; that was the whole secret. Just like chess, only a thousand times more fascinating.

It was just half-past eleven as he drove past the Oval. He had an hour's run before him, and it struck him that he could not have timed it better. Sinclair was dining at Ranelagh that evening, so he wouldn't be remaining too late at White

Lodge. And any way the sooner the thing was done the better. It would enable him to get farther on the Great North Road before calling up his garage.

He left the car in the place he had decided on. Not a soul was in sight; for the last two miles he had seen no one. The house was a hundred yards away almost hidden in the trees, and he strolled towards it quite openly.

There was a possibility that Enid might have altered her mind at the last moment, or that Sinclair had brought someone else down with him. If so, he was not committed to anything; therein lay the beauty—the simplicity of the scheme. He had merely changed his mind about Scotland, and having nothing better to do had run down to see the improvements at White Lodge as Sinclair had suggested.

At the front door stood Sinclair's car, and as Pender stepped on to the drive Sinclair himself appeared.

'Hullo! old man,' he cried. 'I thought you were on the road to Scotland.'

'Changed my mind at the last moment,' said Pender easily, 'so I thought I'd come down and see the house.'

'But where's your car?'

'I stupidly missed the turn out of the village, and got on to the track leading through the copse. It's up there now.'

'Well, it's quite safe there anyway. Let's have some lunch, and then I'll show you around.'

'All alone?' asked Pender.

'Yes, Enid couldn't come.'

He was rummaging in the car for sandwiches, and Pender turned away quickly. So it was the end after all, and at the moment he did not want Sinclair to see his face.

'Come on in. There is enough grub here for a regiment, and I'll search round and get another glass.'

He led the way to the gun-room, leaving his flask on the table. Then he went out, and Pender heard him wandering round the back premises. Now that the actual time had come he felt as cool as ice: it was all so simple and easy. From his pocket he took the little phial, and taking out the stopper he emptied the contents into the flask. Then slipping the empty phial back in his pocket he strolled over to the window.

'This is about the only room in the house they haven't touched,' said Sinclair, as he came in with a glass a few moments later. 'I left everything as it was in here—guns and all. Say when.'

'I won't have any whisky, thanks. Just a little of that Perrier.'

'Well, I've got a thirst on me like the devil,' said the other, mixing himself a drink. 'Get on with the sandwiches.'

Sinclair drained his glass with a sigh of relief, and proceeded to mix himself another.

'They really have made a very good job of it. The extra bathrooms make the whole difference.'

'Excellent,' said Pender. 'I shall look forward to having a go at your pheasants later on.'

His eyes, narrowed and expectant, had seen the sudden half-drunken lurch given by Sinclair.

'Good Lord, Pender,' he cried, 'I feel damned funny.'

'Take another drink. It may be the heat or something.'

'I feel absolutely blotto. It can't be anything—anything —matter—whisky.'

He looked stupidly across the table, and then his eyes closed and his head fell forward. With a gigantic effort he rose to his feet, only to fall back in his chair again. Sinclair slept.

With a faint smile Pender got up: the thing was done. There were one or two small points now to be attended to, but the main thing was done, and more successfully and easily than he had ever dared to hope.

First he took from his pocket a pair of washleather gloves, and picking up his glass he dried it carefully with a clean pocket handkerchief. Then leaving the room he returned it to its proper place in the pantry. Next he took up the flask, and Sinclair's tumbler, and emptied the contents of both down the sink, afterwards replacing them on the table beside the unconscious man. To give the impression that the flask had been emptied would make the accident seem more credible. Just a little too much to drink: just enough to make Sinclair a trifle careless. . . .

Then from his pocket he removed four straps, and still retaining his gloves he fastened Sinclair's hands and feet to the arms and legs of the chair in which he was sprawling. He wasn't quite sure how long it would be before Sinclair recovered from the effect of the sleeping draught, and the binding process must be done before that happened.

And now remained only the final thing. From the glass-fronted cupboard in the corner he took a double-barrelled gun, and into one of the barrels he slipped a cartridge. Sinclair still slept.

For a moment or two Pender hesitated. It would be so easy to do it now. And it would be safer. Everything had gone so wonderfully that it seemed like tempting Fate to delay. There sat the man he hated, unconscious, and at his mercy. He had only to press the trigger and the thing would be done. But where would be the satisfaction in that? He wanted Sinclair to understand—to realize what was going to happen to him. He wanted revenge, and to kill an unconscious man was no revenge. He wanted to see terror dawn on those keen blue eyes: above all, he wanted to speak about Enid.

Half an hour passed and Sinclair still lolled forward in his chair, while Pender sat opposite him—waiting. And then suddenly the sleeper awoke and stared dazedly across the table.

'Where am I?' he muttered, foolishly.'What's happened?'

'You are at White Lodge, Sinclair,' said Pender quietly. 'And I gave you a little drug to send you to sleep which seems to have acted admirably.'

'But why am I bound like this?' He was struggling against the fog in his brain.

'Because, before I kill you, I want to have a talk with you, Sinclair. And I adopted that method to ensure your keeping still.'

Sinclair blinked foolishly. Kill! What the devil was Pender talking about? Kill! Was he mad? Were they both mad?

'Doubtless you feel a little surprised, Sinclair. You wonder if you are still dreaming. But I can assure you that you are not: you are very much awake.'

'Is this some damned silly jest, Pender?' His mind was clearing rapidly. 'If so, it's gone far enough. And what the devil is that gun doing on the table?'

'We will come to the gun in due course, my friend.' Pender leaned across the table, and his teeth showed in a sudden snarl. 'You swine; I can hardly believe that I've got you at last.'

Sinclair said nothing; full realization of his position had come to him. Of course the man had gone off his head; he was alone—bound and powerless—with a homicidal maniac.

'Please don't think that I'm mad, Sinclair,' continued Pender, as if divining his thoughts. 'I can assure you that I've never been saner in my life. This is merely the logical outcome of the intense hatred I've felt for you for years. It started at school, Sinclair. Do you remember on one occasion thrashing me till I was almost unconscious?'

'Because you came for me with a knife,' answered the other quietly.

'I don't care why—but the fact remains that you thrashed me. That started it, Sinclair; I swore then that some day I'd get my own back.'

'In spite of the fact that you shook hands the next day,' said Sinclair scornfully. 'You rotten Dago.'

'So you always called me—all you fellows.' Pender's voice shook with ungovernable rage. 'Do you suppose I could help having South American blood in me? Anyway the rotten Dago has got the upper hand now.'

He controlled himself and went on quietly.

'As I say, that started it, Sinclair. And all through school it was the same. It was Sinclair, Captain of the Eleven; Sinclair, Captain of the Fifteen; Sinclair, Senior Prefect. And it was Sinclair who in his kindly benevolence accorded his divine protection to the rotten Dago. Do you think I liked you for it, you swine? I loathed you all the more. There's no good straining at those straps. They're new and strong.'

'You entrancing exhibition of beastliness,' roared Sinclair. 'Do you mean to tell me that after all these years—after having dined at my house, and eaten my salt—you propose to kill me, because I did better than you at school?'

'Good Heavens, no! I was merely starting at the beginning. I don't deny that frequently I have felt like murdering you. At country houses sometimes when it's been Sinclair who was shooting so wonderfully—and Sinclair who played polo so marvellously — and Sinclair this, and Sinclair that—I could have killed you willingly. But I don't think I should ever have done it but for one thing—Enid.'

Sinclair sat very still; he understood at last. And though no sign of it showed on his face, fear was clutching at his heart. No maniac this, but a dangerous, revengeful man.

'Did you know I asked her to marry me, Sinclair? Of course you do. And she refused. But she might have accepted me in time if you hadn't come on the scene. Always you; always you. She is the only woman in the world, Sinclair, whom I have ever wished to make my wife. And she is yours.'

'So that is why you propose to murder me,' said Sinclair. 'A nice method of disposing of a husband, but as a means of endearing yourself to the widow—a trifle crude.'

He was talking for time—trying desperately to think.

'And do you really imagine, Sinclair, that I shall let Enid discover the truth? You must have a very poor opinion of my intelligence. Your death will be entirely accidental, and when I hear about it in Scotland I shall hurry back to attend the—er—obsequies. I am on my way to Scotland now, you know.'

'You fool,' said Sinclair, harshly. 'They'll catch you for a certainty, and you'll hang.'

'I think not,' answered Pender. 'I have devoted what brains I possess to this problem, and I venture to think—not unsuccessfully. You've no idea how fascinating it is—planning a murder. I won't weary you with the precautions I have taken to cover my tracks, but you can see for yourself two or three little things I have done in this room. My glass removed, for instance; a second glass would certainly give rise to comment. Your flask emptied, serving the double purpose of removing all traces of the drug and giving the impression that you had drunk a little too much. It will help to account for the accident that is shortly going to happen, Sinclair. A strange accident for such a careful shot as you—but these things will happen.'

Sinclair moistened his lips.

'Cut fooling, Pender. This thing has gone far enough.'

'I can promise you it is going considerably farther,' sneered the other. 'Right through to the end, in fact. That gun is loaded, and in a moment or two now I shall put the muzzle under your chin and blow your damned face off. An accident in cleaning will be the verdict, Sinclair, and I'll attend your funeral even as I attended your wedding. And then in time maybe Enid will do what she would have done if you hadn't come on the scene — marry me.'

'You devil.' The veins stood out like whipcord on Sinclair's forehead as he strained and tugged at the straps. And then of a sudden he sat very still: Pender had picked up the gun in his gloved hand. The end was very near, and with his head thrown back and a look of utter contempt in his eyes he waited for it.

'The straps will be off when they find you, Sinclair: the gun on the floor at your feet. No unexpected, unlooked for event out of the blue, such as that fool Cresswell talked about, to save you: nothing to incriminate me.'

The hatred in his eyes was maniacal: the cool scorn on the other's face seemed to drive him to a frenzy.

'You can sneer,' screamed Pender, 'but you won't when the muzzle is an inch from your chin and my finger is on the trigger. This is the position, Sinclair—just as I am now, only it will be your chin, not mine.'

He sat there, the gun between his knees, his chin almost resting on the muzzle.

'Just like this,' he repeated softly.

'Hullo!'

It came from the hall—a man's cheerful hail, and Pender gave a violent start.

'Hullo! Hullo!'

Then a pause.

'2 LO calling.'

But there was no one to listen to the prominent politician's speech on the Near East which continued cheerfully for the next half-hour.

For Sinclair—well, Sinclair had fainted for the first time in his life

And Pender—well, Pender had had his finger—that carefully gloved finger—near the trigger when he gave that violent start. And his chin had been almost resting on the muzzle.

In fact, it was only by his clothes that a few hours later he was officially identified as Pender.

A Hopeless Case

Through the open window came the ceaseless noise of the tree beetles. Occasionally it would be drowned by the coughing grunt of a lion in the distance, or the shrill scream of some animal near by—a scream that showed that death was, as ever, abroad in the land outside. But these were only interludes: life to the man who sat at the table seemed to consist of that eternal, damnable noise.

He was not a very pleasant sight—the sole occupant of the room. His chin required the attentions of a razor; his shirt, which was opened at the neck, could have done with a wash. His riding breeches were threadbare; his boots caked in mud. And yet for anyone with eyes to see one fact would have struck home. Those breeches and boots bore the unmistakable stamp of the West End.

The room was in confusion. Dust lay thick in the corners; a few odd letters littered the table. The lamp had smoked, and half the funnel was black with soot. Against one wall a cupboard minus its doors leaned drunkenly—a cupboard in which unwashed plates and an old teapot without a handle were jumbled together. And, ranged in rows along the opposite wall, empty bottles.

A full one stood on the table by his side, and after a while he picked it up and half filled his glass with whisky. Then he resumed his study of the book that lay in front of him. A strange book to find in such surroundings, and yet one which helped to explain the riddle of the riding breeches. It was a book of snapshots and odd cuttings from newspapers. A few groups cut from *The Tatler* and *The Sketch* were pasted in, and it was at one of these that he was staring.

Bridesmaids; bride and bridegroom; best man—particularly the best man. He was in the uniform of the 10th Lancers and for a long while the man sat there motionless, studying the face on the paper. Good-looking, with clear-cut features; a magnificent specimen of manhood, showing off the gorgeous uniform of the regiment to perfection. Then very deliberately he got up and crossed the room to the broken bit of mirror that served as a shaving glass. Dispassionately he studied his own face, not sparing himself in the examination. And at length he turned away.

'Great God!' he said, very slowly. 'How did it happen?'

And the line of bottles gave answer.

He went back to the table, and started turning over the pages of the book. The regiment on parade; a stately home set in wonderful trees; groups on the moors with keepers and dogs; groups with the women he had known. . . . And at last a simple snapshot of two people—himself and a girl. Pat and self—thus ran the inscription underneath it, and for perhaps a quarter of an hour he sat there motionless, staring at it. Some big insect fussed angrily against the mosquito netting, trying to get at the light; ceaselessly the beetles droned on—but the man at the table heard nothing. He was back in the might-have-been; back at Henley—three years before the war.

Pat! What was she doing now? She'd stuck to him loyally; stuck to him as only a woman can stick to the thing she loves. For it had started even then. The curse was on him: the soul-rotting, hellish curse that had brought him to this. But at last it had had to end: the thing had become impossible.

He had fought. God, how he'd fought! But it had beaten him. No excuse, of course: to be beaten is no excuse for a man. And he could still hear Pat's voice that last time—could still see her sweet face with the tears pouring down it.

'Jim—if you can beat it—come back to me.'

And that was after he had had to send in his papers.

He hadn't beaten it; it had beaten him. And now Pat was married: two children—or was it three? And he—what was he? His family said he was farming in Africa. A pleasant fiction which deceived no one. Least of all himself. He was not farming in Africa; he was a drunken remittance man living on a farm in Africa.

He closed the book, and stared with haggard eyes into the darkness. Why had this girl come to stop at Merrick's farm, and opened all these old wounds? Why had he seen her that afternoon?

She'd reminded him of Pat a little. Cool and dressed in white—riding Merrick's chestnut cob in a way that showed she was used to horses. What the devil did she want to bring all that back to him for? Girls and horses were all part of the life he'd lived a hundred years ago.

'Yes, a trooper of the forces, who has owned his own six horses. . . .'

And he wasn't even that. Just a drunken down and outer, with a father in the House of Lords who paid him five hundred a year on condition that he never set foot in England again.

Cool and dressed in white! Lord! but it was something to see a girl of his own class again. She'd stared at him in faint surprise when he'd spoken; drink doesn't kill a man's accent. And by now she'd know all about him: the Merricks would see to that.

They didn't know who he was; he'd given his name out here as Brown. But they did know *what* he was, and that was all that mattered.

'A drunkard, my dear; a hopeless case.'

He could hear Mrs Merrick saying it. Not that she was a bad sort; quite the reverse, in fact. But she was the wife of a settler who had made good, and she loathed weakness. At first she had tried to pull him round—to make him take an interest in his property. For months she had persevered, and it wasn't until she found out that he wouldn't help himself that she gave up trying. Contemptuously.

And he deserved it: he was under no delusions. But now——He stood up suddenly, and instinctively his shoulders squared. Supposing he took a pull at himself; it wasn't too late. Supposing he, too, made good. Supposing that girl dressed in white——

And suddenly he laughed a little bitterly. Girls dressed in white were outside his scheme of things altogether. Quite deliberately he reached out for the bottle, and tipped what was left into his glass. Then he performed his nightly rite. With meticulous attention to dressing he placed it in line with the others; called the squadron to attention, and then dismissed them.

76

And ten minutes later the man who called himself Jim Brown, having kicked off his boots, lay sleeping heavily on his bed.

He'd shaved when he next saw the girl, and his shirt was clean. She was riding, as before, and he stood waiting for her to come up.

'Good morning,' she said, cheerily. 'What a heavenly day!'

'The one compensation of this God forsaken country,' he remarked 'is that the days generally are heavenly.'

She looked at him steadily.

'Why do you stay if you don't like it?'

'Entirely my duty towards my neighbour,' he answered. 'Think of all the grief and sorrow I should cause if I departed?'

'Is that your bungalow up there?' she said suddenly.

'It is,' he remarked. 'And dilapidated though it looks from the outside, I can assure you the interior is much worse.'

'That's good,' she cried. 'And as I can hardly believe it possible, I'm coming up to see.'

For a moment he hesitated.

'It really isn't in a fit condition——' he began.

'Bunkum,' she answered. 'Do you suppose I've never seen an untidy room before?'

'It isn't altogether that,' he said, slowly.

Then he gave a short laugh.

'Right-ho!' he cried. 'Your sins be upon your own head.'

He led the way in silence, and having tethered her horse flung open the door.

'Behold the ancestral hall,' he announced gravely.

Her eyes travelled round the room, resting for a while on the array of bottles, while he watched her with a faint smile. What was she going to say?

'Get out,' she remarked. 'This is going to be no place for a man for the next hour or two.'

It was so completely unexpected that for a moment or two he could only stare at her.

'Go on—get out,' she repeated, peeling off her gloves. 'You'll only be in the way.'

'You topper,' he said under his breath. 'You absolute topper.'

Then he swung on his heel and left her, not knowing if she'd heard what he'd said—and not caring.

Two hours later he returned to find her sitting on the table smoking a cigarette. And the first thing he noticed was that the empty bottles had disappeared.

'I see you've removed my squadron,' he said. 'It was nearly full strength except for the officers.'

'You mean those dirty old bottles,' she remarked. 'I've buried them outside.'

'Didn't you admire their perfect dressing on parade?' he asked. 'I used to call them to attention every time a new recruit joined.'

She stared at him through the smoke of her cigarette.

'I've been looking at this scrapbook of yours,' she said, calmly. 'I hope you don't mind.'

'Not at all. I fear my library is somewhat deficient. But I need hardly perhaps say that Brown still remains a very good name.'

He glanced round the room: everything was spotless. The shelves of the cupboard were adorned with paper; the plates were washed and neatly stacked; even the teapot seemed to have taken on a new dignity.

'You seem to have been most thorough,' he said gravely. 'Thank you.'

'So you won the Grand Military, did you?' she remarked.

'I believe that in some former existence of mine I had that honour. Incidentally speaking,' he continued, 'I trust that you haven't buried the quick and the dead together.'

'There are a dozen full bottles in there,' she said, pointing to his bedroom. 'I thought they would be more convenient for you if you woke in the night.'

He stood motionless, staring at her. Her face was expressionless: her eyes met his calmly and frankly.

'I deserve that,' he said in a low voice.

'My dear man,' she remarked, 'I don't think you *deserve* anything at all. It's the wrong word. It's not for me to judge. All I say is that it's a pity that being who you are you should be what you are. It seems such a ghastly waste.'

'Some such idea occurred to me when I took the name Brown,' he answered, thoughtfully.

She shook herself a little impatiently.

'How you can have that book here—be reminded day in, day out, of everything that might be yours—and not go mad, absolutely beats me.'

'Sometimes it beats me, too,' he said quietly.

'Good God, man!' she cried, 'can't you try?'

'Good God, girl!' he answered, 'do you suppose I haven't?'

And for a space they were silent, staring at one another. At last she slipped from the table and went up to him.

'Sorry,' she said gently, 'I shouldn't have said that. Look here—can I help? Julia Merrick told me she had done her best—but Julia is married and busy. I'm neither. Shall we have a dip at it together? No slop and slush about it. If you want a drink, have one. I shan't look at you reprovingly. But if we pull together we might be able to keep whisky as a drink—not as a permanent diet.'

He turned suddenly and walked over to the open window. And she being a girl of much understanding lit another cigarette and waited. In her eyes was a look of wonderful pity, but she didn't want him to see it. Something told her that she had started on the right note; that any trace of sentimentality would be fatal. For perhaps five minutes he stood there with his back to her, and only the pawing of the pony on the ground outside broke the silence. Then he swung round.

'Damned sporting offer,' he said, curtly. 'Afraid you'll find it a bit boring, though.'

'I'll chance it,' she said. 'Come over and dine tonight.'

And so the man who called himself Brown began to fight again. For hours he would sit in his bungalow sweating with the agony of it, and with every nerve in his body screaming for the stuff. And sometimes the girl would sit opposite him, holding his two hands across the table and watching him with cool, steady eyes.

His face was haggard; his hands shook uncontrollably when she released them. But he fought on with every gun and rifle he possessed, and the girl fought at his side.

It happened unexpectedly as such things will—in his bungalow one evening. For three hours the girl had been with him, and that particular crisis had passed. They were sitting side by side on the stoep, watching the sun go down behind the distant Drakensburg, and without thought she put her hand on his knee.

'Jim,' she whispered. 'How utterly marvellous!'

And his hand closed over hers in the way there is no mistaking. She turned slowly and stared at him, and then caught her breath at the look in his eyes. She knew instantly what was coming: knew there was no way of stopping it. He was down on his knees beside her, his arms flung round her waist, his face buried in her lap. And for a space he went mad.

Hardly hearing—almost numbed with the suddenness of this new complication—she sat listening to the wild dreams of the man who called himself Brown. He was cured—with her help he had fought and won.

'For God's sake, don't leave me, Beryl!' he said again and again. 'Listen, dear—we'll get married. And now that I'm all right, we'll go back to England under my proper name. I'll get a job—I've got influence. And when they know I'm cured there won't be any difficulty.'

He raised his face, and with blinding clearness she saw him for what he was. Before he had just been a case—a mission: now he was very much a man. A man grown old before his time, with the ineffaceable ravages of drink plain to see: a man with bloodshot, puffy eyes and trembling limbs: a travesty.

And yet, ghastly in its mercilessness though the picture was, in some strange way she seemed to see another one. Shining through this terrible mask she saw the man as he had been— clear-eyed, firm-lipped, with the pride of youth in every line of his body. And a pity that was almost divine took hold of her. She leaned forward and put her hand on his hair—and it was the hair of the man who had been that she touched. She kissed him on the forehead, and it was the forehead of the man in uniform —the man who had won the Grand Military—that she kissed.

And then he, with a little gasp of wonder, seized her hungrily and kissed her on the mouth. And Beryl Kingswood sat rigid: the dream had gone—reality had come back. The man who had kissed her lips was the man who called himself Jim Brown—the drunkard.

He was mad—incoherent with joy. He couldn't believe it: he went on pacing up and down the veranda, painting wild dreams of the future. And every now and then he would stop and kiss the back of her neck—and touch her arm almost humbly.

'Stop and have dinner with me, dear,' he said, 'on this wonderful night of nights. I'll take you back afterwards.'

And because she was incapable of clear thought—because she was dazed by the result of what she had done in that one instant—she stayed to dinner. What was she going to do? How was she ever going to tell him? And gradually as the hours passed the thing began to get clearer. Dinner was over—a meal at which he had proudly drunk orange juice and water. And now, sitting once again on the stoep in the darkness, her hand in his, it didn't seem so very terrible. She would go through with it: she would marry him, and bring him back to what he had been. She had put her hand to the plough—she would not turn back.

'We'll make good, my dear,' she whispered, impulsively. 'We'll make good between us.'

Very tenderly and reverently he bent and kissed her hand.

'You utterly marvellous girl,' he said.

And for a space there was silence, broken only by the ceaseless noise of the tree beetles.

Thus did the man who called himself Brown struggle to the foothills from which a glimpse of Heaven may be got. And Fate ordained that he should remain there for just one week—a week during which only one person mattered, the wonderful girl who had promised to marry him. He got a tablecloth from the neighbouring store, and carefully mended the broken teapot handle with seccotine, so as to be able to give her tea when she came over to see him. He laid in stocks of grub, and got bowls in which he arranged flowers for her benefit. And, perhaps greatest wonder of all, the twelve full bottles under his bed remained full.

Of the other side of the case he knew nothing—how should he? He had not been in the Merricks bedroom on the night they had learned what had happened—the night he had walked over with

81

Beryl after she had dined with him. He had not seen Julia Merrick positively seize her husband as he came in, and almost shake him in her excitement.

'Tom—it's too horrible!'

'It's pretty grim, I admit,' he remarked. 'Still, I don't see what's to be done about it. She seems to have made up her mind.'

'It isn't as if she loved him even.'

'What's that?' said her husband. 'Doesn't she love him?'

'Of course she doesn't. How could she?'

'I dunno. Women do some damned funny things at times. Has she told you she doesn't?'

'Don't be an absolute idiot,' cried Julia Merrick. 'Do you suppose another woman wants to be told a thing like that? You've only got to see them together. Why, he—he almost repels her.'

Tom Merrick yawned hugely.

'Well, my dear—it's beyond me. If he repels her, why the deuce has she gone and got engaged to him?'

'Because she's sorry for him. Because she thinks it her job. Because she thinks she's cured him. Because—oh, a thousand reasons—and not one of them the right one! And from what I know of Beryl, she'll carry the thing through.'

Her husband turned over sleepily.

'We'd better talk it over, my dear. In the morning,' he added, hopefully.

'There's nothing to talk over,' said his wife. 'The thing's unnatural. It's—it's ghastly. Are you asleep?'

'More or less, my dear.'

'Well, become a little less for a moment. Do you honestly and conscientiously believe that that man is cured?'

'Difficult to say,' he grunted. 'Personally, I wouldn't trust him a yard. Think he's a hopeless case. Still, you never can tell.'

'Tom, if Beryl were your daughter—would you allow it?'

'Good God, no!' he cried. 'What an idea!'

'All right,' said his wife, quietly. 'You can go to sleep now.'

And lay awake herself staring into the darkness. Dimly she feared during the past few weeks that some such complication might occur, but never had she dreamed that Beryl would go to the length of promising to marry the man. That he might fall in love with her she had realized was more than likely: many men did fall in love with Beryl Kingswood. But that she would accept him seemed so staggeringly outrageous that she could still hardly believe it.

What to do? That was the problem.

And as the days passed by it became more acute. She was almost frightened of mentioning the matter to Beryl, because it seemed to make her shut up like an oyster. Obviously she didn't want to discuss it; just as obviously her nerves were strung up to the danger point. And Julia Merrick could have screamed with the futility of it.

Her husband was no help.

'What can I do, my dear?' he said, continually. 'They're both of age. If Beryl chooses to marry the man I don't see how we can prevent her. She's her own mistress. She knows the danger she is running as well as we do. He certainly seems to have kept off the drink these last few weeks.'

'Couldn't you have a talk with him as man to man?' she urged. 'Say to him that it isn't fair to marry her until he is *sure*. That he ought to give it a year at least.'

'I'll have a try,' he said, doubtfully. 'But I tell you frankly, Julia, that fellow Brown is a queer customer to tackle. He's got a way of looking at you which says "Go to the devil" plainer than any language. Drunkard though he is, I give you my word that there are times when he makes me feel like a boy in front of a master.'

'He's coming over tonight,' said his wife. 'Get him alone and try.'

But it wasn't necessary; as I have said, Fate ordained that Jim Brown should stay on the foothills for just one week. And that night the week was up. Why he should have approached the Merricks' bungalow from behind instead of going to the front door is just one of those things that happen without reason. But he did—and found himself looking into the room that Julia Merrick called the work-room. Beryl was sitting at the table, and her name was trembling on the tip of his tongue when she looked up and he saw her face. And it seemed as if the world stood still.

He stood there rooted to the spot, staring at hopeless, abject misery and despair. Just for one moment he clutched at the wild hope that she had had bad news. But only for a moment; it wasn't mail day. There could be only one cause —and he knew it. Standing motionless in the darkness he watched this girl who meant salvation to him—watched her as some stranger might have watched her—impersonally. He felt conscious of only one dominant thought—to find out the truth.

Suddenly the door opened and Julia Merrick came in. He saw her pause for a moment, staring at Beryl; then he heard her speak with a sudden rush.

'My dear, now I know. You *can't* do this thing.'

And heard the other answer.

'I *must!*'

He crept nearer the window; he had to hear everything now.

'Why did you do it, Beryl?'

He listened to the girl's puzzled—almost halting— explanation. And because the man who called himself Jim Brown had been a person of much understanding before he became a drunkard, he understood perfectly that which only exasperated Julia Merrick.

'He must be told,' said that lady, decisively. 'If you don't—I shall.'

'If you do, Julia,' said the girl, 'I will never forgive you. I absolutely forbid you to tell him.'

She stood up, facing the older woman squarely.

'Absolutely, you understand. I'm going through with it. I would never forgive myself if I started him off again.'

'I wish to Heaven he'd have another outburst now—before it's too late,' said the other. 'Beryl—the risk is too ghastly. I know he's kept off it for a week or two—but he's a hopeless case. Tom says so. At least, my dear—say that you'll wait a year. Make him prove himself to that extent.'

The girl shook her head.

'No, dear, I won't. I believe I can pull him through if I'm with him the whole time. And I can't be that unless I marry him. My mind is made up, Julia,' she went on, quietly. 'I shall marry him whatever you say. And he's got to go on believing that I'm fond of him, or half my influence will be gone.'

Julia Merrick shrugged her shoulders helplessly.

'So be it, Beryl. It's your choice. But I think you're making a terrible mistake.'

'Perhaps I am,' said the girl. 'But a mistake is better than a sin. And it would be a sin to turn him down now, when he has fought so hard. Let's go, Julia; he ought to be here soon.'

The light went out; the room was empty. She would be in the drawing-room by now—sitting in the chair she usually occupied. He had only to go round to the front door and walk in, and he would see her get up with that grave little smile of hers and hold out both her hands. And she would say:—

'How goes it, old lad?'

And he would answer: 'Quite well, my dear—quite well.'

And she would say: 'Well played, partner.'

Yes—just go round to the front door and walk in. Wipe these last few minutes off the slate—pretend they had never been. A grave smile flickered round his lips—half cynical, half tender. Then, lifting his hand to the salute, the man who called himself Brown turned and walked away into the night.

'I'll come with you, Beryl,' said Tom. Over the girl's shoulder he glanced significantly at his wife. It was ten o'clock, and dinner was long since over—the dinner to which Jim Brown had been bidden and failed to appear.

'All right,' said Beryl, quietly. 'Just as you like.'

In silence they set out on their twenty-minute walk. The glorious African moon made it almost as light as day, and it wasn't until they came in sight of Jim Brown's bungalow that Tom Merrick spoke again.

'My dear,' he said, gravely, 'for God's sake don't be too disappointed if—if——'

'Please don't,' she said. 'I'd sooner not talk.'

It was as they were walking up the rise to his house that they suddenly heard his voice.

'Parade! 'Shun!'

And the girl stopped dead with a little gasp.

'Let me go first,' said Tom Merrick.

'No,' said Beryl, firmly. 'You wait outside.'

She crossed the veranda and pushed open the door. In perfect dressing on the floor stood eleven empty bottles, and on the table in front of him one that was half full. And in front of the eleven was the teapot.

'That gentlemen,' he said, gravely indicating the latter, 'is the commanding officer. Don't you think he's rather a good-looker?'

'Jim,' she said, steadily, 'we were expecting you to dinner.'

'The devil you were, my dear,' he answered. 'That's a bit of a break on my part.'

'What are those doing there?' She pointed to the row of bottles.

'My soldiers, darling,' he explained. 'I took them out for an airing tonight. To spare your feelings, up to date I've kept them in barracks under the bed, but the little chaps insisted on a field day tonight.'

'You mean to say that you've been drinking all this time?'

Her voice was unutterably weary.

'Honesty, my pet, compels me to admit the fact. It was my innate politeness which made me disguise the fact in view of your well-meant efforts on my behalf. Ah! my friend, Mr Merrick, I see. One of those honest pillars of the soil that have made our glorious Empire what it is.'

'So you've lied to me,' she whispered. 'All this while. Oh, my God!'

And just for one brief moment did the man who had tipped eleven full bottles of whisky down the sink that night falter. Then he steadied himself and rode at the last fence.

'My dear,' he said, gravely, 'lie is an ugly word. Shall we say—prevaricated charmingly?'

'A hopeless case, my dear,' said Tom Merrick, as they neared his bungalow. 'He'd gone too far.'

A Hopeless Case

And the hopeless case sat at his table staring with hopeless eyes into the night. The bottle in front of him was empty. At last he rose, and with meticulous attention to dressing he placed it in line with the others. He called the squadron to attention and then dismissed them.

And for a space there was silence, broken only by the ceaseless noise of the tree beetles.

The Man with his Hand in his Pocket

'I'll take one card.'

With the expressionless face of the born gambler, the man glanced at his draw, and laid the five cards face downwards on the table in front of him. Not a muscle twitched as he leaned back in his chair, his right hand thrust deep in his trouser-pocket. So he had played all through the evening, losing with steady persistence and losing highly: losing, in fact as only a man can lose who is holding good cards at poker when somebody else is holding a little better. And now he had drawn one card to three of a kind, and it had come off. There were four eights in the hand in front of him, and they had made their appearance just in time. For Billy Merton knew only too well that the chips by his side represented everything that was left out of a matter of twenty thousand pounds. The play was high at the Ultima Thule Club in Bond Street.

A fat man opposite him had also taken one card, and Merton's keen eye noticed the twitching of his fingers as he laid his cards down. A bad gambler, but having a run of the most infernal luck, this fat fellow. So much the better: he'd probably got a straight at least—possibly a full house. Fours could be ruled out: the fat man was the type who would always discard two if he held three of a kind.

They were playing without a limit, and at length Billy Merton leaned across the table.

'My chips are finished, I'm afraid,' he remarked, with a faint drawl. 'Will you take paper till the end of the hand?'

'Certainly,' said the fat man, in a voice which shook a little.

'Good!' With his left hand Merton scrawled an IOU, quite regardless of the spectators who had collected at the rumour of big play which flies round with such mysterious rapidity. He might have been playing halfpenny nap for all the interest he apparently took in the game.

The fat man saw him at five thousand pounds—which was just four thousand more than Billy Merton possessed in the world. And the fat man laid down a straight flush.

'You're lucky, sir,' said Merton, with a genial smile, lighting a cigarette with a perfectly steady hand. 'I'll just cash a cheque and get you the chips.'

A faint murmer of admiration passed round the onlookers: this clean-shaven, steady-eyed man with the whimsical smile was a gambler after their own hearts. Then in a couple of minutes he was forgotten: players at the Ultima Thule are, in the main, a selfish brand of individual. Possibly had they suspected the utter hopelessness seething behind the impassive face of the man who stood by the buffet eating a caviare sandwich and drinking a glass of champagne, they might not have forgotten him so quickly. But they did not suspect: Billy Merton saw to that. It was only as he turned to help himself to another sandwich that a look of despair came into his eyes. No one could see: the mask could slip for a moment. Ahead lay ruin and disgrace. The cheque could not be met next morning: there was no human possibility of raising the money in the time. And to the descendant of a long race of gamblers there was something peculiarly abhorrent in failing over a debt of honour.

'Bad luck—that last hand of yours, sir.' A thick set, middle-aged man beside him was making a careful study of the various edibles. 'Just came up in time to see the showdown.'

'I have known the cards run better,' answered Merton, curtly.

'I can see that you're a born gambler,' continued the man, 'and being one myself—though not in this particular line—one has, if one may say so, a sort of fellow feeling.' He was munching a sandwich and staring round the room as he spoke. 'The nerve, sir—the nerve required to stake everything on the turn of a card—on the rise or fall of a market—by Heaven, it's the only thing in life!'

Almost against his will—for he was in no mood for talking —Billy Merton smiled.

'Your game is the Stock Exchange, is it?'

'It is, sir—and there's no game like it in the world. Even when ruin stares you in the face, you've still got till next settling day. You've still got a chance.'

'I wish the same thing applied here,' said Merton, with a hard laugh.

'As bad as that, is it?' remarked the other, sympathetically. 'Never mind: the luck will change. I guess there have been times when I've felt like stealing or forging or doing any other blamed thing under the sun to put my hand on some ready money.'

Merton smiled mirthlessly, and said nothing. The point of view coincided rather too unpleasantly with his own.

'And mark you, sir,' continued the stranger, dogmatically. 'I've got a greater respect for a man who wins through, by fair means if possible—but, if not, by foul—than for the weakling who goes down and out. The first, at any rate, is a *man*.'

Again Merton smiled. 'Leaving out the ethical side of your contention, sir,' he remarked, 'there are one or two small practical difficulties that occur to one's mind. It is sometimes as difficult to find the foul means as it is to find the fair. Burglary and forging rank high amongst the arts, I believe, which are not taught at most of the public schools.'

The other man shrugged his shoulders contemptuously. 'Of course you mustn't take me too literally. But'—he thumped an enormous fist into the open palm of his other hand—'there's always a way, sir, if you've got the nerve to take it. Nerve: that's the only thing that counts in this world. Without it—why, you can go and grow tomatoes in the country! Nerve, and the capability of seizing the right moment. With those two assets you come to the top and you stay there.' For a moment or two he stared fixedly at the half-averted face of the younger man; then he gave a jovial laugh.

'Anyway—if you start to recoup your fortunes with journalism—you needn't give those as the opinions of Paul Harker. Not that they aren't pretty widely known, but in this world one must pretend.'

Merton glanced at the speaker. So this was the celebrated Paul Harker, was it? What the devil was it he'd overheard at the club that afternoon about him? Not knowing him, at the time it had made no impression; now he recalled it hazily. Something to do with a woman. He frowned slightly as he tried to remember; then he gave a short laugh. What on earth did it matter? What did anything matter except that cursed cheque?

'Well I'll say goodnight, Mr Harker.' He put down his empty glass. 'It would take a mighty big journalistic scoop to put me straight—bigger even than your ideas on life.'

'Which way are you going?'

'Half Moon Street. I've got rooms there.'

'I'll stroll with you. The atmosphere of this place is fierce.'

In silence the two men got their coats and strolled into Bond Street. The theatres were just over, and a stream of cars were pouring westward with their loads of well-dressed, wealthy occupants. Life—life in London—for people with money! With a cynical smile Billy Merton lit a cigarette. It was what he had promised himself after years in the wilds.

He barely heard his companion's occasional remarks: it was just as they turned into Half Moon Street that it struck Billy that Paul Harker had made some suggestion and was waiting for an answer.

'I beg your pardon, Mr Harker,' he said, apologetically, 'but I'm afraid my mind was wandering. You were saying——'

'I was suggesting that if you've got nothing better to do you should come to my house in Curzon Street. My wife has a spiritualistic séance on. Starts at midnight. Come in and see the fun.'

For a moment Billy hesitated. After all, why not? Anything was better than a solitary contemplation of his own confounded foolishness.

'It's very good of you——' he began, but the other cut him short.

'Not at all. Only too pleased you can manage it.'

'But your wife—— I mean, I'm a complete stranger.' He paused doubtfully by the door of his rooms.

'My wife won't mind,' answered Paul Harker, taking him by the arm. 'Do you good, my dear fellow. Take your mind off.'

It was really deuced good of this fellow Harker. Sympathy of a gambler for a gambler sort of idea. He could only hope that Mrs Harker would see eye to eye with her husband.

'Here is the house, Mr Merton. Come in.' With a smile of welcome Paul Harker stood aside to let the younger man pass.

'I didn't know you knew my name, Mr Harker,' said Billy Merton, as a footman relieved him of his coat.

'I asked who you were at the Ultima Thule. Come on up and meet my wife.' Then, in a hoarse undertone just before they reached the room, he turned to Merton. 'I don't know whether you believe in this stuff; but, for Heaven's sake, pretend to.'

He gave a heavy wink, and Billy smiled. Undoubtedly Paul Harker was quite a pleasant fellow.

There were six women in the room when they entered and one anæmic-looking man.

'Hope I'm not late, my dear,' said Paul Harker, breezily, to a pale, delicate-looking woman who rose to meet them. 'I've brought a friend who is interested in these things. Mr Merton —my wife.'

Billy Merton bowed, and took a chair beside her.

'We hope for some very interesting results tonight, Mr Merton,' she remarked. 'Professor Granger feels confident of getting a tangible materialization.'

'Indeed!'

Mindful of his host's injunction, he nodded portentously. His ideas on what a tangible materialization was were of the vaguest: if it was anything like Professor Granger, he inwardly trusted the experiment would fail.

For a few minutes they continued to talk generalities: then Mrs Harker rose and crossed to the Professor, leaving Merton to his own devices. With some interest he glanced round the room. Heavy black curtains hung over the windows and the door. The furniture was reduced to a minimum, the whole of the centre of the floor being empty. Around the walls were ranged easy chairs draped in some dark material: the carpet, thick and luxurious, was dark also. In fact, the whole room was sombre—sombre and silent.

Curiously he glanced at his companions. In one corner four of the women were talking in low, restrained tones, evidently impressed with the solemnity of the occasion, and involuntarily Merton smiled. They seemed so very earnest—and so very dull. Then he looked at the other woman who was standing by Paul Harker. She seemed of a different type—very far from being dull. Tall and perfectly proportioned, she was dressed in black,

The Man with his Hand in his Pocket

and as his eyes rested idly on the pair it struck him that his host found her far from dull also. And at that moment they both turned and looked at him.

It was the first time he had seen the woman's face, and he found himself staring foolishly at her. She was one of the most beautiful things he had ever seen—beautiful in a sensuous Eastern fashion—and Billy Merton suddenly realized that he was gaping at her like a callow schoolboy. Abruptly he looked away, annoyed with himself at his gaucherie, to find that he was not the only person interested in the lady. For his hostess, though ostensibly speaking to the Professor, was watching her husband's companion with a look on her face which left no doubt as to her feelings on the subject.

'So that's how the land lies, is it?' thought Merton; and the remark he had overheard at the club came back to him. He knew there had been a woman in it.

'Iris, I want you to meet Mr Merton.' His host's voice made him look up quickly. 'Let me introduce you to Miss Sala.'

Merton rose and bowed: on the instant the remark had returned to his memory.

'There will be a crash soon,' a man had said 'with Harker and that Sala girl.'

And now he was talking to the Sala girl, and deciding that if she was beautiful at a distance she was ten times more beautiful close to.

'No,' he found himself saying, 'I've not done much of this sort of thing in England, though I've seen a good deal of what the African native calls *ju-ju*.'

'And it interests you?' Her voice was deep and very sweet.

'Very much,' said Merton. 'I'm most curious to see what is going to happen tonight.'

For one moment the smile seemed to ripple over the surface of her eyes: then once more they were inscrutable.

'It's rather exciting if it comes off,' she remarked, thoughtfully. 'Everything is pitch-dark, of course, and then you hear sighs and groans, and sometimes a hand comes out and touches you.'

'But do you really believe——' began Merton, incredulously.

93

'I don't believe—I know,' said the girl, calmly. 'Why, at one séance I attended a jade necklace I was wearing was wrenched off my neck. The fastening was broken, and all the beads rolled about the floor. And everyone had been bound in their chairs, Mr Merton, before we started.'

Billy nodded discreetly; it occurred to him that he had heard stories like that before.

'You hear something moving round the room,' she continued, 'something you know was not there at the beginning —and won't be there at the end. And sometimes it bumps against you, and then it goes on floundering and moving about the room. It sounds like a sack of potatoes being dragged about at times, and then it changes and you hear soft footfalls.'

Again Billy nodded: he was prepared to listen indefinitely to this sort of stuff when the speaker was Iris Sala.

'It sounds more than rather exciting,' he said, with a grin. 'Let's hope we get the jolly old flounderer tonight.'

For the moment his own trouble was forgotten: he was only conscious of a pleasurable sense of excitement. Not that he really believed in what the girl had said, any more than the average normal person believes in a haunted house. But even the most pronounced sceptic is conscious of a little thrill when he turns out the light in the bedroom which is popularly reputed to be the family ghost's special hunting-ground.

'I think it's very foolish of Mrs Harker to wear those lovely pearls of hers.' The girl was speaking again, and Merton glanced at his hostess. He had not remarked them specially before, but now he noticed that Mrs Harker had three long ropes of large beautifully matched pearls round her neck. 'My jade beads didn't matter very much—though I lost half a dozen at least. But those pearls—why, she might mislay a dozen if the rope was broken, and be none the wiser.'

A jovial chuckle made Merton look up. Paul Harker was standing behind them, and he had evidently heard the girl's remark.

'I'm a Philistine, Iris. Forgive me. I don't somehow anticipate much danger to Rose's pearls.'

'You're wrong, Mr Harker,' she said, gravely. 'You've never seen a tangible materialization. I have—and I know.'

'Anyway,' he laughed, 'there's no use attempting to ask her to take them off, because she won't. And incidentally it looks to me as if the worthy Professor is going to get busy. There's a wild look in his eye.'

'Will you take your seats, please, ladies and gentlemen? The two gentlemen on opposite sides of the room. I thank you.' In a mournful way he contemplated the circle from the centre of the floor. 'I would point out to all of you.' he continued, 'that our experiment tonight is a difficult one, entailing the highest form of will—co-operation and mental effort. If we are successful, I can tell no more than you what form this materialization will take. But I must entreat of you to concentrate with all your power on the one main salient fact of producing a tangible thing: and I must beg you most earnestly not, under any circumstances, to speak while the experiment is in progress. We will now put out the lights.'

And the last thing Billy Merton was conscious of before the lights went out were Iris Sala's grey-green eyes fixed on him with an inscrutable baffling look in them. Even in the darkness he seemed to see them: languorous, mocking, a little cynical. And there was something else—some other emotion which eluded him for the moment. It wasn't sorrow, though it seemed akin to sorrow; it was—yes, it was pity. He moved slightly in his chair, and nodded his head in the darkness. Pity—that was the other message in those wonderful eyes: and the thought brought him back to the reality of his own position.

Paul Harker must have told her, of course: told her that he'd been losing heavily, and she was sorry for him. Even to a millionaire like Harker five thousand pounds on a single hand of poker would seem fairly heavy; and to him—— He gave a mirthless little laugh, which called forth an instant rebuke from the Professor.

'Perfect silence, please.'

Billy Merton lay back in his chair and closed his eyes. His brain was racing with the feverish activity of a worried man. If it had been anything else—anything but a gambling debt. Thank

God his father was dead, and would never know the disgrace of it; but there were quite a number of relations. They'd soon find out; things of that sort can't be kept dark. What a fool, what a damnable fool he'd been!

And it was at that moment that there came a soft bump on the floor, and he heard the woman in the next chair to him draw in her breath sharply.

For a while he stared rigidly into the darkness; then, with a slight frown, he let his body relax. He was in no mood for entertainments of this type: he wished now that he hadn't come. And yet it had been very decent of Harker suggesting it—very decent. Was there a possibility, he wondered—if he made a clean breast of the whole thing to his host—was there a possibility of his lending four thousand? It seemed the only hope, the bare chance of salvation. He'd ask him after this cursed seance was over. The worst that could happen would be refusal. And supposing he didn't refuse? Supposing—— Billy drew in a deep breath at the mere thought.

Thump! thump! Perfectly clear and audible the sounds came from the centre of the room, bringing him back to the present, and he felt the back of his scalp begin to tingle. Of course, it was a trick; and yet he didn't somehow associate the Professor with a vulgar fraud. He had struck him as a well-meaning, conscientious man, who was badly in need of exercise and an outdoor life. Probably dyspeptic.

And if so—if it wasn't a trick—what was it that was now dragging itself about?

'Like a sack of potatoes.' Iris Sala's words came back to him as he sat there motionless.

Suddenly he heard the professor's voice, trembling a little with excitement:

'Who are you? Speak!'

The noise ceased at once; only a long-drawn shuddering sigh came out of the darkness. Then after a minute or two the uncanny dragging noise commenced again: bump—slither —bump. He tried to locate it, but it seemed everywhere. At one moment it was close by, at another it sounded as if it was at the other side of the room.

It was devilish, it was horrible. He put a hand to his forehead; it was wet with sweat. He felt an insane desire to get up from his chair and rush from the room: the only trouble was that he had forgotten the exact location of the door. Besides, he might bump into the Thing on the way.

A frightened cry rang out, and Billy Merton half-rose in his chair. It was a woman's cry: probably the Thing had touched her. The bumping had ceased, he noticed: another noise had taken it's place—a slight gurgling sound, accompanied by a quick beating on the floor, as if someone was drumming with their feet on the carpet. And after a while that ceased also. Silence, absolute and complete, reigned in the room for ten minutes or a quarter of an hour. The Thing had gone.

At length the Professor spoke.

'Are you still there?' There was no sound in answer. 'Manifest yourself now if you are; otherwise the light will be turned up.'

Still there was no sound, though the Professor waited a full minute before speaking again.

'Will you, please, turn up the light, Mr Harker?'

'Certainly.' Paul Harker's cheerful voice came from the other side of the room, as he rose to comply with the request. For a moment or two he fumbled with the switch; then the room was once more flooded with light.

'A most satisfactory manifestation,' began the Professor, only to stop with a look of dawning horror on his face. Scattered around Mrs Harker's chair were scores of wonderful pearls. Sprawling over the arm of the chair was the unfortunate woman herself.

For a moment there was a stunned silence in the room; then with a cry Paul Harker sprang forward.

'She's fainted. I'll get brandy.'

He dashed from the room, as two of the women, reassured by the words, went over to Mrs Harker.

'I knew it was risky wearing those pearls,' whispered Iris Sala in Billy's ear, but he hardly heard what she said. He was staring at the limp form of his hostess through narrowed lids, and suddenly he turned to the girl beside him.

'It's a doctor that's wanted, not brandy,' he said, abruptly. 'Where's the telephone?'

'In the hall,' answered the girl.

He ran downstairs, passing Paul Harker on the way. For what seemed an eternity he stood by the instrument before he could get through. Then he returned to the room above.

'A doctor's coming at once,' he announced breathlessly, and then he stopped dead—just inside the door.

Huddled together in a group at the end of the room were all the women—all save Iris Sala. She was standing by Mrs Harker's chair, with Paul Harker on the other side.

'There is no need for a doctor, Mr Merton,' said Harker, in a terrible voice. 'My wife is dead. And my wife has been murdered!'

'Murdered!' gasped Billy, mechanically.

'Murdered,' repeated Harker. 'Come and see.'

Dazedly Billy walked towards him, to stop and stare foolishly at the woman in the chair. For they had propped her up and laid her head back, and on her throat distinct and clear were the marks of a hand. The four fingers on one side, the thumb on the other, showed up red and angry in the bright light.

'She had a weak heart, Mr Merton,' continued Paul Harker, slowly. 'Any sudden shock, such as a hand grasping her throat'—his voice shook a little—'would have been liable to kill her. And a hand *did* grasp her throat: the hand that tore off her pearls.'

'My god!' muttered Billy. 'It's ghastly—ghastly! Then that thing we heard must have—must have——'

'Must have murdered my wife, Mr Merton. The question is—what was it we heard? I fear we shall find it difficult to persuade the police on the matter of tangible materialization. They deal in more mundane causes.'

And at that moment Billy Merton understood. The relentless voice of the man, the strange look in the grey-green eyes of the girl— it seemed to be triumph now—cleared away the fog from his brain, leaving it ice-cold. He was a man who suddenly sees a flaring notice DANGER, and realizes that there is peril ahead, though he knows not its exact form. And with men of the Merton stamp it is best to be careful at such moments.

'I see,' he answered, slowly. 'You mean that, regarded from the police point of view, the supposition will be that one of the people who were present during the séance tore the pearls from your wife's neck, and in doing so murdered her.'

'Regarded from every point of view,' corrected Paul Harker, harshly.

'Then under those circumstances,' said Merton, grimly, 'the police must be sent for at once.'

With his hands in his pockets he was staring at Paul Harker, while from the other end of the room came an occasional sob from some overwrought woman.

The whole thing was like some horrible nightmare—bizarre, unreal—and the sudden arrival of the doctor came as a relief to everyone. Quickly he made his examination. Then he stood up.

'How did that happen?' he asked, gravely, staring at the marks on the dead woman's throat.

'That man did it!' roared Harker, unable to contain himself longer and pointing an accusing finger at Merton. 'You vile scoundrel! you blackguard! you—you——'

'Steady, Mr Harker!' cried the doctor, sharply. 'Am I to understand, sir, that you did this?' He turned in amazement to Merton.

'You are not,' said Billy, evenly. 'It's a damnable lie.'

'I don't understand,' remarked the doctor. 'Will somebody kindly explain?'

It was Iris Sala who answered, and as she spoke the feeling that he was dreaming grew stronger in Billy Merton.

'We were having a séance, Doctor,' she began, in her deep rich voice, 'trying to get a tangible materialization. The room, of course, was in pitch-darkness, and after it was over and the lights were turned up we found that Mrs Harker was—dead!'

Her voice faltered, and Harker lifted a grief-stricken face from beside his wife's chair.

'But what happened during the séance?' asked the doctor.

'We heard something moving about. A thing that bumped and slithered over the carpet.'

'Pshaw!' snapped the doctor. 'What I don't understand is why this gentleman should be accused of it.'

'Because,' cried Harker, getting up, 'he's in desperate want of money. Look at this!' He fumbled in his pocket, and to Billy's amazement produced the cheque for four thousand he had written at the Ultima Thule. 'I took this cheque tonight in exchange for one of my own—because I liked the look of you. Yes—you wicked villain—I liked the look of you; and I meant to do something for you. I brought him here, never dreaming—never thinking——' His voice broke again. 'He saw my wife's pearls; was actually talking about them just before the séance started—and then when the light went out he must have snatched them off her neck. And in doing so you killed her. And to think I actually heard you doing the vile deed!'

'You deny this?' asked the doctor.

'Absolutely,' returned Billy, grimly.

'I feel that it is partly my fault,' said the girl, in a broken voice. 'I never dreamed, of course, that this man was in want of money. And I told him a foolish story about how some jade beads I once had were snatched from my neck during a séance like this—by the thing that came. But I told it just to frighten him. And I suppose he believed it, and thought he would do the same.' She buried her face in her hands.

'Well, are any of the pearls missing? If so, where are they?' The doctor's question brought Paul Harker to his feet.

'I don't even know how many my dear wife had!' he cried.

'The point seems immaterial,' said Billy, quietly. 'Since I seem to be the object of suspicion, I should be obliged if you would search me, Doctor.'

With a shrug of his shoulders the doctor complied. Methodically he ran through every pocket; then he turned to Paul Harker.

'There are no pearls on this gentleman,' he said, curtly.

'Ah, but he left the room. He left the room to telephone for you. He might have put them in his overcoat.'

'Then we'll send for the overcoat,' remarked the doctor, ringing the bell. 'With your permission, that is, sir.' He turned to Merton.

'By all means,' said Billy. 'Only I would like to state, should they be found there, that I am not the only person who has left the room since the tragedy. Mr Harker has also been downstairs.'

Paul Harker laughed wildly.

'Yes, I know. To get brandy. Before I knew——'

He paused as a footman opened the door.

'Bring this gentleman's overcoat,' ordered the doctor, 'up to this room. And be careful to see that nothing falls out of the pockets.'

With one horrified glance at the motionless figure in the chair, the footman fled, returning almost immediately with the coat.

'This is your coat?' asked the doctor.

'It is,' said Billy.

And then in a tense silence the doctor extracted twenty large pearls from different pockets.

'You murderer!' Paul Harker's voice whispered words seemed to ring through the room, and with a little strangled gasp a woman fainted. The doctor's face, grim and accusing, was turned on Billy, as if demanding some explanation which he knew full well could not be given. And of all those present only Billy Merton himself seemed cool and calm, as, with his hands still in his pockets, he faced the ring of his accusers.

'What have you to say?' said the doctor, sternly.

'One thing—and one thing only,' answered Billy. 'I have read in fiction of diabolical plots: tonight I have met one in real life. But, as so often happens in fiction, one mistake is made, which leads to the undoing of the villain. And one mistake has been made tonight.'

And now his eyes, merciless and stern, were fixed on Paul Harker, and he noticed with a certain grim amusement that a muscle in the millionaire's face was beginning to twitch.

'Mr Harker is a man of nerve: he also believes in seizing the right moment. And tonight struck him as being the right moment.'

'What are you talking about?' snarled Harker.

'For reasons best known to yourself, Mr Harker'—he glanced from him to Iris Sala, from whose eyes the strange look of triumph had mysteriously vanished, leaving only fear—deadly, gripping fear—'you wished to get rid of your wife.'

'It's a lie!' Paul Harker sprang forward, his fist raised to strike.

'You will doubtless have ample opportunity for proving it,' continued Billy, imperturbably. 'By a happy combination of circumstances, a suitable moment—the darkness of a séance — and a suitable motive—robbery—presented themselves to your hand. Acting according to your tradition, you took them. And as far as I can see, Mr Harker, you would have been successful had you also selected a suitable person. Therein lay your one error.'

'Am I to understand,' said Harker, in a grating voice, 'that you are accusing *me*—of murdering my wife? Why—you miserable cur——' He stopped, choking with anger.

'I make no such accusation,' answered Billy. 'All I state is that I didn't.' He turned gravely to the doctor. 'What was the cause of Mrs Harker's death?'

'Heart failure—caused by partial strangulation with the hand.'

'Which hand?'

The doctor looked at him quickly; then glanced once more at the dead woman.

'The right hand.'

'You swear to that?'

'Undoubtedly I swear to it,' said the doctor.

For the first time Billy Merton withdrew his right hand from his pocket, and held it out in front of him.

'The one mistake,' he said, grimly.

The first, second, and third fingers were missing!

For a moment there was a deathly silence; then the doctor suddenly sprang forward.

'Stop him!' he roared.

But Paul Harker had already joined the woman he had foully killed, and in the air there hung the faint smell of burnt almonds. Prussic acid is quick.

The Man with his Hand in his Pocket

An hour later Billy Merton walked slowly along the deserted street towards his rooms. The police had come and gone; everything in the room where the tragedy had taken place had duly passed before the searching eye of officialdom. Everything, that is, save one exhibit, and that reposed in Billy's pocket. And when a man has signed a cheque for four thousand pounds on a total bank balance of as many pence, his pocket is the best place for it.

The Other Side of the Wall

'This afternoon,' remarked the celebrated doctor, 'I have had one of the most salutary lessons of my life.'

He carefully cut the end of his cigar, and his keen, sensitive face seemed unduly serious.

'You've all of you at one time or another,' he went on, 'felt with regard to something you've just done—"That is very good. I, personally, have done it very well. I am a big man, or, at any rate, a distinctly bigger man than my neighbour." Of course, wild horses wouldn't drag such an admission from any of us. Should an acquaintance mention the fact of our bigness we wave a deprecating hand. But we also regard that acquaintance as a distinctly observant fellow, whose own good points we have scarcely done justice to up to date. And we strut a little, and puff out our mental chests, while the gods above laugh. They always laugh—we're so damned comical—but very often we don't hear the laughter. This afternoon, I did.

'It was two years ago almost to the day that a card was brought to me in my consulting room. The name was unfamiliar; the man had not got an appointment, and it was after my usual hours. And for a few moments I debated as to whether I would see him or not. I was a bit tired—I'd had a ticklish operation that morning—and I was leaving London next day on a month's holiday.

'I suppose my indecision was obvious as I turned the card over in my fingers, for my secretary suddenly spoke:

'"I told him, Sir John," she said, apologetically, "that I didn't think you would see him, and that you were going away tomorrow, but he seemed so terribly distressed that I hadn't the heart to refuse to bring you his card."

'"Show him in," I said, and the next moment I was shaking hands with Mr Robert Tremlin.

'He was a man of about forty—clean-shaven, and dark. He was turning a bit grey over the temples, but his whole bearing and appearance proclaimed him an out-of-doors man.

"'It's very good of you to see me, Sir John," he said, as he sat down on the other side of my desk; "but I really am in the most desperate trouble, and I feel I can't go on much longer. It's about my wife."

"'I don't know if you saw in the papers a fortnight ago the account of a terrible motor accident in Devonshire. At any rate, there was one, and the car in question was mine. It contained my wife, and Gerald Weymouth—a very dear friend of us both. He, poor chap, was driving when it happened, and there was no one else in the car. He was taking her over to play tennis with some friends of ours who live about ten miles away, and there is one extremely bad hill to go down. What happened no one will ever know. Gerald was an extremely good driver; moreover, he had often driven the car before. Presumably the brakes failed to act, and the car got out of control on this hill. There's a turn half-way down with a couple of big trees beside the road, and into these two trees the car crashed. Gerald was killed instantaneously, but by some merciful act of Providence my wife was thrown clear. The car slewed sideways after the accident, and she wasn't even cut by the windscreen. She was just pitched over the door—the car was an open one—and landed on her head on the grass. And when the people from a neighbouring house came rushing up they found her there, unconscious, but otherwise apparently unhurt save for a few bruises. The car was like scrap iron, and poor old Gerald was dead."

"'They carried her into their house, Sir John, and telephoned for a doctor and for me. By the time I got there he had already made his examination, and he met me at the door."

"'A miraculous escape, Mr Tremlin," he said, gravely. "Of course your wife is still unconscious, but there is no need to let that alarm you. The great thing is that there is nothing broken, and when she comes to herself again, I think we shall find that beyond a severe shaking, there is nothing the matter. Only in view of the appalling nervous shock she must have had before the crash came, I consider it would be most ill-advised to tell her of Mr Weymouth's death. She will, of course, have to know in time, but until she has fully recovered from the shock she should be kept in ignorance of what has happened. If she asks any questions we can easily say that his leg was broken—or something of that sort—and that he has been taken to a hospital in Exeter."

"'Can I see her, Doctor?" I asked eagerly.

"'Certainly,' he answered. "She naturally won't know you as she is unconscious, but I repeat there is nothing to be alarmed at."

"'So I went and saw her, and then I went out to see what remained of Gerald Weymouth, my greatest friend, Sir John; he'd been best man at my wedding, and now . . . However, I don't want to bore you with all that; sufficient to say that it must have been instantaneous, thank God!'"

"'I must come to the point." My visitor moistened his lips, and I pushed over a box of cigarettes.

"'Smoke if you care to, Mr Tremlin," I said. "I shall see no one else tonight."

'He took a cigarette and lit it, and his hand was shaking.

"'My wife recovered consciousness the following morning, Sir John," he went on after a while. "I wasn't with her at the moment, but the nurse who had been sent for came and told me. We were both in the same house to which she had been taken after the accident; it belonged to friends, and the doctor didn't want her moved. I went at once to her room and found her sitting up in bed. She just stared at me blankly for a moment or two, and then turned to the nurse."

"'Where am I?" she said. "And who is this man? Have I been ill?"

"'I knelt down beside her, and started to explain."

"'There's been an accident, darling," I told her. "You're in the Ashbys' house."

"'But she still stared at me blankly, and after a while it became obvious that I was only distressing her by remaining. So I left the room, and waited until the doctor came."

"'Did she know the doctor?" I asked him.

'Mr Tremlin shook his head.

"'She knew no one; she knows no one now. And this is where I come to the distressing part for me personally. All through this last fortnight she has shown an ever increasing aversion to me. I may say, Sir John, without fear of contradiction, that ours has been a wonderfully happy married life. That's what makes it so hard to understand. I adore her, and I think I can say that she feels the same for me. Or rather felt the same, until this ghastly thing took place. Now she can't bear me in the same room with her."

'"Have you any children?" I asked him.

'"None," he answered

'"And where is your wife now?"

'"Still in the same house with the Ashbys."

'"Well, Mr Tremlin," I said, "from what you tell me, your wife seems to be suffering from a complete loss of memory. Her aversion to you is not an uncommon feature of such cases, so you may reassure your mind on that point. A dislike to those who are nearest and dearest is a frequent symptom of brain trouble, and when memory returns the feeling is blotted off the slate and vanishes like a dream."

'"But when will her memory return?" he burst out. "Sir John, this is absolutely killing me. A fortnight has passed, and there is no trace of improvement. Doctor Rodgers assures me that it is only a question of time, and that we can do nothing except wait. But though I have the greatest faith in him as an ordinary practitioner, a case of this sort is out of his beaten track. It stands to reason it must be. And that is why I've come to you. I was going to ask you to come down and see my wife, but your secretary tells me that you are going on your holiday tomorrow. Well now, I've got an idea. I don't know what plans you've made, but would it be possible for you to spend a few days with me at my house? I can give you some fishing, there are four or five horses it would be a kindness for you to exercise, and there's golf. And then perhaps you could examine my wife, and tell me what you think."

'Well, I hadn't made any plans that couldn't be broken, and the long and the short of it was that I promised to go. The poor devil was pathetically grateful, and we arranged to travel down together the next day.'

The celebrated doctor blew out a cloud of smoke thoughtfully.

'So much for Mr John Tremlin; now for his wife. She was an extraordinarily pretty woman about seven years younger than him, and when you met her there was absolutely nothing to indicate that anything was amiss. Tremlin motored me over to the Ashbys' house the day after I arrived—which necessitated incidentally going down the hill where the accident had occurred. The marks of the car on the trees were still plainly visible, and he showed me exactly where his wife had been pitched to. And, by Jove, you fellows, when I saw the gradient, and reconstructed the accident in my mind, it seemed inconceivable that she should have escaped death! However, that is by the way.

'Doctor Rodgers was waiting for us when we arrived, and he could only shake his head at my host's eager question.

'"Just the same, I'm afraid, Mr Tremlin."

'He turned away wearily.

'"I'll wait for you in the car, Sir John," he said.

'"A very strange case," said the local doctor, drawing me into a room off the hall. "I make no pretensions to be a specialist or expert in brain matters, but I am prepared to stake my reputation on this being no case for an operation. I can find no trace of local pressure anywhere which would account for it."

'"A case of severe shock producing complete loss of memory," I remarked. "And, of course, in such cases the trouble may last for years."

'"Precisely," he answered gravely. "Though naturally, I haven't told him so. It's pathetic, Sir John, quite pathetic. I think they were the most ideally happy couple I have ever met. His devotion to her was almost dog-like, and since the accident it's really been harrowing to see the way he has suffered. With his brain he understands the reason of it; with his heart he can't understand why he, of all people, should have been signalled out for this acute dislike. Because it has turned to that now. To such an extent, in fact, that I have had to forbid him even to see her. And there's another thing too. . . . However, I don't think I'll mention it. I'd like you to see if you notice it youself, or whether it's my imagination. Shall we go up?"

'She was fully dressed, and as we entered the room she turned her head eagerly to look at us. As I've said, she was a strikingly lovely woman, and her whole face was lit up with anticipation. And the next second the look had completely vanished; her expression was quite lifeless again. It was most noticeable, and I seized on it at once.

'"Good morning," I said.

'"Are you expecting someone?"

'"Yes, I am," she answered.

'"Who is it?" I asked.

'"I don't know his name," she replied wearily.

'"Can you describe him? Because perhaps we can get hold of him for you."

'But she seemed to have lost interest in the matter, and I could get nothing coherent out of her at all. She submitted to my examination listlessly, and after a while we went out and left her alone.

'"There's no mistaking it is there," said Rodgers. "I thought it might be my imagination, but I've never seen it so clearly. And I've never spoken about it to her as you did."

'"You mean that look of expectation on her face," I said. "If we could find out who it was and produce him, it might do the trick."

'"Well, it's certainly not her husband," said he grimly. "However, what do you make of the case?"

'I won't weary you with professional shop, beyond saying that I concurred with him over the question of the operation. I could find no trace of pressure anywhere, and I told her husband so. It was a strange case, but by no manner of means a unique one. We were up, so to speak, against a blank wall. All that she knew and remembered was the fortnight or so of her life that lay on this side of it; we had somehow to get her to the other side.

'"Is it going to be a long job, Sir John?" he asked me.

'"There's no good buoying you up with false hopes," I said. "I can't tell you. I don't know. It might be that she will waken tomorrow morning perfectly normal; it might be—years."

'"Oh! my God!" he muttered under his breath.

'"Anyway, the first thing to do is to get her back to her own house. The familiar surroundings there may help her to get to the other side of the wall. And once we've got her there we've taken an enormous step forward."

'So Mrs Tremlin returned to Redlands that day, and I watched her with the greatest curiosity. In fact, that night I went to bed considerably more hopeful. She had walked, for instance, out of the hall straight into the drawing-room and sat down in the chair which, her husband told me, she generally used. She had seemed, in a way, to recognise the servants; at any rate, she had accepted them. And she had gone upstairs to her bedroom without having to be shown the way.

'But there it ended. Amazing though it seemed, she still failed to recognize her husband, and the poor devil was almost distracted. In vain to point out to him the vagaries of the brain; he couldn't get beyond the fact that there must be some glimmerings in her mind of what lay on the other side of the wall, if she could find her own way to her bedroom. And if that was the case, why was the most important thing in her life—her marriage to him—hidden from her?

'I think it was the second day after she came home, that I found her in her husband's study. I'd had to tell him to keep out of the way as much as possible, because, although she no longer displayed actual aversion to him, his presence worried her. She had her meals with us, since my chief idea was that everything should proceed exactly as it had before the accident. And at table she didn't seem to mind him. It was only when he got close to her that she began to get fidgety.

'And now she was standing by his desk holding a big photograph in her hand. There was a queer, excited look on her face as she turned to me, and I was instantly reminded of the first time I'd seen her.

'"Who is this man?" she said.

'As a matter of fact, the very first night I arrived Tremlin told me.

'"That's Gerald Weymouth," I answered. "Do you know him?"

'"Where is he?" she cried, taking no notice of my question. "I want to see him."

'"Is he the man you are expecting?" I said. "The man whose name you forgot."

'"I think so," she answered, passing her hand over her forehead. "It's all so muddled. I seem to remember . . . Gerald Weymouth . . . Gerald . . ."

'Her voice died away, and I didn't press her. To excite a case of that sort is fatal, but it started me off on a new line of thought. And that night I mentioned it to her husband.

'"It may be," I said, "that those few ghastly seconds, whilst the car was dashing down the hill, and she was facing what must have seemed to her to be certain death, have imprinted on her mind a recollection of him. How clear it is, I can't tell—but it's there. And if only she could see Weymouth now it might save her."

'"Since the poor old chap is dead and buried," he said, wearily, "I'm afraid that doesn't advance us much, Sir John."

'"I know all that," I answered. "The point is—how clear is that recollection? Would it be possible to get a substitute?"

'He sat up with the light of hope dawning in his eyes.

'"What do you mean?" he said.

'"It's only a vague idea, Mr Tremlin," I answered. "And I haven't even begun to think out the details. Have you ever heard the story of the man who was driving with his servant along a road he rarely used? And as they went over a rather noticeable wooden bridge, he said to his servant—'Do you like eggs?' And the servant answered, 'Yes, sir.' A few months later he again drove over the same bridge, not having been on that road in the interval. And as the trap got to exactly the same spot where he had put the first question, he said, 'How do you like them.' And the servant answered, 'Fairly hard boiled, sir.'"

'He stared at me as if I had taken leave of my senses.

'"I assure you I'm quite serious," I said. "Whether the story is true or not is immaterial, but it illustrates a very well-known law—the law of Inherent Connection. The second question was put under exactly similar conditions to the first, and although there was a lapse of months between the two—for the fraction

111

of a second that lapse was non-existent in the servant's mind. Subconsciously his surroundings recalled the first question, just as the second was put to him. Now I am wondering if we could do something of that sort in the case of your wife."

"'I'm afraid I must be very dense," he said, "but for the life of me I don't see what you're driving at."

"'I'm driving at this. You'll agree that for a man to ask his servant suddenly if he likes eggs and then to say no more is a peculiar thing to do. And its very peculiarity stamped itself on the servant's mind, so that when identical conditions were repeated, it immediately came to his thoughts. Moreover, it came in such a way, and so naturally, that his answer to the second question was quite spontaneous. Now suppose, Mr Tremlin, we could reproduce the exact conditions which led up to the accident—let us say from the time your wife and Weymouth left the house in the car to the moment when the crash came. *Only this time there will be no crash.*"

'He was staring at me fixedly now; he was beginning to get the idea.

"'Understand; it's only an experiment. It may do no good, but I don't think it can do any harm. And if it's successful, we shall have got your wife to the other side of the wall. She will come up to it, as she did on the day of the accident; but this time she will go through it and come out on the other side."

"'Man," he cried, "do you think there's a chance?"

"'I certainly think there's a chance," I said.

"'But how can we arrange about Gerald?"

"'There lies the principal difficulty I admit. At the same time, I think it quite possible that a reasonable likeness will be sufficient for the purpose if all the other details are exact."

"'He was wearing flannels and a big white blanket coat. And he also had on a pair of motoring goggles. By Jove! Sir John," he almost shouted in his excitement, "if you put on a small black moustache, I believe you could do it yourself. You're greyer, of course—but a hat conceals that; and your eyes are quite different, which doesn't matter either behind goggles. You're exactly the same height and build, and your voices are much the same."

112

'He was pacing feverishly up and down the room.

'"By God, man, you've given me hope. Don't let's dream of failure; don't let's even mention the word. You're going to succeed; I know it."

'And then we set to work to discuss details. The first thing was to get another Panler car—an exact replica of the one that was smashed. He wired for that in the morning. Then we had to find out as nearly as possible precisely what took place before they started. The butler could help there, for Tremlin himself had been out for lunch. So we called him in and explained the situation.

'"I remember perfectly, sir," he said. "Mr Weymouth drove the car up to the front door, which was open. He got out and entered the house, speaking to me as he passed. Mrs Tremlin was in the drawing-room, and Mr Weymouth went to the door and opened it. I heard him say, 'Are you ready, Monica?' Then she came out and I handed her her racket and shoes as I opened the door of the car. I said to her, 'Shall I put them behind, ma'am?' and she said, 'Oh! it doesn't matter; there's plenty of room here.' Then they drove off."

'"A point to remember," cried Tremlin. "There was a tonneau cover over the back seats."

'"That is so, sir," said the butler.

'Well, we sat far into the night discussing details, and by the time I went to bed I was as excited as he was. The whole scheme, which had started as just a vague idea, began to crystallize in my mind; I realized the possibilities. Of course, the fact that I had to play the part of Weymouth was the weak link, but during the next week, under Tremlin's direction, I managed to get his voice more or less. Also we had two dress rehearsals for appearance. We had down a man from London who was an expert in the art of making-up, and with the help of photographs and Tremlin's criticism, he turned me into a very creditable replica of Weymouth.

'And then we had to wait for the right day. I insisted on that; it must be the same sort of weather. The day of the accident had been sunny and warm; as luck would have it we had a fortnight of dull, overcast days. The car had arrived and was being kept in the local garage, from which I had driven it once or twice to get accustomed to it.

'I had left Redlands myself, and taken rooms in the local inn, as I thought it better that Mrs Tremlin should see nothing of me. I formed no part of her pre-accident existence, and that was the atmosphere in which I wanted her steeped.

'And then at last there came the morning when her husband burst in on me at breakfast.

'"It was just such a day as this," he cried, and he was shaking like a man with the ague.

'"Steady, Tremlin," I said, warningly. "We've all got to keep cool."

'And, truth to tell, I wasn't feeling too cool myself. Even with all our carefully arranged details there was still such a lot that must be left to chance. However, there was no question of backing out of it, and so we got on with our final preparations. Tremlin was in such a state of pitiful excitement and agitation that he was banking everything on success. And he had the hardest part, poor devil: he couldn't be there to see what happened. The butler had been carefully coached: the whole staff had been warned just to behave normally.

'The man from London started on my face in the morning, reserving the final touches till after lunch, which Tremlin had with me. But he couldn't eat anything, and it was with a feeling of relief that I saw him go after the meal. He was getting on my nerves rather badly.

'And then at two o'clock I left and drove up to the house. Every detail in the car was correct—side wings, two spare wheels, tonneau cover, everything. The expert from London had done his work well, for the butler gave a positive start as he saw me.

'"Magnificent, Sir John," he whispered. "You're the living image of Mr Weymouth."

'"Where is she" I asked.

'"In the drawing-room, Sir John. I took coffee there after lunch, as you told me."

'So far, so good: that had been one of the many difficulties to contend with.

"'And she has on a similar dress, Sir John: her maid managed that."

"'Excellent,' I said. "You've got the racket and shoes? Then we'll get on with it."

'Nervous, you fellows—I was as nervous as a cat. Would the whole thing, after all the trouble we'd taken, be a ghastly failure? However, there was no use hesitating, so I went to the drawing-room door and opened it.

"Are you ready, Monica?" I said.

'It was the crucial moment, and I saw a look of dawning amazement come into her eyes, to be replaced almost at once by an expression which defeated me. At least, it defeated me in one way only; it defeated me when I saw it on the face of a woman who was devotedly attached to her husband. Except from that point of view, it's meaning was too obvious.

'I stood aside, feverishly trying to think out this new and unexpected development. Then she passed me and walked quite normally towards the car. The butler was splendid: there was not a hint of hesitation in his voice as he opened the door for her.

"'Shall I put them behind, ma'am?"

"'Oh! it doesn't matter; there's plenty of room here."

'And we drove off.

"'Gerry, darling," she said, "I thought you were coming to lunch. You said you would."

'Now here was the devil and all of a predicament. I had assumed that I might have to reply to an ordinary disjointed conversation on general topics, but a love affair, and a serious one, was a different matter altogether. And I was just racking my brains as to what I should say, when she spoke again.

"'I know you couldn't help it, dear heart, but I grudge every moment you're away from me."

'For a moment I was surprised: then I realized that once again luck was with us. She didn't require any answers from me; the answers were already there in her brain. And for the next quarter of an hour I drove in silence, listening to what to all intents and purposes was one person speaking on a telephone.

'It wasn't pleasant, I assure you. It was obvious that Mr Gerald Weymouth had been a pretty useful swine. Certain it was that he had eaten Tremlin's salt, and then done him the greatest injury one man may do another. Certain it was also that he had had no intention whatever of sacrificing his freedom and becoming involved in the meshes of a divorce court. There was no need for his answers to be spoken aloud: they were obvious without that. His career, unnecessary scandal, poor old Bob's feelings—all the old, old stunts rattled off glibly.

'And suddenly a feeling of awe came over me. Just so had this feeling happened a month previously: and even as the man I represented talked of his career, death was five minutes away from him. And then my professional instincts took charge: it was so wonderfully interesting. I hardly heard some of what she said: I was so frightfully keen to see what was going to happen when we got to the hill.

'"Why did you do it, Gerry?" Her voice suddenly arrested me. "I used to love him so much, and now I can't bear him near me."

'The doctor in me noted that point; the strange aversion was accounted for.

'"Of course, I disguise it—but I can't go on. You've—you've bewitched me."

'And now we were at the top of the hill.

'"Gerry—be careful. Not too fast down here. What's the matter—brakes gone—my God! Gerry—turn her, turn her into the bank. . . ."

'I was letting her down pretty fast, you'll understand.

'"Turn her, Gerry." Her voice rose to a shriek. "Slip in a lower gear. Oh, God—you've lost your head! Bob wouldn't have . . . Bob . . ."

'Her weight fell heavily against me—she'd fainted; the car was past the two trees. I pulled up, and laid her on the grass beside the road. Then I ripped off my disguise and brought her round. Now we should see whether it was success or failure.

'She stared at me wonderingly.

'"Who are you?" she said at length.

'"My name is Sir John Caston," I answered. "I'm a doctor."

'"But what on earth——" she stammered in amazement.

'"Listen, Mrs Tremlin," I said quietly, "and I'll explain things. You had a very bad accident some weeks ago, and were thrown out of a car on you head. Mr Weymouth was driving you. . . ."

'"But he's just been driving me. . . ."

'"Oh, no!" I said. "I've been driving you. Perhaps you imagined it was Mr Weymouth. You had a nasty knock on the head, you know, and that produces delusions."

'"But I've been talking to him today."

'I smiled and shook my head, and lied.

'"You haven't said a word since you left the house," I remarked. "You've had a very vivid dream—that's all."

'"I don't understand," she said, wearily.

'"And I don't want you to try to," I answered. "Don't worry your head about it at all. Let's get on back and see your husband."

'"Bob! Yes—Bob wouldn't have lost his head."

'And that was all she said. She got into the car, and we drove back quietly. I talked on outside topics and she answered quite coherently: the thing was a success. She had got to the other side of the wall.'

The celebrated doctor rose and mixed himself a whisky and soda; then he stood with his back to the fireplace, looking down at us.

'An utter complete success,' he repeated. 'Little by little we broke the truth to her, and she took it normally and calmly — even to Gerald Weymouth's death. But the morning I went she asked me a question.

'"That dream, Sir John; that terrible dream, when I thought you were Gerald. You're sure I didn't say anything?"

'"Perfectly sure," I answered calmly.

'And under her breath I heard her say, "Thank God!"

'All that was two years ago, and at intervals I have said to myself—"Good. You did that very well. No one knows her secret, save you: you have restored her to her normal mind, and from information received, they are still a devoted couple. In fact, you are distinctly worthy of a pat on the back." And during

117

those two years the gods have been laughing: this afternoon I heard their mirth.

'I lunched with them both at the Ritz, and afterwards she had to go out shopping. So I sat on, talking to him.

'"Pretty satisfactory, Tremlin," I said, full of the righteous glow of Fin Champagne. "I'm proud of that little experiment of ours."

'"Are you?" he said, with a twisted sort of smile.

'"But dash it, man," I said, aggrieved, "aren't you?"

'He looked at me and his eyes were weary.

'"At any rate, she called for me when she thought the end was coming."

'I positively stuttered at him.

'"What under the sun do you mean?"

'"Only that I was hidden under the tonneau cover at the back."'

The Old Dining-Room

I don't pretend to account for it; I am merely giving the plain unvarnished tale of what took place to my certain knowledge at Jack Drage's house in Kent during the weekend which finished so disastrously. Doubtless there is an explanation: maybe there are several. The believers in spiritualism and things psychic will probably say that the tragedy was due to the action of a powerful influence which had remained intact throughout the centuries; the materialists will probably say it was due to indigestion. I hold no brief for either side: as the mere narrator, the facts are good enough for me. And, anyway, the extremists of both schools of thought are quite irreconcilable.

There were six of us there, counting Jack Drage and his wife. Bill Sibton in the Indian Civil, Armytage in the Gunners, and I—Staunton by name, and a scribbler of sorts—were the men: little Joan Neilson—Armytage's fiancée—supported Phyllis Drage. Ostensibly we were there to shoot a few pheasants, but it was more than a mere shooting party. It was a reunion after long years of us four men who had been known at school as the Inseparables. Bill had been in India for twelve years, save for the inevitable gap in Mesopotamia; Dick Armytage had soldiered all over the place ever since he'd left the Shop. And though I'd seen Jack off and on since our school-days, I'd lost touch with him since he'd married. Wives play the deuce with bachelor friends, though they indignantly deny it—God bless 'em. At least, mine always does.

It was the first time any of us had been inside Jack's house, and undoubtedly he had the most delightful little property. The house itself was old, but comfortably modernised by an expert, so that the charm of it still remained. In fact, the only room which had been left absolutely intact was the dining-room. And to have touched that would have been sheer vandalism. The sole thing that had been done to it was to install central heating, and that had been carried out so skilfully that no trace of the work could be seen.

It was a room by itself standing apart from the rest of the house, with a lofty vaulted roof in which one could just see the smoky old oak beams by the light of the candles on the dinner-table. A huge open fireplace jutted out from one of the longer walls; while on the opposite side a door led into the garden. And then, at one end, approached by the original staircase at least six centuries old, was the musicians' gallery.

A wonderful room—a room in which it seemed almost sacrilege to eat and smoke and discuss present-day affairs—a room in which one felt that history had been made. Nothing softened the severe plainness of the walls save a few mediæval pikes and battle axes. In fact, two old muskets of the Waterloo era were the most modern implements of the collection. Of pictures there was only one—a very fine painting of a man dressed in the fashion of the Tudor period—which hung facing the musicians gallery.

It was that that caught my eye as we sat down to dinner, and I turned to Jack.

'An early Drage?' I asked.

'As a matter of fact—no relation at all,' he answered. 'But a strong relation to this room. That's why I hang him there.'

'Any story attached thereto?'

'There is; though I can't really do it justice. The parson here is the only man who knows the whole yarn—by the way, old dear,' he spoke to his wife across the table, 'the reverend bird takes tea with us tomorrow. But he is the only man who has the thing at his finger tips. The previous owner was a bit vague himself, but having a sense of the fitness of things, he gave me a chance of buying the picture. Apparently it's a painting of one Sir James Wrothley who lived round about the time of Henry VIII. He was either a rabid Protestant or a rabid Roman Catholic—I told you I was a bit vague over details—and he used this identical room as a secret meeting-place for himself and his pals to hatch plots against his enemies.'

'Jack *is* so illuminating, isn't he?' laughed his wife.

'Well, I bet you can't tell it any better yourself,' he retorted with a grin. 'I admit my history is weak. But anyway, about that time, if the jolly old Protestants weren't burning the R.C.'s, the

R.C.'s were burning the Protestants. A period calling for great tact, I've always thought. Well, at any rate, this Sir James Wrothley—when his party was being officially burned—came here and hatched dark schemes to reverse the procedure. And then, apparently, one day somebody blew the gaff, and the whole bunch of conspirators in here were absolutely caught in the act by the other crowd, who put 'em to death on the spot. Which is all I can tell you about it.'

'I must ask the padre tomorrow,' I said to his wife. 'I'd rather like to hear the whole story. I felt when I first came into this room that there was history connected with it.'

She looked at me rather strangely for a moment; then she gave a little forced laugh.

'Do you know, Tom,' she said slowly, 'at times I almost hate this room. All my friends gnash their teeth with envy over it— but sometimes, when Jack's been away, and I've dined in here by myself—it's terrified me. I feel as if—I wasn't alone: as if— there were people all round me—watching me. Of course, it's absurd, I know. But I can't help it. And yet I'm not a nervy sort of person.'

'I don't think it's at all absurd,' I assured her. 'I believe I should feel the same myself. A room of this size, which, of necessity, is dimly lighted in the corners, and which is full of historical associations, must cause an impression on the least imaginative person.'

'We used it once for a dance,' she laughed; 'with a ragtime band in the gallery.'

'And a great show it was, too,' broke in her husband. 'The trouble was that one of the musicians got gay with a bottle of whisky, and very nearly fell clean through that balustrade effect on to the floor below. I haven't had that touched—and the wood is rotten.'

'I pray you be seated, gentlemen.' A sudden silence fell on the table, and everybody stared at Bill Sibton.

'Is it a game, Bill?' asked Jack Drage. 'I rather thought we were. And what about the ladies?'

With a puzzled frown Bill Sibton looked at him. 'Did I speak out loud, then?' he asked slowly.

121

'And so early in the evening too!' Joan Neilson laughed merrily.

'I must have been day-dreaming, I suppose. But that yarn of yours has rather got me, Jack; though in the course of a long and evil career, I've never heard one told worse. I was thinking of that meeting—all of them sitting here. And then suddenly that door bursting open.' He was staring fixedly at the door, and again a silence fell on us all.

'The thunder of the butts of their muskets on the woodwork.' He swung round and faced the door leading to the garden. 'And on that one, too. Can't you hear them? No escape—none. Caught like rats in a trap.' His voice died away to a whisper, and Joan Neilson gave a little nervous laugh.

'You're the most realistic person, Mr Sibton. I think I prefer hearing about the dance.'

I glanced at my hostess—and it seemed to me that there was fear in her eyes as she looked at Bill. Sometimes now I wonder if she had some vague premonition of impending disaster: something too intangible to take hold of—something the more terrifying on that very account.

It was after dinner that Jack Drage switched on the solitary electric light of which the room boasted. It was so placed as to show up the painting of Sir James Wrothley, and in silence we all gathered round to look at it. A pair of piercing eyes set in a stern aquiline face stared down at us from under the brim of a hat adorned with sweeping plumes; his hand rested on the jewelled hilt of his sword. It was a fine picture in a splendid state of preservation, well worthy of its place of honour on the walls of such a room, and we joined in a general chorus of admiration. Only Bill Sibton was silent, and he seemed fascinated—unable to tear his eyes away from the painting.

'As a matter of fact, Bill,' said Dick Armytage, studying the portrait critically, 'he might quite well be an ancestor of yours. Wash out your moustache, and give you a fancy-dress hat, and you'd look very much like the old bean.'

He was quite right: there was a distinct resemblance, and it rather surprised me that I had not noticed it myself. There were the same deep-set piercing eyes, the same strong, slightly hatchet face, the same broad forehead. Even the colouring was similar: a mere coincidence that, probably—but one which increased the likeness. In fact, the longer I looked the more pronounced did the resemblance become, till it was almost uncanny.

'Well, he can't be, anyway,' said Bill abruptly. 'I've never heard of any Wrothley in the family.' He looked away from the picture almost with an effort, and lit a cigarette. 'It's a most extraordinary thing, Jack,' he went on after a moment, 'but since we came into this room I've had a feeling that I've been here before.'

'Good Lord, man, that's common enough in all conscience. One often gets that idea.'

'I know one does,' answered Bill. 'I've had it before myself; but never one tenth as strongly as I feel it here. Besides, that feeling generally dies—after a few minutes: it's growing stronger and stronger with me every moment I stop in here.'

'Then let's go into the drawing-room,' said our hostess. 'I've had the card-table put in there.'

We followed her and Joan Neilson into the main part of the house; and since neither of the ladies played, for the next two hours we four men bridged. And then, seeing that it was a special occasion, we sat yarning over half-forgotten incidents till the room grew thick with smoke and the two women fled to bed before they died of asphyxiation.

Bill, I remember, waxed eloquent on the subject of politicians, with a six weeks' experience of India, butting in on things they knew less than nothing about; Dick Armytage grew melancholy on the subject of the block in promotion. And then the reminiscences grew more personal, and the whisky sank lower and lower in the tantalus as one yarn succeeded another.

At last Jack Drage rose with a yawn and knocked the ashes out of his pipe.

'Two o'clock, boys What about bed?'

'Lord! is it really?' Dick Armytage stretched himself. 'However, no shooting tomorrow, or, rather, today. We might spend the Sabbath dressing Bill up as his nibs in the next room.'

'Sapper'

A shadow crossed Bill's face.

'I'd forgotten that room,' he said, frowning. 'Damn you, Dick.'

'My dear old boy,' laughed Armytage, 'you surely don't mind resembling the worthy Sir James? He's a deuced sight better looking fellow than you are.'

Bill shook his head irritably.

'It isn't that at all,' he said, 'I wasn't thinking of the picture.' He seemed to be on the point of saying something else—then he changed his mind.

'Well—bed for master.'

We all trooped upstairs, and Jack came round to each of us to see that we were all right.

'Breakfast provisionally nine,' he remarked. 'Night-night, old boy.'

The door closed behind him, and his steps died away down the passage as he went to his own room.

By all known rules I should have been asleep almost as my head touched the pillow. A day's rough shooting, followed by bed at two in the morning should produce that result if anything can, but in my case that night it didn't. Whether I had smoked too much, or what it was, I know not, but at half-past three I gave up the attempt and switched on my light. Then I went over, and pulling up an armchair, I sat down by the open window. There was no moon, and the night was warm for the time of year. Outlined against the sky the big dining-room stretched out from the house, and, as I lit a cigarette, Jack Drage's vague story returned to my mind. The conspirators, meeting by stealth to hatch some sinister plot; the sudden alarm as they found themselves surrounded; the desperate fight against overwhelming odds—and then, the end. There should be a story in it, I reflected; I'd get the parson to tell me the whole thing accurately next day. The local colour seemed more appropriate when one looked at the room from outside, with an occasional cloud scudding by over the big trees beyond. Savoured more of conspiracy and death than when dining inside, with reminiscences of a jazz band in the musicians gallery.

124

And at that moment a dim light suddenly filtered out through the windows. It was so dim that at first I thought I had imagined it; so dim that I switched off my own light in order to make sure. There was no doubt about it: faint but unmistakable the reflection showed up on the ground outside. A light had been lit in the old dining-room: therfore someone must be in there. At four o'clock in the morning!

For a moment or two I hesitated: should I go along and rouse Jack? Someone might have got in through the garden door, and I failed to see why I should fight another man's burglar in his own house. And then it struck me it would only alarm his wife—I'd get Bill, whose room was opposite mine.

I put on some slippers and crossed the landing to rouse him. And then I stopped abruptly. His door was open; his room was empty. Surely it couldn't be he who had turned on the light below?

As noiselessly as possible I went downstairs, and turned along the passage to the dining-room. Sure enough the door into the main part of the house was ajar, and the light was shining through the opening. I tiptoed up to it and looked through the crack by the hinges.

At first I could see nothing save the solitary electric light over the portrait of Sir James. And then in the gloom beyond I saw a tall figure standing motionless by the old oak dining-table. It was Bill—even in the dim light I recognised that clean-cut profile; Bill clad in his pyjamas only, with one hand stretched out in front of him, pointing. And then, suddenly, he spoke.

'You lie, Sir Henry!—you lie!'

Nothing more, just that one remark; his hand still pointing inexorably across the table. Then after a moment he turned so that the light fell full on his face, and I realised what was the matter. Bill Sibton was walking in his sleep.

Slowly he came towards the door behind which I stood, and passed through it—so close that he almost touched me as I shrank back against the wall. Then he went up the stairs, and as soon as I heard him reach the landing above, I quickly turned out the light in the dining-room and followed him. His bedroom door was closed: there was no sound from inside.

There was nothing more for me to do: my burglar had developed into a harmless somnambulist. Moreover, it suddenly struck me that I had become most infernally sleepy myself. So I did not curse Bill mentally as much as I might have done. I turned in, and my nine o'clock next morning was very provisional

So was Bill Sibton's: we arrived together for breakfast at a quarter to ten. He looked haggard and ill, like a man who has not slept, and his first remark was to curse Dick Armytage.

'I had the most infernal dreams last night,' he grumbled. 'Entirely through Dick reminding me of this room. I dreamed the whole show that took place in here in that old bird's time.'

He pointed to the portrait of Sir James.

'Did you?' I remarked, pouring out some coffee. 'Must have been quite interesting.'

'I know I wasn't at all popular with the crowd,' he said, 'I don't set any store by dreams myself—but last night it was really extraordinarily vivid.' He stirred his tea thoughtfully.

'I can quite imagine that, Bill. Do you ever walk in your sleep?'

'Walk in my sleep? No.' He stared at me surprised. 'Why?'

'You did last night. I found you down here at four o'clock in your pyjamas. You were standing just where I'm sitting now, pointing with your hand across the table. And as I stood outside the door you suddenly said, "You lie, Sir Henry!—you lie!"'

'Part of my dream,' he muttered. 'Sir Henry Brayton was the name of the man—and he was the leader. They were all furious with me about something. We quarrelled—and after that, there seemed to be a closed door. It was opening slowly and instinctively I knew there was something dreadful behind it. You know the terror of a dream; the primordial terror of the mind that cannot reason against something hideous—unknown——' I glanced at him: his forehead was wet with sweat. 'And then the dream passed. The door didn't open.'

'Undoubtedly, my lad,' I remarked lightly, 'you had one whisky too many last night.'

'Don't be an ass, Tom,' he said irritably. 'I tell you—though you needn't repeat it—I'm in a putrid funk of this room. Absurd, I know: ridiculous. But I can't help it. And if there was a train on this branch line on a Sunday, I'd leave today.'

126

'But, good Lord, Bill,' I began—and then I went on with my breakfast. There was a look on his face which it is not good to see on the face of a man. It was terror: an abject, dreadful terror.

He and Jack Drage were out for a long walk when the parson came to tea that afternoon—a walk of which Bill had been the instigator. He had dragged Jack forth, vigorously protesting, after lunch, and we had cheered them on their way. Bill had to get out of the house—I could see that. Then Dick and the girl had disappeared, in the way that people in their condition *do* disappear, just before Mr Williams arrived. And so only Phyllis Drage was there, presiding at the tea-table, when I broached the subject of the history of the dining-room.

'He spoils paper, Mr Williams,' laughed my hostess, 'and he scents copy. Jack tried to tell the story last night, and got it hopelessly wrong.'

The clergyman smiled gravely.

'You'll have to alter the setting, Mr Staunton,' he remarked, 'because the story is quite well known round here. In my library at the vicarage I have an old manuscript copy of the legend. And indeed, I have no reason to believe that it is a legend: certainly the main points have been historically authenticated. Sir James Wrothley, whose portrait hangs in the dining-room lived in this house at the end of the fifteenth century. He was a staunch Protestant—bigoted to a degree; and he fell very foul of Cardinal Wolsey, who you may remember was plotting for the Papacy at the time. So bitter did the animosity become, and so high did religious intoleration run in those days, that Sir James started counter-plotting against the Cardinal; which was a dangerous thing to do. Moreover, he and his friends used the dining-room here as their meeting-place.'

The reverend gentleman sipped his tea; if there was one thing he loved it was the telling of this story, which reflected so magnificently on the staunch no-Popery record of his parish.

'So much is historical certainty; the rest is not so indisputably authentic. The times of the meetings were, of course, kept secret—until the fatal night occurred. Then, apparently, someone turned traitor. And, why I cannot tell you, Sir James himself was accused by the others—especially Sir Henry Brayton. Did you say anything, Mr Staunton?'

'Nothing,' I remarked quietly. 'The name surprised me for a moment. Please go on.'

'Sir Henry Brayton was Sir James's next-door neighbour, almost equally intolerant of anything savouring of Rome. And even while, so the story goes, Wolsey's men were hammering on the doors, he and Sir Henry had this dreadful quarrel. Why Sir James should have been suspected, whether the suspicions were justified or not I cannot say. Certainly, in view of what we know of Sir James's character, it seems hard to believe that he could have been guilty of such infamous treachery. But that the case must have appeared exceedingly black against him is certain from the last and most tragic part of the story.'

Once again Mr Williams paused to sip his tea: he had now reached that point of the narrative where royalty itself would have failed to hurry him.

'In those days, Mrs Drage, there was a door leading into the musicians' gallery from one of the rooms of the house. It provided no avenue of escape if the house was surrounded—but its existence was unknown to the men before whose blows the other doors were already beginning to splinter. And suddenly through this door appeared Lady Wrothley. She had only recently married Sir James: in fact, her first baby was then on its way. Sir James saw her, and at once ceased his quarrel with Sir Henry. With dignity he mounted the stairs and approached his girl-wife—and in her horror-struck eyes he saw that she, too, suspected him of being the traitor. He raised her hand to his lips; and then as the doors burst open simultaneously and Wolsey's men rushed in—he dived head foremost on to the floor below, breaking his neck and dying instantly.

'The story goes on to say,' continued Mr Williams, with a diffident cough, 'that even while the butchery began in the room below—for most of the Protestants were unarmed—the poor girl collapsed in the gallery, and shortly afterwards the child was born. A girl baby who survived, though the mother died. One likes to think that if she had indeed misjudged her

128

husband, it was a merciful act on the part of the Almighty to let her join him so soon. Thank you, I will have another cup of tea. One lump, please.'

'A most fascinating story, Mr Williams,' said Phyllis. 'Thank you so much for having told us. Can you make anything out of it, Tom?'

I laughed.

'The criminal reserves his defence. But it's most interesting, Padre, most interesting, as Mrs Drage says. If I may, I'd like to come and see that manuscript.'

'I shall be only too delighted,' he murmured with old-fashioned courtesy. 'Whenever you like.'

And then the conversation turned on things parochial until he rose to go. The others had still not returned, and for a while we two sat on talking as the spirit moved us in the darkening room. At last the servants appeared to draw the curtains, and it was then that we heard Jack and Bill in the hall.

I don't know what made me make the remark; it seemed to come out without my volition.

'If I were you, Phyllis,' I said, 'I don't think I'd tell the story of the dining-room to Bill.'

She looked at me curiously.

'Why not?'

'I don't know—but I wouldn't.' In the brightly lit room his fears of the morning seemed ridiculous; yet, as I say, I don't know what made me make the remark.

'All right; I won't,' she said gravely. 'Do you think——'

But further conversation was cut short by the entrance of Bill and her husband.

'Twelve miles if an inch,' growled Drage, throwing himself into a chair. 'You awful fellow.'

Sibton laughed.

'Do you good, you lazy devil. He's getting too fat, Phyllis, isn't he?'

I glanced at him as he, too, sat down: in his eyes there remained no trace of the terror of the morning.

* * *

And now I come to that part of my story which I find most difficult to write. From the story-teller's point of view pure and simple, it is the easiest; from the human point of view I have never tackled anything harder. Because, though the events I am describing took place months ago—and the first shock is long since past—I still cannot rid myself of a feeling that I was largely to blame. By the cold light of reason I can exonerate myself; but one does not habitually have one's being in that exalted atmosphere. Jack blames himself; but in view of what happened the night before—in view of the look in Bill's eyes that Sunday morning—I feel that I ought to have realised that there were influences at work which lay beyond my ken—influences which at present lie not within the light of reason. And then at other times I wonder if it was not just a strange coincidence and an— accident. God knows: frankly I don't.

We spent that evening just as we had spent the preceding one, save that in view of shooting on Monday morning we went to bed at midnight. This time I fell asleep at once—only to be roused by someone shaking my arm. I sat up blinking: it was Jack Drage.

'Wake up, Tom,' he whispered. 'There's a light in the dining-room, and we're going down to investigate. Dick is getting Bill.'

In an instant I was out of bed.

'It's probably Bill himself,' I said. 'I found him down there last night walking in his sleep.'

'The devil you did!' muttered Jack, and at that moment Dick Armytage came in.

'Bill's room is empty,' he announced; and I nodded.

'It's Bill right enough,' I said. 'He went back quite quietly last night. And, for Heaven's sake, you fellows, don't wake him. It's very dangerous.'

Just as before the dining-room door was open, and the light filtered through into the passage as we tiptoed along it. Just as before we saw Bill standing by the table—his hand outstretched.

Then came the same words as I had heard last night.

'You lie, Sir Henry—you lie!'

'What the devil——' muttered Jack; but I held up my finger to ensure silence.

'He'll come to bed now,' I whispered. 'Keep quite still.'

130

But this time Bill Sibton did not come to bed; instead, he turned and stared into the shadows of the musician's gallery. Then, very slowly, he walked away from us and commenced to mount the stairs. And still the danger did not strike us.

Dimly we saw the tall figure reach the top and walk along the gallery, as if he saw someone at the end—and at that moment the peril came to the three of us.

To Dick and Jack the rottenness of the balustrade; to me—*the end of the vicar's story*. What they thought I know not; but to my dying day I shall never forget my own agony of mind. In that corner of the musicians' gallery—though we could see her not—stood Lady Wrothley; to the man walking slowly towards her the door was opening slowly—the door which had remained shut the night before—the door behind which lay the terror.

And then it all happened very quickly. In a frenzy we raced across the room to get at him—but we weren't in time. There was a rending of wood—a dreadful crash—a sprawling figure on the floor below. To me it seemed as if he had hurled himself against the balustrade, had literally dived downwards. The others did not notice it—so they told me later. But I did.

And then we were kneeling beside him on the floor.

'Dear God!' I heard Drage say in a hoarse whisper. 'He's dead; he's broken his neck.'

Such is my story. Jack Drage blames himself for the rottenness of the woodwork, but I feel it was my fault. Yes—it was my fault. I ought to have known, ought to have done something. Even if we'd only locked the dining-room door.

And the last link in the chain I haven't mentioned yet. The vicar supplied that—though to him it was merely a strange coincidence.

The baby-girl—born in the gallery—a strange, imaginative child, so run the archives, subject to fits of awful depression and, at other times, hallucinations—married. She married in 1521, on the 30th day of October, Henry, only son of Frank Sibton and Mary his wife.

God knows: I don't. It may have been an accident.

The Exploits of Bulldog Drummond

Sapper created three series-heroes: Jim Maitland, that monocled wanderer in the earth's furthest corners, who travelled the world armed only 'with a gun and a spare pair of underwear'; Ronald Standish, golfer, cricketer, on occasion cracksman, and sleuth whose methods are decidedly Holmesian; and of course Hugh Drummond.

Both Maitland and Standish are well represented in Sapper's favourite form of fiction, the short story—*Jim Maitland* (1923), *Ronald Standish* (1933), and *Ask For Ronald Standish* (1936), and a single Standish tale, 'The Horror of Staveley Grange', in *The Saving Clause* (1927). Drummond, oddly, is not. Gerard Fairlie wrote a series of Drummond shorts which appeared in, of all places, the *News of the World* in the early 1950s. But what of Drummond's creator, Sapper himself? It's clear that he did contemplate a volume of probably a dozen Bulldog Drummond tales, but unfortunately he died before he could complete the series. Five stories were published in the *Strand* in 1937, three of them posthumously, and they are here presented for the first time in book form.

Lonely Inn

The mist eddied sluggishly over the moors. A slight wind from the north held in it the presage of snow, but at the moment only a cold, clammy drizzle was falling. In the gathering darkness an occasional hill top showed for a minute or two every now and then, only to be obliterated immediately by further waves of the drifting blanket: soon nothing would be visible to the man who stood staring out of the window of the inn.

Behind him a lamp hanging from a blackened beam threw a feeble light into the grey world outside. The light seemed to be caught, stifled, and thrown back at him; now reaching as far as the road, the next instant shut off at the window itself. But with his hands thrust deep in his pockets the man stood motionless with shoulders hunched, and the collar of his travelling coat turned up. Even the sound of the door opening did not disturb him. 'No signs of 'em?' came a harsh voice. 'Not a trace. This damned mist may wreck the whole show.'

The watcher swung round and contemplated the newcomer who was putting some coal on the fire. A green baize apron tied round his waist showed that he was one of the staff. He was, in fact, so far as the male side was concerned, the entire staff — barman, porter, landlord. He finished his task and straightened up. The eyes of the two men met.

'It's unfortunate,' the landlord said. 'And yet it's better than a clear night—if they come.'

'They've *got* to come,' snarled the other, moving over to the fire. 'Otherwise . . .'

He left the sentence uncompleted, and the landlord shrugged his shoulders.

'Got to and this mist don't go together,' he remarked. 'Any car might get ditched on a night like this. And if that happens . . .'

He, too, left his sentence unfinished, and crossed to the bar.

'What are you drinking?'

'Give me a double whisky, and have one yourself. Gosh, what a pestilential bit of country.'

Once more he went over to the window and stood listening intently. As the landlord came across with the drinks, he suddenly leaned forward eagerly.

'What's that?' he muttered. 'Surely that was a car.'

The landlord joined him: they both waited motionless, craning their ears. But save for the faint moan of the wind everything was silent.

'It sounded like a door shutting. Didn't you hear it?'

'I did not,' said the landlord. 'But I was the other side of the room. Anyway, why should they be getting out of the car way down the road? If they've got as far as that, they'd come on to the house. Your whisky.'

The man in the overcoat took the glass and tossed the contents down neat. Then once again he returned to his vigil, having put the empty glass back on the tray. And though the landlord had followed his example he did not immediately return to the bar, but stood contemplating his visitor's back with a curious brooding look in his eyes, and heedless of the fact that his reflection was plainly visible in the glass.

For perhaps three seconds the other took no notice; then he swung round with a curse.

'What the hell are you staring at me for?' he cried angrily.

Again for perhaps three seconds there was silence; then the landlord turned away.

'Getting nervy?' he remarked.

'Nervy be damned. It takes more than a trifle like this to make me nervy, my friend. All that is worrying me is this cursed mist.'

'What's it going to mean to you if they don't come?' asked the landlord curiously.

'Ruin—complete and utter,' said the other shortly. 'And to you it's going to mean the loss of five hundred pounds.'

'I know all about that,' remarked the landlord slowly. 'And I've been wondering if it's enough. Steady, Mr Benton,' he continued, as the other man's face grew purple with rage and the veins began to stand out on his forehead. 'There's no use losing your temper. You're just a bird of passage: this is my home. And people in these lonely parts talk a lot.'

'What the hell will they have to talk about?' The angry colour had died down; Benton spoke almost casually. 'Besides, we've been into all that.'

'Yes, we've been into it,' agreed the landlord. 'But that doesn't prevent one's thoughts. And as I said, I'm wondering if five hundred is enough.'

'Oh, are you?' Benton almost shouted. 'You can't back out now, man.'

'I didn't say I was going to,' said the landlord calmly. 'But when all is said and done the rewards are disproportionate. You, on your own showing, rake in a fortune . . .'

'That's a lie,' snapped the other. 'It's most of it gone already.'

'Have it your own way.' The landlord shrugged his shoulders. 'If you don't rake one in, you prevent the police knowing that you've already raked one out. In other words, you save yourself a nice long stretch, besides losing what is left of the dough, while I'm left here to deal with all the enquiries that are bound to be made, and to answer for what took place on my property. No'—his jaw went out stubbornly—'five hundred is not enough, Mr Benton. It's got to be a thousand.'

For a moment it seemed as if Benton was going to hit the landlord. His powerful fists clenched, and involuntarily he took a step towards him. And then he noted that unostentatiously the landlord had picked up a full bottle of whisky and was holding it by the neck.

'I forgot you were used to a rough house.'

Not very successfully Benton turned his scowl into an apology for a grin. 'Look here—we two mustn't quarrel.'

'I'm not quarrelling.' The landlord replaced the bottle on the shelf.

'We're both in one another's hands,' continued Benton.

'Hold hard. I'm not in your hands—yet. And unless we come to terms maybe I never shall be.'

'Rot.' Benton laughed contemptuously. 'You take things too literally, my friend. I'm not talking about the future: I'm talking about the past. I know that you're up to your neck in debt. I know, and you know, that if I wanted to I could make

Hopkinson foreclose on you right away. And where would you be then? Outside—with your creditors swarming round you. Yes, it's your turn to look sullen now, isn't it?' Shrugging his shoulders, he lit a cigarette.

'Listen to me, Parrish,' he continued quietly, 'and you'll hear some common horse sense. If there's one thing on this earth that I can't stand, it's a fool, and up to date I've never put you in that category. When I said that we were both in one another's hands, I spoke no more than the literal truth. If you refuse to help me, I'm for it. If I refuse to help you, you're for it. In fact, to put it even more shortly, unless we stick together we're both for it.'

'That's as may be,' cried the landlord stubbornly. 'But what I do say, Mr Benton, is this: the proportion isn't fair.'

'Very well,' said Benton after a pause, 'I'll tell you what I'll do. I'll split the difference and make it seven-fifty. And not one penny further will I go.'

'All right.' The landlord's tone was surly, but he knew only too well that Benton's logic was unanswerable. Knew also that in dealing with men of the Benton type there comes a moment when further argument is not only useless but dangerous.

'Seven-fifty it is. In one pound notes.'

'Naturally. You don't imagine I'm going to give a cheque, do you? And it will be up to you to get out of your difficulties in such a way that you don't rouse any suspicions. A little here and a little there spread over a long time will keep 'em quiet, and no questions will be asked. But if you go planking down wads of notes the place will begin to hum like a swarm of bees.'

'You can leave that to me, Mister.'

'I certainly shall,' said Benton shortly. . . . 'Who the hell is that?'

From the road outside had come a sudden shout.

'OK, Hugh. Here's a pub.'

'Do you know that voice?' said Benton quickly.

The landlord shook his head.

'I do not,' he said.

137

'Well, don't forget, you've got no rooms for tonight. We don't want any strangers here.'

The door was flung open, and a tall young man wearing an eyeglass entered the bar.

'Good evening,' he remarked affably. 'If, that is to say, the lie may be pardoned, for I have seldom known a fouler one.'

He advanced to the bar, undoing his coat as he came.

'Alcohol is clearly indicated,' he continued. 'And then more alcohol. A sentiment in which my friend when he arrives will doubtless concur.'

'And where may you have come from, sir?' asked the landlord.

'A motor car two or three hundred yards down the road, which is, at the present moment, more hopelessly ditched than any car I have ever seen. Nothing short of a battalion of men and a traction engine will get her out. We've been trying for ten minutes.'

He turned as the door was flung open again, and Benton glanced quickly at the landlord. This was an unexpected complication, but that worthy could only shrug his shoulders as the newcomer threw his overcoat into the corner. He was a large man, and his temper was obviously not of the best.

'You monstrous excrescence, Algy,' he remarked. 'It's lucky for you that you had a driving licence before they started tests. Where are we, incidentally?' he continued, turning to the landlord.

'Lonely Inn, sir. A quaint name, but it describes it right enough.'

'Lonely Inn! That's the place Peter mentioned, Algy. We've only got ten miles to go.'

'I don't know how the devil you intend to go then, unless you propose to walk. That car is a fixture for the night.'

'Could we be of any assistance?' said Benton, chipping in. 'Perhaps the four of us could get her out.'

'Not a hope,' answered the big man, lowering his whisky. 'My friend Longworth has done his job far too well for that. Nothing short of a breakdown gang with spades would be of the slightest use. Can you put us up for the night, landlord?'

'I'm afraid I can't, sir. I only have three rooms and they're all booked.'

'That's not so good.' The big man pushed over his empty glass. 'The same again,' he said. 'Have one yourself, and you too, sir, if you will. Algy, what are we going to do about it?'

'May I ask where you're making for, sir?' asked the landlord.

'Duncanton Hall. Do you know it?'

'Very well, sir. Belongs to Sir Gerald Moresby. And as you say, sir, it's about ten miles. Would it be any good if I telephoned?'

'We might try. Get through and find out if Mr Darrell is in. If so, say that Captain Drummond would like to speak to him. And if he's not in, ask him to ring me up here when he returns.'

'Very good, sir. I will do so at once.'

He left the bar, and Drummond sauntered over to the fire.

'You are a stranger in these parts?' said Benton politely.

'Complete,' answered Drummond. 'Is this a fair sample of the weather?'

'One gets quite a lot of mists, but not often at this time of the year.'

He paused, listening, as the faint thrumming of an engine came from outside and the white glare of lights shone hazily on the window.

'More fortunate than you, sir,' he continued. 'I wonder if these are my friends.'

He walked over to the door, and as he did so the landlord entered from behind the bar.

'You're through, sir,' he said to Drummond. 'The gentleman is on the 'phone. Would you come this way?'

Drummond followed him, and a moment or two later he heard Peter Darrell's voice at the other end of the wire.

'Listen, Peter,' he said. 'That raging blight Algy has ditched the car, and it's impossible to get her out tonight. Do you think you could come over and get us? We're at Lonely Inn.'

'But, my dear old boy,' came the answer, 'you can't see your hand in front of your face here. I doubt if any car would ever get through tonight. Why don't you both stop there? I'll come for you tomorrow morning.'

'There isn't a room vacant. They've only got three and they are full up.'

'What's that? Only three rooms. Don't talk tripe. To my certain knowledge that blackguard Parrish has eight.'

And at that moment Drummond saw a shadow on the floor by the door leading out of the bar. The landlord was listening. From the room came the sound of voices, one of them a woman's, and a faintly puzzled frown wrinkled his forehead.

'Hullo! Are you there, Hugh?' Peter's voice came through again.

'Yes, I'm here, Peter. I'm just thinking what is the best thing to do.'

Why had the landlord lied over the number of rooms? Why had he tried to turn away perfectly good trade? And why did Peter allude to him as a blackguard?

'Well, old man, it's impossible to get to you tonight.' Peter's tone was definite. 'If by any chance it lifts later, I'll come over. But it won't.'

'I understand, Peter—perfectly.' The frown had gone: a faint smile twitched round his lips. 'And never forget, old boy, that out of the most unlikely oysters there sometimes emerges a pearl. Did you say anything? Merely a hiccough! Good. Well, Algy and I will expect you when we see you.'

He replaced the receiver, and strolled back into the bar, to find two newcomers. One was a scholastic-looking grey-haired man with a slight stoop. He wore pince-nez and at the moment was warming his hands by the fire. The other was a girl, whom Algy was contemplating with considerable favour. She was young—nineteen or twenty at the most—and a well fitting jumper and skirt showed off her figure to perfection. She glanced up as Drummond came in, and then continued her remarks. And it was obvious that she was not in the best of tempers.

'Anyway, where is Tiny?' she demanded of Benton.

'I'm afraid he has not arrived yet. And though I don't want to be despondent, I'm afraid, with this mist, there's a chance he won't be able to manage it. Still there's plenty of time yet. Now I think I'd better go and put your car away for you.'

'That's very good of you, Harold,' said the grey-haired man. 'Mary has had all the driving she wants today.'

'Why did he ever suggest we should come to this beastly place, Daddy?' she cried as Benton left the room.

'It's central, my dear. Convenient for Tiny and us and him. Don't forget he's a busy man. And no one could have foreseen this mist.'

'Grim, isn't it?' said Drummond. 'You were luckier than us, sir. We got ditched about three hundred yards down the road.'

'I saw the car as we passed,' cried the girl. 'What bad luck!'

And at that moment Benton put his head round the door.

'Would it be of any use to you, sir,' he said to Drummond, 'if before I put Mr Patson's car away I towed you out? I have a rope.'

'I wouldn't dream of troubling you,' answered Drummond affably. 'She is quite all right where she is for the night. My friend is coming over from Duncanton Hall if he can. If not, we shall have to make shift in the bar here.'

'You know Sir Gerald?' said the grey-haired man as Benton withdrew.

'Slightly,' answered Drummond. 'A great friend of mine is staying with him, and we are supposed to be putting up there on our way down from Scotland.'

'A charming man. My daughter and I have met him two or three times.'

'You come from this part of the country?' asked Drummond.

'About forty miles away,' said the other. 'This is a rendez-vous for us and my daughter's fiancé with my solicitor, Mr Benton.'

For a moment or two Drummond studied him through half-closed lids. A delightful old man, he reflected; of the type who tells his life-history to complete strangers. And apparently his daughter thought so too.

'Really, Daddy,' she remarked, 'I don't think those details can interest anybody else.'

She gave Drummond an apologetic little smile, which he returned. And then his eyes fixed themselves on the landlord who was busy doing nothing behind the bar.

'And where is this gentleman going to sleep?' he asked. 'I understood you had only three rooms.'

'If he comes, sir,' cried the landlord obsequiously, 'I shall turn out of my room, of course. You see I have other rooms, but they are not furnished.'

'Oh,' Drummond grunted non-committally, and joined Algy at his table. The girl and her father were talking by the fire, to be joined a few moments later by Benton.

'I don't think, Algy,' said Drummond in a low voice, 'that mine host is a very clever man. Did you notice what he said? "If he comes." Why "If?"'

'The mist, old fruit: the mist.'

'The mist didn't come down till an hour ago. Up till then therefore he must have assumed that the fiancé was arriving. And yet he has taken no steps to provide a certain guest with a room.'

'What are you getting at, Hugh?'

'At present, nothing. Peter alluded to him over the 'phone as a blackguard, and said that to his certain knowledge he had eight rooms. Which may or may not mean anything. He may have said blackguard as a term of endearment, and he probably has no idea how many rooms there are. At the same time . . .'

He lit a cigarette thoughtfully, his eyes on the group by the fire.

'I wonder if I'm fancying things, Algy,' he continued. 'Or is the wish father to the thought?' he added with a grin. 'But I'm inclined to agree with the girl. In these days of easy travel why choose a damned awful pub like this for a business rendezvous? Ah! The girl and Pop are going upstairs with the landlord. I think I'll lead Mr Benton up the garden path a little. Come over to the fire.'

'It will be fortunate for us if Miss Patson's fiancé does not turn up,' he remarked. 'It will solve the question of accommodation.'

'I don't think you had better rely on it,' said Benton. 'He will get through if he possibly can.'

'But with only three rooms it's going to be a bit awkward for him,' went on Drummond.

'Three rooms! Er—three rooms! What the deuce . . . Er — Parrish!

The landlord appeared in the bar.

'Parrish—what on earth did you mean when you said three rooms? You meant—four. There's one for Mr Montgomery.'

'I was giving up my own, sir, to him,' said the landlord after a pause.

'Ah, yes: of course, of course. Your own. I'd forgotten,' said Benton.

'You ought to keep a reception clerk here, you know,' said Drummond blandly. 'Someone whose masterly brain could co-ordinate this seething mass of visitors, without mine host being in doubt up till the last moment as to where the angels are going to watch over him.'

'Fortunately for him,' said Benton, with a laugh, 'I don't think he'll be left wondering for long tonight.' He was staring at the window as he spoke. 'The mist is definitely lifting, though I never thought it would. And that means that Mr Montgomery will certainly arrive, and that you will be able to reach Duncanton Hall.'

He was right: already some stars were showing and the night was almost clear.

'How very lucky for all concerned,' said Drummond quietly, and as he spoke the telephone rang. 'Very lucky indeed,' he repeated as the landlord went to answer it. 'And so I shall never know the answer.'

'The answer!' Benton looked at him. 'What to?'

'The great problem. Where should we have slept if the mist had continued?'

'Mr Darrell, sir,' said the landlord, coming back. 'Wanted to know what it was like here. I told him, and he's coming over right away.'

'Thank you,' remarked Drummond, and fell silent, staring at the fire, whilst Algy watched him curiously. Benton had left the room and the landlord was busy behind the bar.

'What's stung you, Hugh?'

'The first time the landlord said three rooms Benton said nothing, although on their own showing four were needed.

143

Presumably he'd ordered them. But when I said three rooms to him he got hot and bothered. Four were necessary and he didn't know the landlord was turning out his. Moreover, when the landlord said it Mr Montgomery had not been mentioned: when I said it he had. Get me, Algy?'

'Not quite'.

'There was no necessity to account for Mr Montgomery until the girl mentioned him. And they hadn't rehearsed that bit so far as we were concerned.'

'But why was there no necessity to account for Montgomery? Supposing he'd turned up.'

'Suppose my foot. Don't you see, Algy, that the only possible reason which would have kept Benton quiet when the landlord said three rooms instead of four was the knowledge that Parrish was turning out of his—if the show was above-board. And he didn't know it until the landlord told him a few minutes ago.'

'But what does it lead to, man?'

'That Montgomery is not coming at all. That only three rooms have been booked, and when I cornered the landlord all he could say was what he did. For if he had then mentioned a fourth, that would have been available for you and me. And they don't want you and me here.'

'I say, old boy, it's a bit far fetched, isn't it?'

'Is it? You think it over. I don't like it, Algy. That man Benton may be a solicitor, but if he was mine I'd change my firm. No—I don't like it. Father strikes me as a dear old chap, but he'd be a child in the hands of those two.'

'What do you propose to do about it?'

'I haven't got as far as that—yet. We'll see what Peter thinks.'

But Peter Darrell, when he arrived a quarter of an hour later, was not very helpful. And even Drummond, after the suitcases had been taken out of the stranded car, had to confess to himself that it looked a bit thin. When actually repeated to someone who had not been there, the whole point of the number of rooms seemed to fall flat.

'When I called Parrish a blackguard,' said Peter, 'it was really only a figure of speech. Admittedly the man hasn't a good reputation, but it's principally because he's in debt all over the place. And admittedly that inn hasn't a good reputation either, but that is largely due to the stories from the past, and is nothing to do with the present man. There were two or three mysterious murders and disappearances in days gone by. Come on, old boy, let's push back before there's any chance of the mist returning. After all, what can happen to the lady? You surely aren't suggesting that the wicked solicitor has taken her there to wreak his evil will on her?'

'I'll lay six to four he gets a cauliflower ear if he has,' remarked Algy with a grin. 'Tread on it, Peter: I want a cocktail.'

All perfectly logical, Drummond agreed, and yet, try as he would all through the evening, he could not shake off his feeling that something was wrong. Absurd to imagine that Benton and the landlord intended any violence to old Patson and his daughter: retribution would be immediate, especially now that Algy and he had been to the inn. Equally absurd to imagine that Benton was trying any funny stuff. And yet . . . back it came again and again. Why such a rendezvous? Why that discrepancy about the rooms? And at last he could stand it no longer.

'Peter,' he said, 'I may be several sorts of an ass. But I can't help it: I've got to be sure. Now Moresby knows the Patsons slightly. I want you to ring up Lonely Inn, ostensibly for Moresby, and ask to speak to Miss Patson or her father. Say anything you like about hearing that they are in the neighbourhood, etc., but find out if Montgomery has arrived.'

'OK, Chief,' said Peter resignedly. 'And if he has?'

'Make a noise like a hen and ring off. Then come back and we'll play slosh.'

Peter left the hall, and Drummond glanced round the house party. It was a large one, and he was fully conscious that he was not pulling his weight. But he couldn't help it: once the other matter was settled everything would be different. And then he saw Peter coming towards him and knew the answer before he spoke.

'The gentleman has not arrived,' said Peter briefly. 'I spoke to the girl, and she said that they can't understand why he hasn't 'phoned if he was hung up.'

'Algy!'

Drummond beckoned to Longworth, who came over and joined them.

'Montgomery has not arrived at Lonely Inn, nor has he telephoned. It is now half-past ten and the night is clear. That settles it.'

'Merciful heavens!' cried Algy. 'Settles what?'

'Go and change,' said Drummond briefly. 'Coming, Peter? We'll sneak out by a side door, and get off as soon as possible.'

'Lights out, Peter. We'll leave the car here and walk.'

A quarter of a mile ahead of them a solitary light from one of the top windows of Lonely Inn was shining over the moors. The wind had dropped; the night was fresh and pitch dark. The road stretched in front of them—a smudged grey streak: from somewhere in the distance came the faint music of water over stones. Save for that everything was uncannily still.

They were all wearing rubber shoes, and had there been a spectator he might have thought that three phantoms were abroad that night. Not a sound heralded their passing, they loomed up and were gone. And when they were still a hundred yards from the inn, the light in the top window was extinguished. A narrow beam across the road, however, now became visible. The bar was evidently still occupied.

The curtains were drawn, but an open chink gave them a clear view of the interior. Benton was standing with his back to the fire; the landlord was in his usual position behind the bar. And though he was still quite sober, it was obvious that he had had enough.

'Her light's just gone out,' the landlord said, and the words came clearly to the watchers through the open window. 'Let's get on with it.'

'Everything ready outside?' asked Benton.

The landlord nodded and bent down behind the bar. And
when he straightened up he had in his arms a mongrel sheep
dog.

'Don't forget to switch out the light in the passage,' continued Benton. 'I'll go up to my room now.'

'What the devil!' breathed Drummond. 'Don't say we're
mistaken after all.'

'We,' muttered Algy gloomily. 'I like that.'

But Drummond had faded away like a ghost, and when they
found him he was in a corner of the yard at the back. On the
opposite side a candle was flickering in a stable, and as they
watched it they could see a man's shadow dancing fantastically
against the wall as he moved.

'The landlord,' whispered Drummond. 'He's taken the dog
over there.'

After a few moments the candle was blown out, and they
heard the stable door open and shut. Then steps came across
the yard, and the back door closed. The landlord had retired
for the night.

'Really, old man,' said Peter peevishly, 'I'm getting a bit fed
up with this. For heaven's sake let's get back to bed. What's
stung you now?'

From the stable came a mournful howl, but Drummond was
standing motionless, peering in front of him, and his grip had
tightened on their arms.

'Stay where you are,' he muttered, and vanished into the
darkness.

'Has he gone loopy?' asked Algy. 'Can you see anything?
And listen to that dog.'

Howl after howl was coming from the stable—the piteous
cry of a dog in misery. And suddenly a light went on in one of
the rooms upstairs and they saw the girl outlined against it by
the window. Saw a dark figure in the yard below—a figure
which vanished like a wraith into the shadows by the back
door.

For a while the girl stood there; then she withdrew into the
room. But Peter was not watching her; he, too, was now
staring in front of him. And at last he turned to Algy.

147

'Look about three yards from the back door,' he whispered. 'Out into the yard. Do you see what I mean? That dry square in the middle of the damp stones . . . I can spot it now the light is on. Is that what Hugh meant?'

But now voices were coming from the hotel, though the light upstairs had been extinguished as abruptly as it had been switched on. Then they heard the key turn in the back door, and Benton's voice.

'Be careful, Miss Patson. Straight ahead. That cursed land-lord must be drunk.'

And then, shrill above the howling of the dog—so unexpectedly that they both started forward—a woman's scream rang out, a scream that was followed two or three seconds later by a splash that seemed to echo hollowly up from the depths. For the moment the dog had ceased howling, startled into silence. Then windows were flung up; lights were switched on. And in the middle of it all Drummond joined them. In his arms he was carrying the girl, and in the faint light they could see his set white face and blazing eyes.

'Get the car, Peter,' he said tersely. 'We'll wait for you in the bar.'

From the yard came Benton's voice shouting 'Miss Patson; Miss Patson,' and from above the landlord's gruff shout, 'What's the matter?' Then came her father's agonized call: 'Darling—what's happened?'

They met the old man running down the stairs, and Drummond beckoned him into the bar. Then he put down the girl by the dying embers of the fire. She was now shivering uncontrollably and her eyes never left his face.

'Your daughter is quite safe, Mr Patson,' he said quietly. 'And as there is not much time, would you please tell me exactly what and who Mr Benton is. And why you are all here?'

'To meet her fiancé, and discuss settlements. Mr Benton has charge of her money : he's my solicitor.'

'Ah!' said Drummond softly. 'I see.'

'You fool!' came Benton's shout from outside. 'The well is uncovered—she's fallen in.'

148

'Precisely,' said Drummond even more softly. 'The well is uncovered: but she hasn't fallen in.'

'I don't understand, sir,' cried the old man pitifully.

'I fear you will soon, Mr Patson,' said Drummond gravely. 'Only too well.'

'It was the the dog howling, Daddy,' said the girl, her eyes still fixed on Drummond, 'Mr Benton asked me if I could do anything— he came to my room.'

'He did, did he?' Drummond's face was expressionless.

'And then this gentleman picked me up in the darkness and I screamed . . . What was that splash?'

'A sack of potatoes I kicked down the shaft,' said Drummond. 'Recovered the body, Mr Benton?'

Standing in the doorway was the solicitor. His eyes roved over the group by the fire. He seemed to have difficulty in swallowing. But at length he forced himself to speak.

'Thank Heavens!' he muttered. 'I was afraid that . . .'

'Yes', said Drummond politely. 'You were afraid that? . . .'

'That Miss Patson had fallen down the well.' With a great effort he pulled himself together. 'That fool Parrish had forgotten to put back the boards.'

'Quite,' drawled Drummond. 'So I perceived. Oh, Peter—I want to introduce you to Miss Patson, and her father . . . Mr Darrell . . . He has a car outside, Miss Patson, and I want you and Mr Patson to put on some clothes and then go with him to Duncanton Hall for the night. Then, Peter, would you come back for Algy and me.'

'But, really,' said the old man doubtfully, 'it's a little late, isn't it?'

'Go along, Daddy,' cried the girl. 'Go and get dressed.'

She watched him leave the room, then she rose and came over to Drummond.

'It would be stupid to thank you,' she said in a low voice. 'Why are you waiting here?'

'For a little chat with Mr Benton,' answered Drummond with the suspicion of a smile. 'Now trot along and get your things.'

* * *

'A merciful thing, sir, that you happened to be there,' said Benton ten minutes later. The car had gone, and he and the landlord were both in the bar.

'What brought you back I can't imagine,' he continued in a voice that despite all his efforts shook a little from time to time as he glanced at the big silent man who was staring at him unwaveringly from the fireplace. 'One can only be thankful that something did.'

'Can't imagine how I came to leave it open,' muttered the landlord uneasily.

And suddenly Drummond spoke.

'You are in the legal profession I believe, Mr Benton,' he remarked suavely.

'I am,' said the other.

'A profession which demands proof above everything else. A pity, isn't it, that I have no proof.'

'What of?' Benton was licking his lips.

'That you and your brother swine have been guilty of an attempt at the foulest and most damnably cold-blooded murder I have ever thought of.'

'How dare you, sir?' shouted the solicitor, starting forward. 'How dare you say such a thing?'

'Whether you ever notified Mr Montgomery at all,' continued Drummond impassively, 'is doubtful. You planned to get that girl and her old father here alone. You wanted to kill her because I should imagine you couldn't face any inquiry into her money affairs. So you staged an accident, Mr Benton. A dog which you knew would howl if left in the stable; a tender-hearted girl; a dark night; an open well. Just an accident, Mr Benton; a terrible and regrettable accident, with no one to blame. But unfortunately for you I have a strange gift of seeing in the darkness, and I spotted the top of the well.'

'It's a cursed lie,' said Benton thickly. 'Your statements are libellous, sir. You can't prove a word of them.'

'I know I can't,' remarked Drummond placidly. 'And it's such a pity for you that I do know that.'

'What do you mean?'

150

'Well, if I was foolish enough to charge you with this accusation before the police, I am sure that my action would fail, and I should be heavily mulcted in damages.'

'Glad you're beginning to see some sense.'

'Yes. But it's a pity for you all the same. Because, although I can't prove my case, I *know* it's true. So what are we going to do about it?'

'I don't know what you are, but I'm going to bed.'

'Oh, no, you're not, Benton,' said Drummond softly. 'Not yet, at any rate. You see, I hate not to support a worthy profession, and since I can't bring my case against you, I'm going to give you a case to bring against me. I cannot do what I would like to do, and throw you both down the well yourselves: the Board of Health people would certainly object to the water being polluted. And so I am going to do the next best thing, and give you a magnificent example of drumhead justice. Or injustice—as you like to put it. I see your accomplice has bolted, but never mind. I'll attend to him later.'

'My God!' screamed Benton, staring fascinated at a face chalk-white with cold fury. 'Here—keep off! Mercy! Have mercy!'

And the next spoken word came from Algy two minutes later.

'Steady, old Hugh! You'll kill him.'

Like a man coming out of deep water, Drummond looked up from the job in hand and blinked. Then he flung what was left of Benton into the corner and shook himself.

'That would never do, Algy,' he said dreamily. 'We don't want to lose him—yet. Now for the landlord.'

But that was a different story. They went through every room in the inn, but of Parrish there was no sign. Somewhere on the moors that worthy was lying up—waiting till it was safe to return. And so it was only Benton that Peter Darrell inspected with a professional eye half an hour later.

'Definitely one of your better efforts, old boy,' he remarked approvingly. 'The right one will, possibly, turn a richer green than the left, but I don't think he really deserves to be symmetrical.'

The Mystery Tour

The landlord of the Angler's Rest contemplated his preparations with pride. Underneath a huge tree was set a long table, groaning with good fare. Cold salmon and cucumber, meat pies and salad, with a Stilton cheese as the central *pièce de résistance*, went to make up a meal of much merit—a meal which he felt did credit to the famous hostelry he owned.

The order had been somewhat of a surprise. Well known though he was for the excellence of his food, his principal customers were fishermen. Through his land there flowed the Weldron, which, as all the fishing world knows, is one of the best trout streams in the south of England. and since the cost of a rod is considerable, it followed that most of his guests were men of means and leisure, who like peace and quiet in which to tell their lies. So that he wondered how this sudden influx would be viewed by the three who were staying with him at the moment.

And it had indeed been sudden—so sudden that he contemplated with justifiable pride his response to such an unexpected commission. Only four hours in which to prepare a genuine old English spread for thirty people was asking a good deal. And that was all the time he had been given. At four o'clock that afternoon a car had drawn up outside his hotel, and from it had descended a well-dressed and pleasant individual who had ordered dinner for thirty at eight o'clock. And it was to be no ordinary dinner, since it was no ordinary party. Simple and plain the food might be, but it must be of the very best. For, as the gentleman had pointed out, the atmosphere of a hundred years ago could be obtained with the genuine article just as well as with tinned salmon and tough beef, and with far more beneficial results to the digestion. And when he had proceeded to pass over a tenner as advance payment before getting back into his car, mine host had wasted no time.

'Great heavens, Jackson! What is this ghastly thing I see before my eyes? Have you got a charabanc party coming?'

He swung round: three men, their footsteps noiseless on the grass, were standing behind him contemplating the long table with horror.

'Not a charabanc, Captain Drummond,' he said. 'Money no object, sir. Old English fare, and of the very best. They're coming at eight.'

'You'd better give 'em that trout you stunned, Hugh,' said one of the three. 'Have you ever seen Captain Drummond fish, Jackson? Or I should say, "Have you ever heard him?"'

'Can't say as I have, Mr Darrell.'

'It sounds like a gramophone record—the departure of a troopship. First there is a loud crack and a branch behind him is torn off. That is followed by a medley of oaths, and the noise of a large cable hitting the water. Then the waves begin to break all round you.'

'My dear Peter,' said Drummond languidly, 'your insults leave me cold. I caught a fish—true, not a large one. But alone I did it.'

'I should damn well think you were alone,' remarked Darrell. 'I was a mile from you, and only great agility saved me from drowning in the bore you started.'

Drummond waved a vast hand.

'Beer, Jackson, beer. Lots of beer. And then tell us about your party. Algy, don't finger the food, you filthy beast.'

Algy Longworth returned from the table, his mouth full of meat pie.

'Definitely good, old jolly-belly,' he assured the landlord. 'Tell the varlet to feed those to me at dinner.'

'But joking apart,' said Darrell as the landlord went inside, 'what has the silly ass let us in for? It's sacrilege on an evening like this.'

'It is life,' answered Drummond, taking a pie himself. 'Life in this land of ours today. Here we sit, 'neath the old oak tree, surrounded by our trophies of the chase. The sun is sinking in the west; the shadows lengthen, throwing into gentle relief the rugged beauty of our features. All is peace; nought is heard save the gentle babble of the brook. . . .'

'Sit on his head,' said Algy. 'That's Eliza having a bath.'

'Where did I get to? Brook. . . . The babbling brook. And what does the future hold for us? Is it pleasing converse with fair ladies and brave men clad in knightly armour telling of glorious deeds in derring-do? Is it Dick Turpin bidding us ride the road with him as darkness falls? No, sir, it is not. It is the descent upon us of hordes of women, clasping grubby-nosed and puling brats to their bosoms, whilst from their foul conveyance a portable abomination will give us the fat stock prices. England, my England.'

'Beer, sir?' said the landlord at his elbow.

'Tell me, old friend of my youth,' continued Drummond, as he took a tankard, 'where is the spirit of adventure today? Rich and riotous adventure. . . . Does no red blood still flow in our veins? Passing over my battle today with that monster of the deep. . . .' He peered into his creel. 'By the way, where the hell is my fish?'

'Hidden under the third blade of grass,' said Darrell. 'Look here, Jackson, what on earth induced you to wish a beanfeast on us?'

'It's a funny sort of beanfeast, gentlemen, that stumps up a tenner in advance.'

'Worse and worse,' cried Algy. 'It's a gathering of absconding goose-club treasurers.'

'Hardly that,' came a suave voice. 'I can assure you, gentlemen, that our guests will not trouble you in the slightest.'

With a smile and a little bow the speaker crossed to the table and inspected the contents.

'He's the gentleman who gave the order, sir,' said the landlord in a hoarse aside to Drummond before joining the newcomer at the foot. 'The best I could do, sir,' he remarked, 'at such short notice.'

'And a very good best too,' said the other approvingly. 'Let us have plenty of ale and cider. And whisky for those who prefer it.'

He lit a cigarette and sauntered back to Drummond's bench.

'What a charming spot!' he remarked.

'Very,' agreed Drummond shortly. 'So quiet as a rule.'

Once again the man smiled.

'I see that you fear the worst,' he said. 'And I admit, gentlemen, that you will have to put up with a party of thirty for an hour or so. But I can promise you that there will be no banana skins or orange peel thrown about, and that everybody will be strictly sober. You will excuse me?'

With another bow he turned and went indoors, leaving the three men to their beer.

'That man,' said Drummond apropos of nothing, 'is not English. Algy, you hound of hell, go in and get these refilled. The whole staff is running round in circles over this damned party.'

'What about feeding somewhere else, Hugh?' said Darrell as Algy went obediently. 'The prospect is not inviting.'

'Not a bad notion, Peter. Let's lower another can and think about it. Though I admit I'm curious to see who the preparations are for.'

'We'll give 'em the once over and then push off,' suggested Darrell. 'Don't slop the beer, Algy.'

'Slop be blowed,' said Algy, putting down his tankard. 'Look here, you boys, our foreign friend seems a bit curious about us.'

'What's that?' cried Drummond.

'I was getting the drink through the hatch place, and he was round the corner in the bar having a quick one with Jackson.

'"You know them, Mr Jackson?" I heard him say.'

'"Very well, sir," answered the old boy. "Mr Darrell often comes here to fish, and the other two gentlemen are friends of his."

'And then Eliza gave me the tankards and they saw me, and shut up. But why should the organizer of this bun-worry be interested in us?'

'Why indeed?' agreed Drummond thoughtfully.

He relapsed into silence as Darrell gave him a warning kick under the table: the gentleman in question was approaching.

'I have just heard from the landlord,' he said, 'that you are frequent visitors here. And so I felt I must really come and express my regrets at this invasion of your privacy.'

'Don't mention it,' said Drummond. 'We are full of curiosity. . . . Now was that genuine?' he continued as the man moved away. 'Or was it an endeavour to explain his curiosity, knowing he'd been overheard in the bar by Algy?'

'We ought to know soon,' said Darrell. 'Here are the competitors arriving.' And then he gave a grunt of disgust. 'Good Lord!' he cried. 'It's one of those confounded Mystery Tours.'

'What are they?' asked Algy vaguely.

'My dear man, they've been going for years. You buy a ticket and get into a bus, which then starts off for some unknown destination. . . . You finally arrive at Stonehenge at dawn, where you are bitten all over by mosquitoes and the other passengers.'

The luxurious motor-coach drew up opposite the door. In front was a notice—MYSTERY TOUR: behind, standing by the open door, was the organizer of the party. And with languid interest they watched the guests descend—an interest which became slightly more animated during the process. For by no stretch of imagination could they visualize the occupants of the coach biting one another at Stonehenge. Or throwing banana skins about. For almost before a babel of voices broke out to proclaim their nationality it was obvious that the party consisted of well-to-do Americans.

The majority consisted of young people, but there was a leaven of older ones who were evidently parents. And from the fragments of conversation that came drifting to the ears of the three spectators it was clear that one and all of them were tickled to death with the whole performance. In fact, when the oldest inhabitant of the village, clad in a smock, appeared at the door of the inn, smoking a long clay pipe, a positive cheer went up from the younger members of the party.

'Ladies and gentlemen, will you please be seated.'

The voice of the organizer rose above the general hum of conversation.

'Sit where you like,' he continued. 'I am sure you can all sort yourselves out better than I can. And now,' he went on when all the chairs were occupied, 'I am just going to say a few words before our worthy host begins to serve the dinner. On our trip

156

over in the *Begonia*, you were good enough, sir,'—he turned to a grey-haired man on his right—'to bet me that I would not stage for you something out of which you would get a kick. That I think was your exact phrase.'

'Sure,' agreed the American.

'You were good enough to say that you would put yourselves unreservedly in my hands. And I asked you to assemble at Hyde Park Corner this afternoon, and get into the motor-coach which would be awaiting you there, so that you could embark on a mystery tour. I gave strict instructions to the driver and his mate that they were not to tell you where you were going—not even this half-way mark. Because I can assure you, ladies and gentlemen, that I should not consider I had seriously tried to win my bet if this was the finish of my entertainment. That comes later.

'But since we poor mortals must feed, I decided to try and introduce—even to such a prosaic thing as dinner—a certain novelty: to give you something as far removed from the Ritz and Claridge's as I could. And mercifully our fickle climate has been kind.

'Ladies and gentlemen, I want you to throw your minds back into the past. Seated where you are under that same tree, were the men who watched the beacons light on the hills yonder, as the Spanish Armada approached our shores over three hundred years ago. Seated where you are under that same tree were the men who awaited the latest news of Bonaparte. And they were eating the same fare as you will be eating tonight; and drinking the same. No cocktails, ladies and gentlemen: I forbid it. There is English ale, English cider, and I have stretched a point over Scotch whisky.

'There stands the inn as it stood then; there flows the stream as it flowed then. Nothing has changed save that you came in a motor-coach and not on horseback. You are dining in a little piece of untouched England.'

'If he says "God save the King",' whispered Drummond, 'I shall burst into tears.'

He was saved that, however: a burst of applause signified that the oration was over.

157

'What's stung you, Peter?' Drummond asked. For Darrell was staring thoughtfully at the table, his forehead wrinkling in a frown.

'You see that elderly grey-haired woman sitting two from the end,' he said, and Drummond nodded. 'I'm trying to think where the devil I've met her. . . . Somehow or other she's connected in my mind with cricket . . . Wait: it's coming. . . . That team I went out with to America two years ago. . . . It was then I saw her. . . . In Philadelphia. . . . Mrs . . . Mrs . . . I've got it: Mrs Walmeyer.'

'Who is Mrs Walmeyer?' asked Algy.

'Wife of Mr Walmeyer, the grey-haired bird who made the bet, and who is one of the ten richest men in the States. Her pearls, which she's got on now—incidentally she is reputed even to have her bath in 'em—are insured for five hundred thousand dollars. And the rest of her stuff is in keeping.'

'None of 'em look as if they were qualified for the dole,' said Drummond as he rose and stretched himself. 'But they seem harmless enough, so let's feed here if there's anything left to eat. I'm going to wash.'

He lounged indoors, leaving the other two over their beer.

'Going to introduce yourself to the girl friend?' asked Algy.

Darrell shook his head.

'Not I,' he said. 'I don't suppose for a second that she'd remember me, and I'd hate to butt into the party. You know, I rather take off my hat to that fellow, whoever he is. I'll bet it's a novelty to this crowd.'

'Depends on the second part of the programme,' said Algy. 'What's stung Hugh? I want my dinner.'

And at that moment they saw Drummond beckoning from the door.

'Boys,' he said happily as they joined him, 'I have impinged on a fairy. Going up to my room I became aware of a faint but delightful scent. And as I stood sniffing the ozone, a door suddenly opened and I perceived a positive peach framed in the light. ' Is that you, Paul?" she said.

'I assured her that to my undying regret it was not, but I naturally placed what poor services I could render at her disposal. She thanked me adorably, and I asked her if she would like me to teach her fishing tomorrow. She seemed to think it was a capital idea, and on that high note of optimism we parted.'

'Was she a member of the party?' asked Algy.

'No, dear boy, she was not. I at once looked out of my window, and found that the mystery tour was all present and correct.'

'When did she arrive?' demanded Darrell.

'That is not the point. When will she leave?'

'On the spot, when she sees you by daylight,' said Algy. 'What have we got to eat? Your trout?'

'And you have the frightful gall to tell the poor child you'll teach her to fish?' Darrell gave a hollow laugh. 'If I did my duty, I'd summon the police.'

'Jealousy, jealousy,' said Drummond sadly. 'Jackson, old host, bring some of the fish Mr Darrell bought in the village this afternoon.'

They sat down by an open window, from which they could see the table outside. Dinner, there, was nearly over, and the younger and more impatient members of the party were beginning to agitate for the next item on the programme. They were clamouring for a hint as to what it was going to be. But the organizer was adamant. Smilingly he shook his head; everything would be discovered in due course. The whole show would be ruined if it was given away beforehand.

'But I can promise you all,' he said, 'that it will come up to your expectations. If it doesn't,' he added with a shrug of his shoulders, 'I lose my bet. Now—are we all ready?'

There came a pushing back of chairs, followed by a general exodus towards the motor coach.

'And we shall never know,' said Drummond, 'whether he wins his bet or not. But the ghastly thought that assails me is that he is Paul. That laden tomorrow with American dollars he will insist on attending my fishing lesson . . . My God!'

The other two stared at him in amazement, for he had jumped to his feet and was staring out of the window like a man possessed. And the next moment he had left the room.

'What's the matter with him?' said Algy bewildered, and Darrell shook his head.

'No good asking me,' he answered. 'Here he comes again.'

Gone was the Drummond of a few moments before, and they looked at him even more bewildered.

'Listen to me,' he said curtly. 'The two drivers on that coach have been changed. They're not the same men that brought it down from London.'

'What of it?' cried Algy feebly.

'They never send four men on a coach, you fool: only two. Why have they been changed? And who has taken the original men's places?'

He swung round as the landlord came in.

'Jackson—where are the two men who brought down the coach? I saw them having their dinner a quarter of an hour ago.'

'A dreadful thing, sir, has happened.' The worthy man was wringing his hands. 'They've both of them drunk too much. Luckily there were two others here who were qualified to take their places.'

'Very lucky,' snapped Drummond. 'Let me see the two originals.'

And most assuredly they had drunk too much if appearances were to be believed. Snoring stertorously, they were sprawling over a bench, and Drummond took one look at them.

'Drugged, or I'm a Dutchman,' he cried to Darrell. 'And you don't drug men for fun. Get the car, Algy, and jump to it!'

He let out a bellow of laughter.

'Adventure, boys: rich, riotous adventure after all.'

'But what's the game, Hugh?'

'That, old lad, remains to be seen. All that matters at the moment is that Paul—if it is Paul—has abducted a perfectly good party of American millionaires. Look here, Jackson,' he continued as Algy sprinted out of the room, 'what did these two sportsmen have to drink?'

'A pint of beer each, sir.'

'Was it laced with anything?'

'Not that I know of, sir.'

'Even if it were doped with gin, Hugh,'.said Darrell, 'one pint wouldn't produce *that* effect.'

'I agree. And where did the two substitutes spring from?'

'They'd been here some time, sir. And when Mr Verrinder saw what had happened they volunteered to drive instead.'

'Is Verrinder the name of the man who organized the show?'

'That's right, sir. Mr Paul Verrinder.'

Drummond smiled.

'And the lady upstairs?'

'A friend of his, sir. She went off in a car with another gentleman about ten minutes ago. Is anything wrong, sir?' he added anxiously as Algy appeared in the doorway to say the car was ready.

'That's what we're going to find out, Jackson. Did anyone drop a hint as to where they were going?'

'I heard the lady say something about it being five miles beyond Romsey, sir.'

'Good. We should overtake 'em by then. Come on, boys.'

They tumbled into the car, and set off in pursuit. It was a quarter of an hour before they saw the lights of the coach in front of them. Drummond at once slowed down. To overtake the party would be fatal; to sit close on their tail might arouse the driver's suspicions. And so with dimmed lights he kept two or three hundred yards behind, only drawing nearer when they came to Romsey itself.

The coach took the Winchester direction, and Drummond fell back again. From now on more care was necessary, since the actual destination was unknown. And so when the coach suddenly swung right handed along a narrow road, he was only about a hundred yards behind.

For two miles they continued, then once again the coach swung right—this time through lodge gates into a drive flanked on each side by an avenue of trees. And very cautiously, with lights extinguished, Drummond swung in after them.

In the distance they could see the dim outline of a big house against the sky. It was in darkness, as was the lodge; evidently the place was empty. And as Drummond turned the car on to the grass verge and ran her in between two trees he chuckled joyfully.

'What the devil is the game, chaps? Or can it be that the show is genuine?'

The party had dismounted by the time they reached the house: the motor coach, lights switched off, was standing by the front door. And keeping in the shadows of the trees, the three of them skirted round the edge of the drive.

Suddenly Drummond paused, his hand raised warningly. From close by had come the sound of voices and a short laugh; then two figures loomed up and disappeared in the direction of the house.

A moment or two later Drummond came upon a fast sports car carefully hidden behind some shrubbery.

'Can it be that it just grew here?' he continued. 'Or is it for a rapid getaway? In either event, I think we will tune it up.'

He opened the bonnet, and under the ministrations of three experts the car gave up any claims to fastness. In fact, its maximum speed would now be that of a cart-horse towing it. Then conscious of work well done they continued their progress towards the front door.

It was open, and they cautiously entered the hall. Practically empty of furniture, the house smelled of disuse. In front of them they could dimly see the stairs, with a stained glass window at the top: on each side doors opened into lofty rooms empty as the hall. And then from the back of the house they heard Paul Verrinder's voice.

'Ladies and gentlemen.'

'Come on,' whispered Drummond. 'The curtain is going up.'

'Ladies and gentlemen,' continued the voice, 'you are now in the banqueting hall of Strathray Place—one of the seats until quite recently of the Earls of Strathray. Above us, at the far end of the room, is the musicians' gallery, untouched since the terrible tragedy that took place over a century ago.'

Without a sound Drummond and his friends crept towards the door and stood outside. A faint light filtering in through the mullioned windows on to the floor only seemed to throw into greater darkness the rest of the room. And when for a moment the voice ceased, a sudden nervous giggle from some girl came almost as a relief.

'Silence, please!' Verrinder was speaking again. 'It is essential that you should try to attune yourselves to the atmosphere of the place. And to help you I will tell you the story of that night. For in the room where we now stand a very strange drama was being enacted.

'Picture to yourselves a long table, on which burned countless candles. It was laid for a party of thirty. The historic Strathray plate was adorning it in all its magnificence. The major-domo and the footmen stood motionless in their places, though had one looked at them closely, one would have noticed that here and there a finger twitched, a jaw clenched unnaturally. For grim things were in the air that night, and the men sensed it.

'Seated at one end of the table was their master—the eighth Earl. Dressed in the height of fashion, with the candlelight glinting on his aquiline features, he seemed to be enjoying some secret joke as his eyes wandered from one to the other of his two companions, who sat on each side of him. The remaining chairs were empty.

'On his right was a beautiful girl; on his left a young man, whose plainer clothes betokened a less exalted rank than that of his host. A handsome youth with sensitive hands and face, he kept shooting little glances first at his host and then at the girl opposite, who kept her eyes fixed steadily on her plate.

'Slowly the meal dragged on, each course ushered in with the pomp and ceremony habitual to the household, but it was noticeable that the only one of the three who spoke was the earl. And after a while he frowned.

'"You are silent, my love," he said suavely to the girl. "I trust nothing ails you."

'"I thank you, no my lord," she answered. "But I am wondering what can have happened to your lordship's other guests."

'"Surely, my dear, the company of your husband and Mr Ludlow is ample compensation for the absence of others. What say you, Mr Ludlow?"

'"That I greatly appreciate your lordship's hospitality," said the young man.

'"Long may your appreciation continue," remarked the earl. "Put the wine upon the table." He signed to the major-domo. "And then begone. And now we can talk undisturbed," he continued as the servants left the room. "I understand that you are a musician, Mr Ludlow."

'"In my poor way," said the other with a bow.

'"Excellent. I did well to countermand the players. And since you too, my love, perform so charmingly upon the harp I shall be privileged to listen to a duet later."

'The eyes of the two young people met, held for an instant and then fell apart. But in that instant the message had flashed between them. The earl knew. How he had found out that they loved one another did not matter; he knew.

'"A duet played in the musicians' gallery with an audience small but most appreciative. Incidentally, my dear wife, small though the audience may be, it will be larger than many you have both played to."

'"I don't understand you, my lord," she whispered through dry lips.

'"Don't you?" he sneered. "Then your brains are hardly in keeping with your beauty."

'He clapped his hands.

'"Bring Mr Ludlow's violin," he ordered the servant who had appeared. "And her ladyship's harp."

'"My lord," stammered the youth. "I am not in the mood . . . I . . ."

'"To play with a lady! Zounds, Mr Ludlow, what an ungallant remark! But I fear I must insist."'

Paul Verrinder's voice ceased, and even as it did so a faint light began to illuminate the musicians' gallery and a little sign of expectation whispered through the party. For there, seated by the rail, clad in the costumes of a bygone day, were a girl and a man.

'Play!' the harsh voice rang out again. 'Play—damn you — your last duet!'

But no music followed. Instead there came a splintering

crash, and the two figures seemed to fall through the floor of the gallery into the darkness below. Two dreadful thuds: the dying twang of a violin string: then silence—save for a sardonic laugh.

'The last duet! Admirably played.'

For a moment there was a stupefied silence, then pandemonium broke loose. Women screamed, men shouted for lights. So that it was not surprising that in the general uproar the noise of a sharp struggle near the door passed unnoticed. And when Paul Verrinder's voice rose above the tumult calling for silence the struggle was over.

'Ladies and gentlemen, be silent, I beg of you. Everything is quite all right. Neither of them is hurt. Look!'

He switched on a torch, and there, carefully placed under the floor of the gallery in such a position that it had been invisible was a net. On the floor lay two dummies, a harp and a violin: the two performers had disappeared. And as the full realization of how they had been spoofed dawned on the party, a burst of applause broke out.

'Gee! Mr Verrinder,' cried Walmeyer, 'that gave me one of the nastiest turns I've had for some time. I sure thought there had been an accident.'

'And do I win my bet, Mr Walmeyer?'

'You certainly do. It was worth all of five thousand dollars. And if you call round to the Porchester tomorrow I'll have the greatest pleasure in handing 'em over.'

'But surely,' came a cheerful voice, 'the entertainment is not yet over, Mr Verrinder?'

And at that moment the headlights of a car shining through the windows lit up the room clearly. The whole party swung round. Standing at the top of the three steps leading down into the banqueting hall was Hugh Drummond. In his hand he held a small bag, the sight of which caused Paul Verrinder's face to turn a delicate shade of green.

'Who the blazes are you?' said Mr Walmeyer.

'Just a helper in the party,' answered Drummond affably.

'I've seen him before,' cried one of the men. 'He was having dinner at the Angler's Rest.'

'Quite right,' said Drummond. 'And now, Mr Walmeyer, I gather from what you said a few moments ago that the entertainment up to date has been worth five thousand dollars.'

'That is so.'

'Well, if we can give you a further entertainment, where the thrill will, I think, be as great—even if not from the same cause—as the one you have already had, would you be prepared to make that five thousand, ten?'

'Yes. I would,' answered the American after a pause.

'You see, Mr Verrinder thinks of everything. And supposing something had gone wrong with the admirable little play he staged for you tonight, he had another card up his sleeve. Shall I begin—er—Paul?'

'Of course,' said Verrinder, contorting his face into a smile.

'Now your pearls, Mrs Walmeyer,' continued Drummond. 'You know—I don't see them round your neck.'

Her hands flew to her throat.

'John!' she screamed. 'They've gone.'

Drummond held up his hand.

'Please don't be alarmed! Peter! Mrs Walmeyer's pearls, please. Will you hand them to the lady . . . Thank you. And now exhibit B.'

He groped in the bag and extracted a bulky pocket book.

'Someone seems to have lost this. Marked J.B.W. Any claims?'

'My wallet,' howled John B Walmeyer.

'And mine's gone . . . Mine too . . .' came in an excited babble from the other men.

'Sort them out, gentlemen . . . Peter, put the collection on the floor. Now, Mr Walmeyer,' he continued as the others crowded round the bag, 'I leave it to you to decide whether we deserve that extra five thousand dollars or not. My friend here, Mr Algernon Poltwhistle, the most famous pickpocket entertainer in the world, was specially hired by Mr Verrinder tonight, to put the finishing touch to the evening's performance . . . Algernon Poltwhistle. . . .'

He pushed Algy forward, who bowed deeply.

'His other well-known trick is a life-like imitation of bath water running away, but as the hour is late, and he wishes to get back to his wife and eight children, we will not call on him for that. However, Mr Walmeyer, as I see that you have considerably more than the sum at stake in your pocket book—may I be permitted to extract ten thousand dollar notes?'

John B Walmeyer looked at him with shrewd blue eyes: then he looked at Verrinder. And then, like little Audrey, he laughed and he laughed and he laughed.

'What are you going to do with the ten thousand?' he asked, when he had recovered.

'It will come in most handy for Mr Poltwhistle's ninth child,' answered Drummond blandly.

'Help yourself,' said John B Walmeyer resignedly. 'And may heaven preserve me from being anywhere in the neighbourhood when he has his tenth.'

'A most satisfactory ending, Paul, to a charming evening,' remarked Drummond a few minutes later.

The mystery tour had departed on its way back to London, amidst general hilarity, after voting the performance a howling success.

'There is one thing, however, that I would like to know,' he continued 'How did you propose to do your own getaway? It wouldn't have been long before someone spotted that he'd been robbed.'

'By car, confound you,' said Verrinder with a grin. 'Along with two drivers of the coach. I was going to leave the whole outfit here.'

'A little difficult,' remarked Drummond. 'We have already attended to it.'

'The devil you have. Incidentally, what have you done with Joe Parkins?'

'Is he the engaging gentleman who pinched the stuff?'

Verrinder nodded.

'I dotted him one, Paul. My fist crashed against his jaw. He's in a flower bed outside. But a little arnica, or one of those excellent advertised preparations should soon put him right.

Ah! And here is the fair accomplice. My congratulations, angel face. Is the fishing still on?'

The girl lit a cigarette.

'What put you wise, big boy?' she asked.

'Drugging the drivers, darling.'

'It was a risk, I know,' she said. 'But if we were going to leave the crowd here it had to be done.'

And then she looked at him curiously.

'Why didn't you give us away?'

'Because I haven't enjoyed myself so much for a long while,' said Drummond with a grin. 'Most reprehensible, I know—but there you are.'

'What about the ten thousand bucks?' cried Verrinder.

'What, indeed?' said Drummond grinning still more.

'Damn it—you might go fifty-fifty. I've paid for the dinner, and the coach, to say nothing of mugging up English history till I was faint from brain fag.'

Drummond roared with laughter.

'Nothing doing, old boy, absolutely nothing. Your sole reward must be the consciousness of tomorrow's good deed.'

'What do you mean?' cried Verrinder, looking puzzled.

'Acting on your instructions, Paul, I shall tomorrow send ten thousand dollars to one of the Village Centres for Disabled Soldiers and Sailors. Unless, of course, you have another charity you fancy. Well . . .?'

'I leave it to you,' said Verrinder resignedly. 'I suppose my overdraft in Paris is not on the approved list.'

The Oriental Mind

Hugh Drummond sat at beer. Outside, a pea-soup fog drifted sluggishly against the club windows; inside, the most crashing bore in Europe was showing signs of vocal labour. It was therefore with feelings of considerable relief that, over the rim of his tankard, he saw Algy Longworth approaching. Anything was preferable to the bore, so he waved a large hand benignly.

'You may approach the presence, Algy,' he remarked. 'Do you feel as lousy as you look?'

'I thought I should probably find you drinking yourself to death in here,' said Algy. 'I will join you in a pink gin.'

Drummond beckoned to a passing waiter.

'And to what do we owe the pleasure of your visit?' he asked.

'Can you lunch today, old boy?'

'Who with and where?'

'Me and a wench.'

Drummond looked at him suspiciously.

'Where's the catch?' he demanded. 'If she's the goods you don't want me, and if she isn't I don't want her.'

Algy grinned.

'Not this outing, laddie. You just listen while I hand out all the dope that I know myself. Have you ever heard me mention Marjorie Porter?'

'Probably,' said Drummond resignedly. 'But don't let that deter you.'

'This morning I got a letter from her,' continued Algy. 'It was written from her home in Norfolk, and she asked me to give her lunch at the Berkeley today. She went on to say that it was urgent, and . . . wait a moment. I'll read you this bit.'

He produced a letter from his pocket.

'She says: "Haven't you got a friend who is very strong, and likes adventure? Do bring him too if you can. I really do want help."'

Algy replaced the letter, and finished his drink.

'There you are, my boy. Damsel in distress appealing for assistance. What about it?'

'So far,' said Drummond, 'you have our ear. But I'd like to get the form a bit better. Who is this Marjorie Porter?'

'A damned nice girl. Her father and mother both died when she was a kid, and since then she has lived with her uncle, one John Greston, at Macklebury Hall. He had a son, whom I never met and who died out East some months ago. There was something a bit odd, so I heard, over the matter, but I haven't seen Marjorie since then, so I really don't know the facts.'

'And this John Greston. Have you met him?'

'Once: years ago. He's a great big giant of a man, and he must be rising sixty.'

'So you've got no idea what's stung the girl?'

'Not an earthly. But I know her well enough to feel sure that she wouldn't have written what she did without good cause.'

'All right, old boy,' said Drummond. 'You can count me in. I'll be at the Berkeley at one.'

He was a bit late, and when he arrived Algy was already there talking to a very attractive girl. And having been duly introduced the three of them went in to lunch.

'It strikes me, my pet,' said Algy, after he had given his order, 'that you'd better begin all over again. All that Hugh knows is that you live with Uncle John in Norfolk.'

'It's really very sweet of you, Captain Drummond,' she said, 'to listen to the troubles of a complete stranger, but honestly I am most terribly worried.'

'Cough it up, Miss Porter,' said Drummond. 'If you only knew, you're really doing a kindness to two great lazy brutes who are both bored stiff with life.'

'Did Algy tell you about my cousin? Uncle John's son.'

'I mentioned it,' said Algy. 'And incidentally, my dear, that was a thing I wanted to ask you. What happened?'

'What did you hear?' asked the girl.

'That he'd died somewhere out East.'

'He committed suicide, Algy,' she said quietly. 'And that was the beginning of all the trouble. Did you ever meet Jack?'

'I don't think I did.'

'He was an awfully nice creature, but terribly weak where women were concerned. He was the apple of Uncle John's eye—Aunt Mary died when he was about six, and I suppose that threw the two of them together. At any rate, they were inseparable until about a year ago, when Jack fell in love with a woman at least ten years older than himself. Which might not have been so bad if she'd been a decent sort.

'I only met her once, when he brought her down to Macklebury Hall; and what Jack saw in her was beyond my comprehension. She was a hard-bitten gold-digger of the most blatant description, and she didn't even take the trouble to be civil to him. She was good-looking in her way, and she certainly knew how to put on her clothes, but having said that you've said all. She ordered him about like a dog, but he just didn't seem to see it. He was completely infatuated.

'Uncle John, of course, was furious, and when Jack announced his intention of marrying her there was the most appalling row, which ended with Uncle John telling him straight out that if he did he'd cut him off. As you perhaps know, Algy, Uncle John is a very wealthy man, but the threat produced no effect at all on Jack. What was money compared to the woman he loved, etc.? So my uncle had a brainwave and wrote the same ultimatum to the dame. And you can take it from me that that acted quicker than a dose of dynamite. She dropped Jack like a hot potato, and left for a long trip to the East to soothe her outraged nerves.'

'How long ago was all this?' asked Algy.

'Eunice Radnor sailed just twelve months ago. Jack, despite all we could do to stop him, followed by the next boat. He was mad with his father for having written to her, and they had one row after another before he left. Which made it all the worse for Uncle John when he heard about the tragedy.

'At first the news was very skimpy; just a bald telegram announcing that Jack was dead. Then came a letter from the head of the police in Ceylon giving the details. It appeared that she had got off the boat at Colombo, and was living in an hotel there when Jack arrived a fortnight later. How he found out she was disembarking there we don't know: he may have wirelessed her boat or something. At any rate, he tracked her down and went to see her. And what happened at the interview we don't know either, of course.

'According to the hotel boys very high words were heard coming from the room, and one swore that he had heard two men's voices inside. But this she denied absolutely when questioned later. At any rate, Jack was seen to leave the hotel in a state of great agitation—the interview had taken place after dinner—and no one seems to have seen him alive again. Four days later his body was found at the foot of some cliffs a few miles from Colombo, and he had evidently been dead for some time.'

'Then he may have slipped over,' remarked Drummond.

'Just what I said to my uncle, Captain Drummond, to try and soften the blow. But I'm afraid he didn't believe it, any more than I did. What happened, I fear, is obvious. Jack tried to persuade her to change her mind, and when she wouldn't he just went out and took his own life.'

'I wonder if there *was* another man,' said Algy thoughtfully.

'More than likely, I should think,' remarked the girl. 'And several at that.'

'And it broke your uncle up?' said Drummond.

'Completely. He began to blame himself for the whole affair. Said that if he'd handled the matter differently Jack would still be alive, and all that sort of thing. And nothing that I said seemed to have the slightest effect. Then a month ago Hubert Manton suddenly appeared on the scene.

'Hubert Manton is another cousin, but a distant one. And I don't think I've ever met anyone to whom I took such an instant dislike. Apparently he's been abroad all his life: in fact I, actually, had never heard of him. But Uncle John explained who he was, and raised no objections to the brute parking himself on us. He certainly raised no objections to doing so, and there still is at Macklebury Hall. He brought a native servant with him, whom you suddenly come on unexpectedly round corners, and who terrifies the rest of the staff out of their

172

senses. Personally, I think he is infinitely preferable to his master, but that's neither here nor there. He is called Chang, and he was pathetically grateful to me the other day when I bound up a bad cut in his hand. You poor dears,' she added with an apologetic smile, 'must be wondering when I'm going to get to the point.'

'Not a bit,' cried Algy. 'Tell it your own way, my pet.'

'The first thing that happened took place two days after this Manton man arrived. I was wearing india rubber shoes, and so when I went into the library, I made no sound. And there, to my surprise, standing with his back to me, was Chang. He was holding a photograph in his hand, and studying it closely. It was a photograph of Jack.

'"Do you know that gentleman, Chang?" I said on the spur of the moment.

'He nearly dropped the frame, he was so startled: then he put it back on the table.

'"No, Missie," he said. "Chang not know gentleman."

'And at that moment Hubert Manton came in, so that he overheard Chang's reply. He said something in native dialect that I couldn't understand, and Chang slunk out of the room. Then he apologized to me for the servant being in the library at all and the matter passed off. In fact, it was such a trifling thing that I forgot all about it till a week later, when I was up for the day in London.

'I was walking along Piccadilly past the Ritz when the lights went red and the traffic stopped. And just as I got abreast of a taxi I happened to glance inside. There, to my utter amazement, I saw Hubert Manton and Eunice Radnor. They neither of them saw me, and I hurried past for fear they should. The last thing I wanted to do was to meet that woman again. But once I was out of sight I began to do some pretty hectic thinking.

'You see, Uncle John had told Hubert Manton about the tragedy, and the Radnor woman's name had been mentioned. Why, then, had he concealed the fact that he knew her? Was it because he thought it tactful not to let Uncle John know that she was back in England? Or was there some other reason? And if so, what could it possibly be?

'I puzzled and puzzled all the way back in the train, until suddenly a wild idea flashed into my mind. As I told you, I'd forgotten about Chang and the photograph: now the episode came back. Had Chang been lying when he said he didn't know Jack? For if that was the case, something very funny was in the air.'

She paused and lit a cigarette and the two men waited in silence.

'You see, Captain Drummond,' she continued, 'Chang has never been to England before this time, and the only occasion Jack ever went abroad, except to Switzerland, was the fatal trip to Ceylon. So that if Chang had recognized the photo, the only time he could have seen Jack was in Colombo. Further, Chang has been in Hubert Manton's service for years, and if Chang was in Colombo it was more than likely that his master was also. So could it be possible that Hubert Manton was lying when he said that he was in China at the time of Jack's death? Was his the other man's voice the boy thought he heard in the room? I tell you, Algy, my brain began to reel with all that it implied.

'I tried to reason myself out of it; to tell myself that I'd built up the whole thing on the supposition that Chang was lying. But all the time that other question came hammering back; why had Hubert Manton kept the fact that he knew Eunice Radnor a secret? I wondered if I should tell my uncle; drop out a remark casually at dinner that I'd seen them together in London. But some instinct warned me not to: if there was something going on, I could be of more use if I kept my knowledge to myself.

'And then began the other thing which is what finally made me write you, Algy. Even Simmonds, the butler, remarked on it to me. My uncle seems positively to dislike me near him, and what is even worse than that, he's very queer at times. I've found him muttering to himself, and he's developed a sort of strange nervous twitch in his left eye. He spends the whole of his time with Hubert Manton in his study. I've often heard them talking far into the night. And one day I tackled the Manton thing on the subject, because I think Uncle John ought to see a doctor. Would you believe it, he assured me he'd noticed nothing unusual. Why, a child could see that my uncle is not normal. So obvious is it, in fact, that for the past week I've locked my bedroom door each night. And two nights ago I was glad I'd done so.

'I'd fallen asleep when a sound woke me. The fire had died down, but there was still just enough light to see across the room. And the handle of the door was slowly turning. I watched it, fascinated, too terrified even to call out and ask who was there. Then, when whoever it was found the door locked, he gave it up and I heard footsteps going softly away down the passage. And the next morning, I wrote to you, Algy.'

'And a deuced sensible thing to do, darling. What do you make of it, Hugh?'

'Well, one thing sticks out a yard. Whether Miss Porter is right or wrong about Manton, something must be done about her uncle's condition. Can't you get the local pill to come and vet him?' he went on, turning to the girl. 'Ask him to lunch, so that it doesn't seem a professional visit.'

'I can try,' said the girl doubtfully. 'But I'm afraid it wouldn't do much good. All he could do would be to prescribe some medicine, and Uncle John would immediately throw the bottle at his head. He loathes doctors.'

Drummond smiled.

'I see,' he remarked. 'Well, can't you go away for a time? Either your uncle's condition will improve, or he'll get so bad that he will *have* to be seen by a doctor.'

'I could do that, but I don't want to,' she said. 'I hate the thought of leaving him alone with Hubert Manton.'

'Then what do you suggest yourself, Miss Porter?'

'I was wondering, though I know it's a terrible lot to ask, if you and Algy could possibly come down and tell me what you think yourselves. You're men of the world, and you'd know far better than I whether I'm talking rot or what you think I'd better do.'

'My dear soul,' said Drummond, 'I'd be only too delighted to come down, and so I'm sure would Algy. But it's not quite so easy as that. What possible excuse have we got for suddenly appearing on the scene? I'm a complete stranger, and I gather Algy hardly knows your uncle at all.'

'I realized that difficulty, Captain Drummond, and I've thought of a way round it. Couldn't you stage a breakdown near the gate, and then walk up to the house to ask if you can use the telephone? I'll be in the hall and recognize Algy. Then if you time it for about a quarter to eight the least I can do is to ask you to stay to dinner. I know it's an awful sweat, and I'm positively ashamed at asking you to do it, but it would be such a comfort to me to have your opinion.'

'Don't you worry about that end of it, Miss Porter,' said Drummond. 'It's no sweat or bother at all. I was just wondering if we could improve on your scheme, and I don't think we can. It's simple and direct, and what could be fairer than that? Now, when do you go back?'

'This afternoon by the three-fifteen.'

'Then, since there is no good delaying, we'd better do it this evening. OK with you, Algy?'

'OK by me.'

'Then at a quarter to eight, Miss Porter, you can expect to see us on the doorstep with our tongues hanging out.'

'A nice child,' he continued to Algy, after they had put her into a taxi, 'but for the life of me I don't quite see what we're going to do about it. Even if Uncle John gets the jitters at dinner and Manton eats peas with a knife, I don't see that we're much further on. However, if it eases her mind, it gives us a nice trip into the country. Away, hellhound—you offend me. And you may call for your Uncle Hugh at four o'clock.'

The plan worked without a hitch. At half-past seven a car might have been seen to stop a few yards away from the entrance to Macklebury Hall—a car from which the two occupants immediately emerged to delve under the bonnet. And five minutes later, well satisfied with their handiwork, they turned into a long drive which led through an avenue of trees up to the house. On one side they passed stabling sufficient for a dozen horses; on the other a lake, complete with swans, lay placid in the still evening air. A house reminiscent of the old spacious days: too often now, alas, a drug upon the market.

Their ring was answered by the butler, over whose shoulder they could see Marjorie Porter talking to a man.

'My compliments to your master,' began Drummond gravely, 'and would you ask him . . .'

'Algy!' cried the girl incredulously. 'What on earth are you doing here?'

'Good Lord! If it isn't Marjorie.' Algy waved delightedly. 'Look, darling: the bus has died on us outside the gate. Can we ring up the local tinker, and tell him the dread news? And by the same token, meet Captain Drummond. Miss Porter.'

'Of course you can ring up, Algy. Simmonds, show Mr Longworth the telephone. And you must both stop to dinner.'

'That's very nice of you, Miss Porter,' said Drummond. 'It seems lucky that we broke down where we did.'

'And where are you making for?' asked the man.

'Oh, I forgot,' cried the girl. 'Mr Manton: Captain Drummond.'

The two men bowed slightly.

'Hunstanton,' said Drummond. 'A few days' golf seemed indicated.'

He was conscious that Manton was studying him closely; he was also conscious that there was no necessity for him to return the compliment. For Manton was an almost perfect example of a type he knew well—the hard-bitten crowd who live by their wits. And some of them are charming, and some of them are not: but all of them want watching.

'All set,' cried Algy, coming back into the hall. 'The local gear crasher is sending up a minion. I hope Mr Greston is in good form, Marjorie.'

'Not too good, I'm afraid, Algy,' she answered. 'I was talking to Mr Manton about him just before you arrived. I'm very worried. I wish I could persuade him to see a doctor.'

'At the moment, my dear Marjorie,' said Manton, 'I'm afraid you can't. You know his views on doctors generally, and though I agree that he seems a little nervous and irritable this evening, it would only make him worse if you suggested it. I'll just go along and tell him we've got guests for dinner.'

'A little nervous and irritable!' cried the girl furiously as he

177

left the hall. 'Captain Drummond, I don't believe he wants my uncle to see a doctor.'

'Was Mr Greston worse when you got back?' asked Drummond.

'Yes. At least, I think so. There's such a queer look in his eyes.'

'I wonder,' began Drummond thoughtfully, only to break off as he saw Manton returning.

'My uncle wants me to apologize for him,' he said as he joined them, 'but he thinks he will have his dinner in his study.'

'I do hope we're not being an infernal nuisance,' remarked Drummond to the girl.

'Not a bit,' she answered. 'Have you told Simmonds?' she asked Manton.

'I have. And now what does anybody say to a drink? Sherry? Gin and French? Will you fellows help yourselves?'

'I'd rather like to wash my hands, if I may,' said Drummond. 'Messing about with a car doesn't improve them.'

'Of course. How stupid of me not to have thought. I'll show you both the way.'

'What do you make of it, Algy?' remarked Drummond when Manton had left them. 'Can there be anything in the girl's idea that Manton doesn't want his uncle to see a doctor?'

'Ask me another, old boy. He certainly doesn't seem to want to see us.'

'Or Manton doesn't want him to.'

'But what's the motive, Hugh? What's the great idea?'

Drummond was whistling softly under his breath. 'I'd very much like a glimpse of Mr Greston,' he said at length.

'Short of gatecrashing the study, I don't see how you're going to get one,' remarked Algy as he dried his hands. 'Incidentally, what do you think of Manton?'

'I don't,' said Drummond. 'But I'm flummoxed the same as you, Algy. What's the great idea? If it is Manton who doesn't want the old man to see a doctor or to see us, what is his object? He can't be poisoning him: the Manton breed don't murder. Or are we both barking up the wrong tree, and making a mystery

178

where no mystery exists? Don't forget that we're basing every-thing on what the girl has told us. And she, bless her heart, may be exaggerating without meaning to in the least.'

'I don't think she is, Hugh,' said Algy decidedly. 'I believe that there is some funny stuff going on. But what or why, has me guessing.'

'Then what are we going to do about it? We can't make any excuse for stopping on after dinner when the car is repaired. Moreover, I don't see that we're going to find out anything more if we do. We've already vetted Manton, and we're not going to see the uncle.'

'Let's wait and see,' said Algy. Something may happen. And in the meantime I require alcohol.'

They went back into the hall to find Manton alone.

'I fear,' he remarked as they joined him with their drinks, 'that my dear little cousin is worrying herself unnecessarily over her uncle. I suppose you know about the tragedy of his son?'

'Yes,' said Algy. 'Very sad, wasn't it?'

'Well, there is no doubt that since then he has been a little queer and moody. Like tonight, for instance. He just felt he didn't want to meet strangers. But it's no case for a doctor. In fact, with a man of my uncle's temperament, a doctor would only make matters worse.'

'Quite,' remarked Drummond. 'Over things like that I think that a man is generally the best judge. Algy was telling me about the son while we were washing. A terrible thing. What happened to the woman?'

'I don't know at all. She must, I gather, have been a pretty poor specimen.'

'I was told her name once,' said Algy.

'Yes, I heard it too,' remarked Manton, 'but it slips my memory. Careful: here's my cousin.'

The girl was coming down the stairs, and the men made way for her by the fire.

'Would you get me a glass of sherry, please, Hubert?' she said.

'With pleasure,' he answered, crossing the hall.

And as he did so, like a flash, she handed Drummond a note, with an imperative sign for him to put it in his pocket. That she was upset about something he could see, but when Manton returned with the sherry, she was talking ordinary banalities about plays. And shortly after they went in to dinner, the note still unread.

He got his chance over the fish. Algy, who had seen the whole thing, had cornered Manton; and under cover of talking to the girl Hugh read the contents.

'My bedroom door has been tampered with. The key won't turn.'

Drummond's face was quite expressionless as he continued his dinner, though his brain was working at pressure. He realized at once that that simple little statement put everything on a very different basis. Whatever he might have thought before, by no possibility could the girl be exaggerating over such a point as that. The matter had definitely assumed a very sinister aspect.

That Hubert Manton had been monkeying with the key for purposes the reverse of honourable he dismissed as unlikely. The gentleman was certainly not a fool, and if ever a cast iron certain raspberry was assured over tricks of that sort, the present case was it. No: he felt convinced that that was not the reason. So what was it?

The native servant—did he supply the clue? Possibly: possibly not. The uncle? Again possibly: possibly not. And the more he thought about it, the more clear did it become to him that there was only one method of solving the problem—to let the problem solve itself after suitable precautions had been taken. And to do that it was essential that no suspicions should be aroused.

The first difficulty was to get a word with the girl alone. The conversation had become general, but in any case he was too far away for her to attempt to say anything at the table. And it was not until the port had circulated that the problem was solved by the sudden appearance of Chang, who whispered something to his master.

'Excuse me,' said Manton, rising. 'My uncle wishes to see me about something.'

'May Allah be praised,' said Drummond as he left the room. 'Listen: there's not a moment to be lost. Can we get into your room from outside, Miss Porter?'

'Yes. If Algy gets on your shoulders he can reach the balcony outside the window.'

'Good. When you go to bed, show a light so that we shall know the room. Get undressed and go to another room. Lock yourself in. Got that?'

'Yes.'

'Algy, you have a married sister at Hunstanton who knows Miss Porter well. Ask Miss Porter to go over and stay with her tomorrow for a few days to play golf. Do it in front of Manton. Your sister is not on the 'phone, so we can't fix it tonight. All set?'

'All set.'

'And you're to accept, Miss Porter.'

'Right.'

'That's simply grand,' said Algy as the door opened and Manton returned. 'Mary will love to see you again, my pet. Come over tomorrow and bring your mallets. We'll have some foursomes and you stop as long as you like.'

'Going on a visit, Marjorie?' remarked Manton as he sat down.

'Mr Longworth is suggesting that I should go over and stay with his married sister whom I was at school with. I'd love to, Algy.'

'If only the old girl was on the 'phone we could have fixed it for you to come with us tonight,' continued Algy. 'But as it is, we'd better make it tomorrow. You don't happen to know,' he went on, turning to Manton, 'if they've brought the bus up?'

'It's outside the door. Magneto trouble, I gather.'

'Then I'd better go and pay the warrior,' said Algy.

'And we had better push on,' remarked Drummond, 'or Mary will be wondering what's become of us. A thousand thanks, Miss Porter, for feeding us. And we'll be seeing you tomorrow. Goodbye, Mr Manton. I hope Mr Greston will be quite recovered by the morning.'

'What's the game, Hugh?' said Algy as they spun down the drive.

'The note that girl passed me said that her door had been interfered with and she couldn't lock it,' answered Drummond. 'I don't like it, Algy. So there is only one thing to do. Take her place in her bedroom tonight and see if anything happens. By letting it be thought that she is leaving tomorrow, it may precipitate matters.'

'So she wasn't exaggerating,' said Algy thoughtfully. 'I suppose it's safe leaving her there now.'

'I can't think that anything is likely to occur until the staff has gone to bed. Have you got any rope in the car? You have? Good. Then we'll park the bus somewhere and go back to the house. And when the time comes, you get on to the balcony first, fix the rope, and I'll swarm up.'

They had not long to wait, and luckily the night was warm. Just after eleven had struck from a church in the distance a light went on in a room on the first floor and they saw the girl framed in the window. Then she withdrew and they could see her shadow as she moved about.

'Give her ten minutes,' muttered Drummond, 'and then we'll get in.'

But ten minutes passed; fifteen; twenty, and the light still remained on, though no longer was there any sign of her shadow.

'She can't be taking all this time,' said Drummond uneasily. 'We'll have to chance it, Algy. Can't help it if she's not in a rig to receive visitors.'

They crossed the lawn swiftly, and Drummond hoisted Algy on to his back. And a moment later Algy was astride the parapet outside the window.

'All right,' he whispered. 'She's gone.'

He paid out the rope and Drummond joined him.

'Why the devil did she leave the light on?' he muttered. And then he gave a sudden gasp. 'My God! Look there.'

Sticking out from the other side of her bed were her legs. She was lying on the floor in her dressing-gown, and as they dropped on their knees beside her they each gave a sigh of relief. For she was not dead, but her breathing was heavy and stertorous. And on the table beside the bed stood a tumbler of milk, half drunk.

'Drugged,' said Drummond shortly. 'Which complicates matters a little. Not knowing the house, we can't put her in another room.'

'We'd better lift her on to the bed, anyway,' remarked Algy.

'I don't think so,' said Drummond. 'If anything is going to happen that's where they would expect her to be. We'll put her in that cupboard, and then we will await developments, which are bound to occur. They can't have doped her for nothing.'

The cupboard was amply big enough, and they made her as comfortable as they could with cushions. Then, switching off the light, they took up their positions in the corner between the cupboard and the wall. And only just in time. Hardly had they got there when the door opened and someone came cautiously in.

'Missie. Missie. Wake up. Wake up.'

'Chang,' breathed Drummond.

'Missie. Wake up.'

The beam of a torch flashed on the bed, and they heard a little gasp of astonishment. Then it travelled round the room, pausing for a moment on the chair where her clothes were thrown. Came a chuckle, and as silently as he had come Chang withdrew, though to their surprise he did not close the door.

'We're certainly in the front row of the stalls,' muttered Drummond. 'What on earth is that peculiar noise?'

From the passage outside there came sounds as of a sack being pulled along. They came to the door and into the room. Then they heard a heave, and the creaking of the bed as something heavy was put on it. Once again came a chuckle, and the door was softly shut. Chang had departed.

'This requires investigation,' whispered Drummond, taking his own torch out of his pocket. 'My sainted aunt!' he muttered as the light picked up the bed. 'Look at that.'

Lying there, in what appeared to be a drunken stupor, was Hubert Manton.

'This, my dear old Hugh,' remarked Algy at length, 'is beyond my form. Why should Chang deposit the unconscious body of his master on Marjorie Porter's bed?'

'I'm thinking that we shall know before the night is much older,' said Drummond gravely. 'Help me to put Manton on the floor. As I said, I don't think that bed is going to be a healthy place.'

They laid him down on the floor, so that the bed came between him and the door: then they again took up their position in the corner by the cupboard. The curtains were eddying in the faint breeze; save for that the house was silent. And then suddenly a board creaked in the passage outside.

'It's coming.'

Another creak, nearer this time; then the handle was softly turned, and the door began to open. Suddenly it was flung wide, and something bounded into the room. They heard a terrific thud on the bed, and Drummond switched on his torch. Confronting them was a huge, gaunt man holding a crowbar in his hand. His eyes were wild and staring, his face was twitching. And after blinking at the light for a second or two he twirled the crowbar round his head as if it was a walking stick and hit at the torch furiously.

Drummond side-stepped coolly; all the instincts that go to make the perfect fighting machine were alert. And there was need for them to be: an immensely powerful madman is not a pleasant customer to handle.

The maniac lunged again at the darkness behind the torch, and Drummond saw his chance.

'Light, Algy,' he said quietly, and dived straight at the big man's knees, bringing him down with a crash just as Algy switched on. The crowbar flew across the floor, but the madman was not finished. He scrambled to his feet and rushed at Drummond, but at that game there could only be one result. A straight left caught him on the point of the jaw and he went down as if he had been poleaxed.

'And this is the poor devil whom Manton described as being a little nervous and irritable,' said Drummond grimly. 'Just lash his legs, Algy, with our bit of rope: I'm taking no chances with

184

that gentleman. And then we'll get on with it. It seems to me that much remains to be elucidated over this night's work.'

'And it seems to me,' remarked Algy, 'that Chang is the man to do the elucidation. What's the game, you black devil?'

The native was standing in the doorway staring in amazement at the bound man. Then he glided round the bed and saw Manton. And involuntarily Drummond took a step towards him. For as he looked at his master there came into his face an expression of such rage and hatred that he almost ceased to be human. But it vanished as quickly as it came, and when he turned to the two men he was once again the impassive oriental.

'Did you drug Miss Porter, Chang?' said Drummond sternly.

'No, master. Him drug Missie.' He pointed at Manton.

'And who drugged him?'

'Chang. Chang know everything. Him want big man kill Missie, so him gave big man native drug and tell him lies about Missie. Him say Missie bad woman, and big man believe because of drug.'

'But why did he want big man to kill Missie?' asked Drummond incredulously.

'Big man hang: Missie dead. Him get money.'

'And even if they hadn't hanged him they'd have put him in Broadmoor,' said Drummond to Algy. 'Go on, Chang.'

'Him meet white lady Colombo. Him knew white man in picture downstairs.'

'So the girl was right,' said Drummond. 'Did him kill white man in Ceylon?'

'Chang not know that.'

'And why didn't you tell someone about all this sooner?'

'Chang hate him. Chang want him killed. Chang love Missie. Chang see Missie not hurt. When Chang found Missie not here, Chang thought Missie in other room.'

'Truly,' said Drummond, 'the mind of an oriental is tortuous. What happened to Uncle John doesn't appear to have come into the reckoning at all. Algy, find the telephone and ring up the police. If we don't get that swine Manton fifteen years for this I'll eat my hat. My only regret is that we didn't leave him on the bed.'

Wheels Within Wheels

The front door of No. 3, Bridgewater Square opened suddenly, and from it there issued a discordant volume of sound and a large man in evening clothes. At any hour of the day or night such a thing was unusual in that ultra respectable locality; at two a.m. it was not only unusual but a definite outrage. And yet what else was to be expected when the Dowager Countess of Betterby had been unwise enough to let her house for the season to Mrs van Ranton of Baltimore, U.S.A.?

Mrs van Ranton was a young and vivacious American, whose husband, as was only proper, was cornering something in his native town in order to supply the wife of his bosom with the means to keep her end up in London. And since the dear fellow was succeeding most admirably, Mrs van Ranton decided to give a party which was a party. It was to be a party which would linger in the memory of the guests as a knock-out, and to do the little lady justice she had succeeded. It was a wow from the word go.

Now it is not my intention to describe the performance in any detail, since, save as a foundation, it has nothing to do with what follows. But even the most unintelligent reader will demand some reason for Hugh Drummond's presence in Bridgewater Square in the middle of a fine July night, wearing a large false nose of crimson hue. He will demand even more reason when it has to be truthfully stated that Drummond was quite unaware of his adornment.

To say that hardy warrior was 'sewn' would be an exaggeration. Possessing, as he did, a head of teak, even Mrs van Ranton could not accomplish that miracle. But honesty compels the narrator to admit that he was not in a condition where his presence would have been welcomed at the mid-term celebrations in a girls' school. Let us leave it at that.

The door closed behind him; the noise died down. And for a while he stood there contemplating the row of empty cars and wondering why he had left the party. A slight indiscretion during a game of sardines, inaugurated by Algy Longworth, had passed off better than he had anticipated; the trouble was he could not remember who the girl was or where he had asked her to lunch. And now, with the cool air beating on his brow, he wondered whether he ought not to return and settle these two trifling points. But it was difficult. Eighty wenches: betting seventy-nine to one against sotting the winner. Not good enough.

A cat joined him, a friendly cat—and at two a.m. in Bridgewater Square a man needs friendship. It proves that life is still extant in an apparently dead world. And Drummond was on the verge of stroking the new arrival when there came from the distance a most unexpected sound. He straightened up and listened. There was no doubt about it: someone was running, and running fast. And the next moment the runner came in sight.

The cat vanished; alone Drummond awaited the onslaught. It came with an abruptness that left him bewildered. He had a fleeting vision of a white-faced man whose breath was coming in great sobs; he felt a paper thrust into his hands; he heard a gasped-out sentence—'Take it to Scotland Yard'—and he was alone again. The runner had disappeared round the other end of the Square.

Drummond blinked thoughtfully. The matter required consideration. From inside No. 3 there still came bursts of hilarity, but his mind no longer toyed with the seventy-nine to one chance. Why should a man run in a condition of great distress through Bridgewater Square in the middle of the night? And to do him justice there is but little doubt that, given sufficient time, he would have solved the problem correctly had it been necessary. It was not; the solution appeared almost at once in the shape of three more men running swiftly towards him.

He put the paper in his pocket and again awaited the onslaught.

'Hey, you!' cried the first. 'Has a guy passed running this way?'

'Why,' said Drummond solemnly, 'should I reveal the secrets of my heart to a complete stranger?'

'Aw! cut it out, Bill,' muttered one of the others. 'The bloke's tight. Let's get on.'

'An extremely offensive utterance,' remarked Drummond as a window above was flung up, and the voices of happy revellers came to their ears. 'Almost libellous. Dear me! How distressing.'

It was a charlotte russe that descended from the stratosphere, and it burst, by superb chance, on the first speaker's head.

'An albatross without a doubt,' said Drummond sympathetically. 'How true it is that the rain it raineth upon the just and the unjust alike. However, as I think it is more than likely that there will be an encore, I will wish you all a hearty good night.'

'Have you seen a man running?' snarled the leader, plucking macaroons from his ears.

'You remind me of the old song, "Have you ever seen a dream walking?"' said Drummond reminiscently. 'Have you a moment? If so, I will sing it to you. No? Well, perhaps you're right.'

He watched them vanish round the corner, and waited till the sound of their footsteps had died away. Then, his hands thrust deep in his trousers pockets, he started to saunter homewards. What story lay behind the runners of Bridgewater Square? Who were the pursuers and who the pursued?

Suddenly it struck him that he had not yet looked at the paper, and he paused under a street lamp. It was a dirty little fragment torn hurriedly from a cheap notebook, and on it three words were scrawled in pencil: 'Rest House, Aldmersham.' And having examined both sides, and satisfied himself that there was nothing more, he replaced it in his pocket and walked on.

On the face of it a harmless enough communication in all conscience. And yet a man with bursting lungs, running for his life, had deemed it of sufficient importance for Scotland Yard. At which stage of his reflections he frowned.

Running for his life! If he was any judge of men and matters that was no exaggeration, and he had done nothing about it. It was true that until the pursuers appeared on the scene it had not struck him that way. It was true that the man had come and gone so quickly that there had been no time to do anything. But for all that, Drummond had an uneasy twinge of conscience that his performance had not been too good; that the brain had not functioned with that speed which he had a right to expect. And why?

Came the measured tread of a policeman; he would make inquiries.

'Officer,' he remarked as they met, 'I would hold converse with you. And what, may I ask,' he continued, 'are you laughing at?'

'Your nose, sir. Most refreshing.'

'An unusual epithet to apply to the organ in question,' said Drummond with dignity. 'It is a poor thing doubtless, but . . .'

He paused as his hand encountered the obstruction.

'I perceive the cause of your hilarity,' he remarked. 'I appear to be wearing a false one.'

'I should hope so, sir.'

'What do you mean—you hope so?'

'Only, sir, that if that was real you'd better stick to milk for a bit.'

'I take your meaning,' said Drummond, removing the offence. 'And to tell you the truth I am constrained to cry —*touché*. As man to man would you say I was tight?'

'Oh, no, sir! Slightly oiled, if I may say so.'

'That accounts for it,' remarked Drummond with great relief. 'I feared it might be softening of the brain. Listen, my trusty rozzer: unless I'm much mistaken there's some dirty work afoot. Some five minutes ago a man raced through Bridgewater Square, with three others hard on his heels. I detained the pursuers for a space, but I should think the betting is that they caught him. And I don't think they wanted to kiss him good night.'

'Your name, sir?' said the policeman curtly, pulling out his notebook.

'Hugh Drummond: 87, Half Moon Street.'

'Which way were they going?'

'From north to south.'

'Would you know them again?'

'I should know the man they were after and at any rate one of the other three.'

'Thank you, sir. Good night. I know where to get you if I want you.'

The constable disappeared almost at a run, and Drummond resumed his way.

'Slightly oiled,' he murmured sorrowfully to himself. 'Slightly oiled. And at my time of life. Disgraceful. It must have been the orange juice in that Bronx. Very dangerous fruit.'

It was at ten o'clock the following morning that his servant Denny awoke him with his early tea, and the news that a couple of cops were in the sitting-room.

'One of 'em's an ordinary peeler,' he added. 'The other is that inspector bloke we've worked with in the past.'

'Give them something to smoke and drink,' said Drummond. 'I'll be with them as soon as I've shaved.'

Fate had been kind: his hangover was of the mildest. And five minutes later he stepped into the sitting-room to find Inspector McIver and his friend of last night. Moreover, their faces were grave.

'Good morning, boys,' he remarked. 'Sherlock Holmes deduces that developments have occurred.'

'Murder, Captain Drummond,' said McIver quietly, and Drummond paused with a cigarette half-way to his mouth.

'Is that so?' He stared at the inspector. 'And the victim is the runner of Bridgewater Square?'

'That must, of course, be confirmed later,' said McIver. 'On the face of what you told Constable Baxter it seems more than likely, but you will be able to settle it definitely. I will now tell you what has happened. Following your information, Baxter went through Bridgewater Square, and along Taunton Street into Milverton Square. Not a soul was in sight, and he was beginning to be afraid that the trail was cold when he saw something sticking out from an area gate. He walked up to it to find that it was a man's leg: the man was on the steps inside —dead. Across the pavement lay a trail of blood. It was obvious that the body had been dragged from near the gutter to where it was then lying.'

'How had he been killed?' asked Drummond quietly.

'Stabbed in three or four places. He was only just dead: the blood was still flowing. And of his assailants there was no trace; the Square was quite deserted. So Baxter summoned assistance; took the body to the station, and here we are. For *if* the dead man is your runner of last night—and it seems almost certain that he must be—you are the only man who has seen the murderers. Now can you give us any further details? And then I will ask you to get dressed and come with us to view the body, which, incidentally, I have not yet seen myself.'

Drummond was frowning.

'I'm sorry about this,' he said at length. 'I blame myself very considerably. Whoever the poor devil is I feel I ought to have prevented it. But, as Baxter has doubtless mentioned in his report, I was a bit on last night. And the brain didn't function with its usual lucidity. I'd been to a party at Mrs van Ranton's —No. 3. And it was just as I left that it happened. The pursued man dashed up to me—and gave me a bit of paper with instructions to take it to Scotland Yard. . . .'

'Hold hard,' cried McIver. 'Have you got it?'

In silence Drummond handed it over. 'I was coming to see you this morning about it,' he remarked. 'Hullo, McIver—you seem excited!'

'Aldmersham,' muttered the inspector. 'I wonder if it is possible. Go on, Captain Drummond, and cut it as short as possible. The sooner we see the dead man the sooner I'll know.'

'There's not much more to tell,' said Drummond. 'I had barely recovered from the hare's arrival when the hounds hove into sight, who paused to demand if I had seen a man running.'

'You would recognize them?'

'As I told Baxter, the leader is the only one I'd swear to. A swarthy, powerfully built man of about my height. I'd know him again at once, even though his features were obliterated almost immediately. You see,' he explained, 'we were still just outside the house, and the party was in great heart. At any rate someone bunged a charlotte russe out of an upstairs window, and by the mercy of Allah it burst on the leader's head.'

'Charlotte russe!' cried Baxter excitedly. 'Is that one of them things full of cream?'

'Very,' said Drummond. 'And sponge fingers and things.'

'Proof, sir,' said Baxter to the inspector. 'There was a great smear of white cream on the dead man's coat.'

McIver nodded. 'Go on, Captain Drummond.'

'That's all. They departed at speed, and Baxter knows the rest.'

'I see,' said McIver. 'Could you come with us at once?'

'Give me ten minutes to get dressed and I'm at your service. Got any line on it, McIver?'

'Just this,' answered the inspector. 'If the dead man is the man who gave you this paper, which I think almost certain, and if the dead man is the man I believe he is, which I think very possible, we're on to one of the biggest things we've tackled for some months.'

'Excellent,' said Drummond. 'You'll find beer in the sideboard.'

The body had been placed in a small mortuary attached to the district police station, and one glance at the dead man's face was sufficient for Drummond. It was the runner of the previous night.

'Is that your man?' asked McIver.

'It is,' said Drummond.

'And mine too. So I was right, Captain Drummond: we're on to something very big. Did you find anything in his pockets?' he continued, turning to the sergeant in charge.

'Nothing, sir, of the slightest importance. Some loose money, and a cheap watch. Do you know his name, sir?' he added curiously.

'I do,' said McIver. 'Or one of 'em. At the moment, however, he had better remain an unknown man, at any rate so far as those gentlemen are concerned.'

He glanced through the window at a couple of youths, metaphorically sucking their pencils, with reporter written all over them.

'It's a pity, Captain Drummond,' he continued thoughtfully, 'that the man who did this job last night saw you. They had to, naturally, as you saw them, but I'd give a lot to have 'em pointed out to me without their smelling a rat.'

'A rather tall order, McIver,' said Drummond. 'Like looking for a needle in a bundle of hay.'

'No, sir, that's where you're wrong. The location, sooner or later, of the needle is clear—the Rest House, Aldmersham. But if you spot them, they'll spot you, and that's what I want to avoid. Not that I mind you being recognized,' he went on cheerfully. 'You're quite capable of looking after yourself. But it will show we're after 'em.'

'I'll guarantee to disguise myself,' began Drummond, only to pause as he saw a grin spreading over Baxter's face. 'Good Lord!' he cried, 'I'd forgotten that. Listen, McIver, the wicket's good. As I told you, last night was a little damp. Now when I saw these blokes, I was standing under a lamp with an opera hat on, so that my face was in shadow. In addition to that I was wearing a large false nose, of which Baxter is more qualified to speak than I.'

'I'll bank on it, sir,' said the constable. 'They wouldn't recognize the captain again. They only saw him for a second, and he won't be in evening clothes next time.'

'You're sure of that?' snapped McIver.

'Dead sure.'

'And are you willing to help, Captain Drummond?'

'More than willing,' said Drummond quietly. 'It's true I don't know that poor devil in there, but I have a very definite feeling that if I had acted differently he wouldn't be dead. Wherefore I would like to play.'

'Good. Then we must have a little talk. Come in here.'

He led the way into an inner office and closed the door.

'It's the age-old story of drug trafficking,' began McIver, 'but on an unprecedentedly large scale. You probably haven't followed matters, but since the Geneva commission was set up facts and figures have come to light which prove that far from diminishing the trade is increasing. Cocaine and heroin particularly. The price of the stuff is decreasing in order to get more addicts, but they can still make enormous profits because it's being manufactured secretly all over the East and Near East.

'Six months ago Paris got in touch with us: they were trying to get on to the western European gang of distributors. And since the Paris and London underworld are far more closely interlocked than most people think, we worked together. It soon became obvious that a new and very dangerous crowd were at work—new, because all the usuals were accounted for: dangerous, because of the vast amount of stuff that was coming through, and because of the skill with which they covered their traces.

'But three months ago they made one slip. A tiny one, it's true—but it narrowed our field of search for their headquarters down considerably. From a possibility of anywhere in England, we became tolerably certain that we could concentrate on the eastern counties. But nearer than that we couldn't get, though we caught some of the smaller fry and pumped 'em dry. Honestly, I don't believe they knew themselves.

'And then he appeared on the scene.' McIver jerked his thumb towards the mortuary. 'Half French, half English—he spoke both languages fluently. He was wished on to me by the Sûreté, and we took him for what he was worth. Name of Esmer, which was as good as any other, but what his motive was we didn't inquire. Not, I venture to think, a very exalted one: he was a gentleman with a sultry past if I'm any judge. But he offered to help us, and we didn't say no. It was his funeral—and that's what it's turned out to be.

'Evidently he knew the gang and managed to link up with them. I should say he'd been mixed up in the dope traffic himself in the past, so he had no difficulty over that. And consequently he got in with the men at the top, sufficiently to get information he passed to you.'

'Where is Aldmersham?' asked Drummond.

'Suffolk. About ten miles from the coast. But it wasn't only that that made me suspect before I saw the body. I thought I recognized the writing, even though it was a mere scrawl. In any event, we now know where we stand. The Rest House at Aldmersham is a red spot on the map. Whether it's *the* red spot remains to be seen.'

'By me?' said Drummond.

McIver nodded.

'If you're on,' he said. 'Though of course we shall be in the vicinity; very much so. But in view of their record up to date I'm under no delusions about these gentlemen. They're a swift crowd, and although we don't know them, I'm pretty certain they know the classic features of most of the Yard. And if they saw me at the Rest House, it would be a case of goodbye for ever. We've got to have 'em pointed out to us without their knowing it. And if in addition to that we can catch 'em with the stuff on 'em, we're home. So, once again, are you on?'

'You bet I'm on,' said Drummond. 'I haven't had any fun for a long while. What are your ideas on the plan of campaign?'

McIver rang a bell and the sergeant entered.

'Find out at once full particulars of the Rest House at Aldmersham,' he said. 'And when we know those we'll decide, Captain Drummond.'

'Will you be able to run these swine for murder?' asked Drummond.

McIver shrugged his shoulders and lit a cigarette.

'Not much to go on up to date,' he said. 'But one never knows. I should have liked to have seen the charlotte russe episode,' he added irrelevantly.

'You would,' agreed Drummond as the sergeant came back.

'Eight bedrooms, sir. Fully licensed,' he announced. 'Good reputation and crowded at this time of the year with cyclists and hikers.'

'Excellent,' said McIver. 'What about a bicycle tour, Captain Drummond?'

'Great Scot!' cried Drummond. 'I hadn't bargained for that.'

'Or you can hike,' said McIver kindly. 'Shorts and a nice knapsack. However, I leave it to you.'

'Thanks awfully, old boy.'

'Not at all, not at all. Having arrived there you will engage a room and make it your headquarters.'

'Hiking every day?'

'But never going far from the Rest House. You might be an artist. However,' he continued hurriedly, 'once again I leave that to you. I will arrange for some youngster of ours to be there too. He will make himself known to you by asking you for a match. If and when our birds turn up you will let him know by asking him for one. And he will pass that on to me. After that events must shape themselves. But I want to catch 'em, Captain Drummond—with the stuff.'

'So do I, McIver. And we will.'

The Rest House at Aldmersham was certainly crowded when Drummond and Algy Longworth arrived at six o'clock that evening. Quite rightly contending that the cause of the whole affair was Mrs van Ranton's party, his attendance at which was directly due to Algy, Drummond had insisted on that young gentleman accompanying him.

'Variety, you scourge, is the salt of life,' he had remarked. 'After the caviare of Bridgewater Square, we go to the ham and eggs of great open spaces in Suffolk. So put on your shorts, if you own any, and we will join the great army of hikers. It's all right,' he added consolingly. 'We do all but the last mile by train.'

They found an empty table in a corner of the verandah, and proceeded to take stock of their surroundings. And it would have been hard to imagine a setting less likely to harbour crime. Young men and maidens clad in varying degrees of shorts were taking nourishment. Strange noises from an open window proclaimed that the Hosh-Bosh sextette had jumped a claim on Regional. And in one corner two very dreadful women in plus fours were eating boiled eggs. Just a little bit of unspoiled England. . . .

'Beer,' said Algy faintly. 'Beer at all costs. It isn't,' he went on plaintively, 'that I dislike legs. Far from it. But a permanent diet of this would send any man into a monastery screaming for mercy. There should be a law passed on the matter. The wearing of shorts and other dangerous practices related thereto. No woman having a knee of greater circumference than a yard is ever to be permitted to show it in public: penalty imprisonment. If said knee is scalded red in the sun the penalty to be amputation.'

A waiter brought them their beer, and at the same moment a pleasant-looking youth rose from a neighbouring table and came over.

'Excuse me, sir,' he said to Drummond. 'I wonder if I could trouble you for a match. Thank you. You'll hold him if he comes, won't you, sir. Until the inspector has seen him.'

'Our ally, Algy,' remarked Drummond as the youth sat down again. 'And there, I take it, is the proprietor.'

A stout and smiling man was standing in the doorway leading into the house, regarding the scene complacently. Aesthetic quibbles on legs concerned him not. His mental range began and ended with the capacity of the human stomach for food. And on that standard all was well.

He caught Drummond's eye and came over to the table. A room? Certainly. He could manage that for them with ease. And if they had a car there was a garage attached to the house, with a competent man in charge. Just been opened.

He strolled away and Drummond lit a cigarette.

'Lower your beer, Algy,' he said, 'and we'll do our little tour of inspection. On the face of it,' he continued as they threaded their way through the tables, 'mine host has no appearance of a criminal. One cannot quite visualize him as the centre of a dope gang.'

'They probably use the place unknown to him,' answered Algy. 'One can hardly think of an atmosphere that would afford a better blind.'

They rounded a corner. In front of them stood the garage. It was, as the landlord had said, evidently a new addition, and they walked over to the entrance. Three baby cars were in the yard, and a small empty van with the back axle jacked up and minus its rear wheels. And they were just turning away again when a man emerged from a workshop at the back carrying a spare wheel. He stared at them for a moment; then he stood the wheel up against the running board of the van and came towards them.

'Looking for anything, gents?' he remarked.

'No, thank you,' said Drummond affably. 'This is new since my friend and I were last here.'

'Opened last May,' answered the man, shading his eyes with his hand and staring up the road.

'Pretty busy?' continued Drummond.

'So-so,' said the man. 'Varies, you know; it varies. Good evening.'

With a nod he turned away and went back to his workshop, to come out again shortly with another spare wheel which he placed by the first. Then, apparently conscious of arduous work well done, he sat down on the running-board of the van and lit a cigarette.

'Nothing doing here,' said Drummond swinging on his heels. 'Let's go and sample the bar.'

'Anything you like,' said Algy cheerfully, 'so long as I don't see those female plus fours again.'

'You'll see something a damned sight more interesting,' said Drummond curtly. 'Here's our man.'

A big Bentley had drawn up by the petrol pump, and the garage attendant had appeared hurriedly.

'That big fellow driving,' continued Drummond. 'know him a mile off. MFF236. So far, so good. Let's get hold of McIver's warrior.'

The young plain-clothes man was still at the same table, and he glanced up as Drummond approached.

'Just getting out of that Bentley,' said Drummond quietly. 'The tall, dark man.'

He strolled on towards the bar, followed by Algy. McIver's man promptly vanished, and the driver of the Bentley, with passenger, was evidently bound barwards also.

'So we've got to keep him for a while, Algy, until McIver has given him the once over. Now, as I get it, if there's anything in this place at all, he'll either be picking the stuff up here or dropping it. Otherwise there's no meaning to the performance, since no one would come here for fun.'

'Which means that there's a confederate in the house,' said Algy.

'Probably. Steady the Buffs! Here he comes.'

The first thing that became apparent was that the visitor had been there before. He called the barman 'George,' and was greeted as Mr Margiter in reply. And having given Drummond and Algy one brief uncompromising stare, in which no shadow of recognition lurked, Mr Margiter ordered two double whiskies.

'Trade good?' he asked in a harsh domineering voice which was obviously natural.

'Very, sir,' answered George. 'Nothing to complain of.'

'Then you're luckier than most of us,' said Margiter with a laugh, which turned into a snarl of anger as Drummond bumped accidentally against his arm and spilled his drink. 'Confound you, sir! Don't be so infernally clumsy.'

Drummond turned round very slowly.

'Are you speaking to me, my good man?' he said in a drawl so offensive that it would have provoked sudden death at a pacifist meeting.

Mr Margiter put the remains of his drink on the counter, and his face turned a full red.

'Did you call me "my good man"?' he remarked softly.

'Gentlemen, gentlemen!' George was dancing up and down in his agitation, but he might have been a fly on the wall for all the notice anyone paid him. His companion was plucking at Margiter's coat. Algy, wise to the ways of Drummond, suppressed a happy grin. And at the same time felt the tingle in his veins which is born of murder in the air.

'I did,' said Drummond casually. 'But now that I've seen you more closely, I withdraw the phrase in its literal sense.'

The veins stood out on Margiter's forehead. A vicious back-hander nearly knocked over his friend, who was muttering feverishly in his ear. Margiter was dead to caution. So dead that there was nothing real in his universe save a yokel in grey flannel trousers and an old tweed coat, who had deliberately gone out of his way to insult him. He failed to notice the watchful glint that had come into the yokel's eyes; and when a

199

vicious left-hander missed its objective by a foot he failed to read the writing on the wall.

He swung a right haymaker, and then something that felt like a pile driver hit him straight in the mouth, so that he staggered back, spitting blood, into the arms of his friend just as the door opened and a stern official voice rang out.

'Now then—what's all this?'

Inspector McIver was standing there, giving Drummond a glance without a trace of recognition.

'Can't have brawling here, gentlemen. Stop it you, sir,' he roared, as Margiter showed further signs of wanting to go on, 'or I'll take you in charge. I'm an Inspector of Police.'

With a gigantic effort Margiter pulled himself together.

'Yes,' continued McIver, staring at him thoughtfully. 'And I'm just wondering where I've seen you before,'

'Professionally?' cried Drummond happily. 'Has he murdered his wife?'

And through half-closed eyes, he saw that the second man had turned very white.

'I don't understand you,' said Margiter, now completely in control of himself. 'Why should you have seen me before?'

He lit a cigarette with a perfectly steady hand, and Drummond wondered. Was McIver bluffing, or did he really recognize the man? In either case, what was the idea? If he wanted to catch them actually with the stuff, why warn them to start with?

'Why should you have seen me before?' repeated Margiter with rising warmth. 'Put as you put it, it seems to me a damned libellous remark.'

'In fact, I'd like to question both you gentlemen,' continued McIver unperturbed, and his gaze shifted to Drummond.

'I trust you haven't seen me before,' said Drummond in alarm.

'Maybe not. But if my suspicions are correct we shan't be strangers in the future. What were you two men fighting about?'

'I accidentally upset his drink, Inspector,' remarked Drummond, and McIver snorted.

'Don't play the fool with me, sir,' he said sternly. 'It won't pay you. Now where's the stuff?'

'The stuff?' echoed Drummond blankly.

'The dope. You're running a load of it between you, and that's what you were fighting about. Moreover, I'm going to find it.'

'I think, Inspector,' said Margiter solicitously, 'that the Suffolk sun must have gone to your head. My friend and I arrived here ten minutes ago: our car is outside. If you wish to, you are at perfect liberty to search us and the car.'

Drummond still failed to get McIver's idea: did he really imagine the stuff *was* in the car? Or on Margiter? And the humorous point was that Margiter was now treating him as an ally. 'Well, Inspector,' he said. 'Are you ready?'

Margiter began to turn out his pockets, until McIver stopped him.

'We'll have a look at your car,' he said curtly. 'You stay where you are, sir.' He turned to Drummond, who bowed.

'Your slightest wish is law, Inspector,' he remarked amiably. 'I'll have a look for the hiding-place in here.'

He watched the three men troop out; then he crossed to the window which opened on to the garage. And having got there he paused, an unlighted cigarette half-way to his mouth.

'Come here, Algy,' he said curtly. 'Another van has arrived.'

'What of it?' remarked Algy as he joined Drummond.

It was true: another van, identical with the one that had been in the yard, was now there. And the back wheels were being changed. It was one of those vans that had double wheels on the rear axle, and against the running-boards they could see three wheels propped up on each side.

'Most interesting,' said Drummond thoughtfully. 'Our friend in charge of the garage must be a prophet. How,' he continued even more thoughtfully as Algy stared at him, 'did he guess that the two spare wheels he brought out while we were watching him would be required? You note that they no longer adorn the side of the original van, and they are just being put on van number two. Let us see what happens to the two wheels that have just come off van number two.'

For a few minutes they watched in silence, and Drummond's frown grew more pronounced.

'Is this a new game?' he said, as the van, the change completed, drove away, leaving its own two wheels behind. 'Is it conceivable?' he went on half to himself, 'that . . . Come on,' he cried suddenly. 'It's sheer guess work, but it's worth following up. We will jape with them, Algy, and see if we strike a bull.'

He strode over to a table and picked up a large bowl of castor sugar. Then he left the bar, followed by a completely bewildered Algy Longworth, and walked towards the Bentley.

'Are you satisfied now, Inspector,' Margiter was saying with a sneer. 'Or would you like me to have the engine taken down?'

'Don't worry,' cried Drummond. 'I know where the dope is.'

For the fraction of a second Margiter's face grew strained. Then as Drummond produced the sugar-bowl from behind his back he laughed heartily.

'In the bar, Chief Constable,' continued Drummond. 'Right under our noses. Snow, my dear fellah: cocaine by the pound. Have some.'

He offered the bowl to McIver, and Margiter laughed even more heartily.

'Do you good, Inspector,' he said jovially. 'And now, if you don't mind, I'll be getting along. How much was that petrol?' he called out, and the garage man approached.

'Twelve and eight, sir. I suppose you aren't by any chance going past Durnover's garage just this side of Ipswich?'

'I am. Why?'

'I was wondering, sir, if you would mind dropping these two spare wheels there. They were lent to a van, and . . .'

'Put 'em in the back,' said Margiter, getting into the driving-seat. 'And another time, Inspector, I think it would be better if you didn't jump to such farcical conclusions.'

'Quaite,' remarked Drummond, emerging from behind the car. 'Quaite. In fact, McIver, it was most reprehensible of you,' he continued as the car drove off. 'What are you going to do now?'

'Search this place for the stuff.'

'I'll bet you a well-earned pint it's not here,' said Drummond with a grin. 'And I'll bet you another that I know where it is.'

'Where?' snapped McIver.

In the car. Summon the Baby Austin, old sleuth hound, and we will chase the Bentley.'

'Don't be a fool, Captain Drummond,' said McIver. 'How can we possibly overtake it?'

'Yet a third pint is now on,' grinned Drummond. 'I'll bet you we find the Bentley stationary by the road within three miles.'

'Whereabouts in the car is it?' said McIver as their driver drew up beside them.

'Those two spares,' answered Drummond. They boarded the car and started in pursuit.

'Not a place one would think of looking when they were actually on the van wheels. The inside one of each pair: always changed at the Rest House. And I'll bet that Durnover's garage would be a bit surprised if they were handed in . . . What did I tell you, McIver?' He was pointing ahead. 'The third pint is OK. There's the Bentley.'

'How the deuce did you do it?' asked McIver curiously.

'A little jest of my own,' said Drummond. 'Never known to fail.'

They drew up behind the stationary car, as Margiter, white with rage, emerged from under the bonnet.

'What the hell do you want now?' he snarled.

'Those two spare wheels,' said McIver calmly, and things moved.

Margiter's hand shot to his pocket, but he was up against two past-masters in a scrap. A few seconds later, his hands hand-cuffed behind him and his gun in McIver's pocket, he was leaning up against the car panting, with his companion by his side.

'It's there all right,' he said sullenly. 'But if only this damned car hadn't died on me you'd never have got it.'

'I know,' remarked Drummond sympathetically. 'That's what I wanted the castor sugar for. Incidentally, I didn't really think it was snow,' he went on brightly. 'In fact, I don't suppose cocaine would have acted. But castor sugar in the petrol tank is wonderful. Gums up the jets marvellously. Stops any car within a mile or two, and it's funny how few people know it.'

203

'So that was it,' said Margiter softly, staring at Drummond with a look of recognition dawning in his eyes. 'Where the devil have I seen you before today?'

Drummond grinned happily.

'An albatross, without a doubt,' he murmured.

Thirteen Lead Soldiers

'You mustn't touch them, Uncle Hugh, because they're still wet. Mr Stedman is going to paint some more when he comes back.'

Hugh Drummond—uncle by courtesy—looked down at the small boy on the floor. Around him was strewn the litter inseparable from small boys, be it trains, aeroplanes or hairy bugs. In this case the central motif consisted of tiny soldiers, with paints and brushes and pools of multi-coloured water. In addition there were boxes of infantry, and cavalry, and guns all of a dull grey colour, whilst in a tray, resplendent in scarlet, stood some freshly painted heroes.

'Mr Stedman says it's far more fun to paint them oneself,' explained the proud owner. 'And he says it doesn't matter if there is no full dress any more.'

'I quite agree with Mr Stedman, Billy,' said Drummond. 'Red looks much better than khaki, doesn't it? That's a good-looking Highlander next door to the General on the horse.'

'Yes. I've got some more of those. They're Cameron Highlanders.'

'Not Camerons, old man. They might be Gordons.'

'Mr Stedman said Camerons,' persisted the boy. 'Didn't you?'

He looked up as a tall, dark man entered the room.

'Didn't I what, Billy?'

'Say these were Cameron Highlanders. Uncle Hugh says they're Gordons.'

'Only after they're painted, son,' said Drummond. 'Before they're painted they might be any Highland regiment.'

'But Mr Stedman painted him and he said he was a Cameron. Why can't he be a Cameron?'

'Because he's got the wrong coloured kilt on, old man. I might stretch a point and say he was a Seaforth, but I can't allow Cameron, I'm afraid. You see, that kilt gives the gen-

eral impression of being dark green, or even black, whereas the
Cameron kilt strikes one as red.'

'The complete Scotsman, I see,' said Stedman with a smile,
and Drummond glanced at him. There was no friendliness
behind the smile.

'Even to the extent of always saying, "Guid nicht the noo,"'
he answered placidly.

'The colour of a kilt seems a somewhat trifling matter to
worry the child's head with.'

Drummond raised his eyebrows and laughed: friendliness
was even less marked.

'I don't suppose that it would materially affect Billy's future
career if he was told that the Archbishop of Canterbury always
preached in purple pyjamas,' he remarked. 'At the same time,
if you are painting soldiers and thereby giving the child a little
lesson in things military, it does no harm to get such trifles as
facings and kilts correct.'

He lit a cigarette and strolled over to the window.

'The rain has stopped: I think I shall take exercise. I suppose
the great ones are still conferring?'

'They are,' said Stedman shortly, and with an amused glance
at him Drummond lounged out of the room. One of those
tedious individuals, he reflected, who hate to be found wrong in
anything. And yet able, presumably, or he wouldn't have his
present job.

'Algy, you noxious blight,' he remarked to Longworth,
whom he found in the hall, 'you may accompany me to the
village. The evening paper should be in by now, and I want to
see if I've backed my fifteenth consecutive loser. Tell me,' he
continued as they walked down the drive, 'what do you think of
the man Stedman?'

'I don't,' said Algy, 'if I can help it. Why?'

'I just wondered. We have been chatting on kilts and things,
and I don't think he was amused. Incidentally painting toy
soldiers is a new game for a grown man, isn't it?'

'It is. But the kid seems to like him. And I suppose it was
decent of the fellow to go all the way to Manchester to get
unpainted ones. What's this about kilts?'

'Nothing of importance,' answered Drummond, halting for a moment and looking back at the house.

'What a magnificent old pile it is.'

Outlined against the westering sun the towers and battlements of Oxshott Castle stood out dark and sombre. Trees as old as the house flanked it on each side. In front lay a lake placid as a sheet of glass. And as they looked four men came through the front door and strolled across the drive.

It was easy to recognize them even at that distance. Slim and upright, their seventy-years-old silver-haired host, Lord Surle, came first, with the Frenchman, the Comte de Dinard. Behind them, the smoke from their cigars almost motionless in the still air, were the Belgian, M Meteren, and Sir Charles Dorking. And as they disappeared round a corner of the house Drummond gave a short laugh.

'It's quaint, Algy, you know, when you think of it,' he said. 'At this moment the fate of Europe is quite possibly being settled. And Stedman is painting toy soldiers for Billy, and you and I are going to see who won the two-thirty.'

Algy looked at him anxiously.

'You'll be quoting Ella Wheeler Wilcox in a moment, my lad,' he remarked. 'What you want is beer in a large can. And what has stung you now?' Drummond, his eyes narrowed, was staring down the drive towards the lodge.

'I'd know that walk anywhere,' he said. 'If that isn't our old friend Andrews of Scotland Yard, I will consume my headgear. Now what the deuce is he doing here?'

They strolled on and a few moments later the three men met.

'Good evening, gentlemen,' cried the jovial faced inspector cheerily. 'I was hoping I might see you.'

Drummond glanced at him in surprise.

'Very kind of you, old lad,' he remarked, 'and the same to you. But may I enquire how you knew we were here?'

'Because I suggested that you should be asked,' answered Andrews calmly. 'When discussing the house party with his lordship it transpired that he knew both you and Mr Longworth very well. So, as I say, I suggested that he should send you invitations for the weekend.'

207

'Again very kind of you,' said Drummond, looking even more surprised. 'But why?'

'Because I may want your assistance,' replied the inspector quietly. 'What about a pint at the "Barley Mow", and I'll tell you the lay of the ground.'

'A brave thought, bravely spoken,' said Drummond. 'By the way, d'you know what won the two-thirty?'

'Moonlight. Sharpshooter second.'

'Hell!' grunted Drummond. 'Another fiver down the drain. I shall soon be known as the bookmaker's friend.'

They entered the bar, and found it empty.

'What about that table over in the corner?' suggested Drummond. 'I am frankly very curious, Andrews, to hear why you should have discussed the party with Lord Surle.'

'I suppose you're aware, Captain Drummond,' said the inspector, as they sat down, 'that some very important discussions are on foot at the present moment between England, France and Belgium.'

'I am,' replied Drummond.

'That being the case, has it struck you as strange that a reporter isn't lurking behind every bush at Oxshott Castle?'

'It had not struck me up to date,' admitted Drummond. 'But now that you mention it, I get your meaning.'

'The reason why they're not there,' continued Andrews, 'is that this conference has been kept a profound secret. The Press, of course, know that Meteren and the Comte de Dinard are in England. They know further that they are not over here to enjoy the English climate, but for the express purpose of meeting Sir Charles. And since the one thing the statesmen wished to avoid at the present stage of affairs was publicity, this weekend was arranged at Lord Surle's suggestion. The whole plan was kept completely dark, and the very fact that there are no reporters here proves that we succeeded.'

He paused and took a pull at his tankard, while the others waited in silence.

'Yes, Captain Drummond,' he repeated, 'we succeeded—so far as the reporters are concerned—which, believe me, is no mean feat. But we have not succeeded entirely. Some unauthorized person knew of this conference four days ago.'

'At any rate he seems to have kept the information to himself,' remarked Drummond. 'Incidentally, how did you find out that somebody knew?'

'I'm coming to that,' continued Andrews. 'Four days ago when I went to my office in the morning I was as certain as a man could be that everything was all right. The only people who knew about the weekend were Lord Surle himself, the three statesmen and their confidential secretaries—Mr Stedman and the other two—and, of course, myself. I had fixed all the staff work over cars and, as I say, I felt quite confident that all was well. So you can understand how I felt when I received a letter by the second post that blew my optimism sky high. It was undated, bore no address, and naturally was not signed. And it ran as follows: 'Guard the Comte de Dinard at Oxshott. Guns are useless.'

He took another pull at his beer.

'Short and pithy, you'll agree,' he went on, 'and it gave me the devil of a jolt. To trace the writer was, of course, an utter impossibilty even if there had been time. And there we were, confronted with the fact that what we thought was a close secret was nothing of the sort. So I went off post-haste to see Lord Surle. Should we alter the arrangements—postpone the conference, or what? Well, postponement was out of the question: Monsieur Meteren has to be back in Brussels on Monday. To alter arrangements would have been difficult, since the Comte had just flown back to Paris and was only returning that night, in time for the conference. So we decided to carry on, and do as the anonymous writer had suggested—guard the Comte And it was then that I took the liberty, when I found out that Lord Surle knew you both, of asking him to invite you. Your methods, Captain Drummond, may at times be irregular, but there are few people I would sooner have beside me if there's any trouble about than yourself.'

'Very nice of you to say so,' said Drummond. 'I should like to play.'

'The trouble is,' continued Andrews, 'that I have no idea what the game is likely to be.'

'It's just possible,' put in Algy, 'that the letter is a hoax.'

'Possible, but not likely, Mr Longworth. And even if it were, it doesn't alter the fact that somebody, inadvertently or otherwise, has spilt the beans. Because it's preposterous to think that any of the other seven people in the know could have sent me that note. No: I don't think that letter is a hoax. It is, I believe, a definite warning, sent by someone who has found out about this weekend, who knows that an attempt may be made on the Frenchman's life, and whose conscience has pricked him. You see, there's no secret about the fact that there is a large section of people in France, and in other countries too, who would rejoice if the Comte was out of the way.'

'Has he been told about it?' asked Drummond.

'He has. And pooh-poohs the whole thing. Takes up the line that if people in his position paid any attention to threats of that sort they might as well chuck up the sponge straight away. Which is quite true. But the last thing I or Lord Surle want is that the chucking up should occur here.'

'Naturally,' agreed Drummond. 'You've got some men down, I suppose?'

'Four,' said Andrews. 'They're in the grounds now. They'll be in the house tonight.'

'"Guns are useless." I wonder what that means. Poison?'

The inspector shrugged his shoulders.

'Possibly. But unless he eats or drinks something different from everybody else the whole house party is for it.'

'Thanks,' said Drummond with a grin. 'What about the servants?'

'Been with his lordship for years. Besides, it is inconceivable that one of them should have sent the note, or given the show away. It would mean that Lord Surle himself had been indiscreet, otherwise they could never have known.'

'Still *somebody* has given it away,' remarked Drummond. 'And assuming what you've said to be correct it must be one of you eight.'

'My own belief is that it's the Comte himself,' said Andrews. 'Quite unintentionally, of course. He's one of those men who is reckless to the point of foolhardiness where his own safety is concerned. For all that, he's got to submit to some safety measures tonight, whether he likes it or not.'

'Are they hush-hush?' asked Drummond.

'Not from you,' said the inspector, 'though I don't want you to pass them on at present. But he is not going to sleep in the room he occupies now. He will dress for dinner there, and then just before he goes to bed a strange defect will be discovered in a fuse. Or else Lord Surle will tell him the truth point-blank. He will sleep in another room, with one of my men outside his door, and I shall spend the night in his present one. Which may lead to us finding out something.'

'You evidently take this as dead serious,' said Drummond.

'I do. But in any case it's just as well to be on the safe side. And I think my arrangements, simple though they are, give the maximum of security with the minimum of inconvenience. If trouble comes from the outside it finds me: if it comes from the inside it has to pass one of my men.'

'And what do you want us to do?'

'Keep your eyes open during the evening for anything that strikes you as being suspicious. I shall be on hand in one of the sitting-rooms, if you want to get hold of me. And if the phrase, "Guns are useless," means anything in the nature of a rough house, you won't want any prompting,' he added with a grin as he rose. 'No, I won't have another, thanks. I must go and inspect my myrmidons. Probably see you later.'

'So that's why we were honoured, Algy,' said Drummond as the door closed behind the inspector. 'I had hoped that my advice was going to be asked on high matters of state, but life is full of disappointments. However, if we've got to do the Sherlock Holmes stunt, more beer is indicated. And then we'd better toddle back. But one wonders,' he continued as another tankard was put before him, 'why the letter writer was so cryptic. Having gone to the trouble of saying what he did, why the dickens didn't he say more? Didn't he know himself, or what stung him?'

'It's that that made me suspect a hoax,' said Algy.

'You frightful liar,' remarked Drummond dispassionately. 'You never thought of the point till I mentioned it. Now mop up your ale, and wipe your chin, and then you must go back and change your dickey. And for heaven's sake don't tell old Dinard that French story of yours or all Andrews's precautions will be wasted. Though I admit,' he added brutally, 'that death could only be regarded as a merciful release from listening to it,'

Any setting less suggestive of violence or murder than Oxshott Castle that night it would have been hard to imagine. They had dined in state in the large banqueting hall, a dinner which reflected credit on even Lord Surle's far-famed chef—and the conversation at times had been amazingly indiscreet. It had taken the three diplomats a certain amount of time to understand the reason for Drummond's and Algy's presence, since by tacit consent no allusion was made to the threatening note. The Comte especially appeared to think that Algy was mental—a skeleton in the family cupboard and Drummond his keeper — but the fact did not prevent him making one or two remarks that Fleet Street would have paid thousands for. And Meteren was not far behind in frankness.

No women were present, and no other guests had been asked in. And as the meal progressed, Drummond found himself so absorbed in the glimpses—the human, scandalous glimpses —that lie at times behind the wheels of state that he almost forgot the real reason for his presence. And then, the drawn curtains—drawn ostensibly to keep out the mosquitoes—with the motionless bulges behind them on each side of the open window would bring him back to reality. For the bulges were two of Andrews's men, and two more were outside the door.

He was sitting between the Belgian minister and Mark Stedman, who seemed to have quite recovered from his temporary irritation of the afternoon.

'I had no idea, Captain Drummond,' he said over the port, 'that you were such a friend of Lord Surle's.'

'Hardly the way to put it,' smiled Drummond. 'His eldest son, who married my first cousin, and I were at Sandhurst together, and the old boy has asked me to shoot several times. Hence grandson Billy calls me Uncle.'

'Quite. I thought you were a sort of unofficial bravo brought in to help to protect our guest.'

'You're perfectly right: I am. I should not be here but for that anonymous threat.'

'What is your opinion about it?' asked Stedman.

'I haven't one,' said Drummond frankly.

'I saw Inspector Andrews before dinner,' Stedman remarked, 'and he seems equally at sea. However, he is neglecting no precautions. Would it be indiscreet to ask what is your rôle?'

'Not at all,' answered Drummond. 'Since neither Andrews nor his merry men can actually join the party, my job is to keep my eyes skinned in the room itself for anything unusual that may happen.'

'But what *could* happen?' said Stedman with an amused smile. 'It sounds like a stage thriller: a secret death-dealing ray or something ridiculous of that sort.'

'It does rather, I admit,' agreed Drummond. 'Certainly nothing could appear further removed from anything of that sort than the table at present.'

'And yet,' said Stedman thoughtfully, 'it is an amazing thing how science has helped crime, though it sounds rather as if I was contradicting myself.'

'It has helped the detection of crime just as much,' Drummond argued.

'I wonder. I agree with you, of course, over crude commonplace crime, but in those cases the criminal is not availing himself of science, whereas the detective is. The crime I am alluding to belongs to a higher category, and of necessity must be murder.'

'Why of necessity?'

'Because in burglary or forgery, let us say, however much science is employed in the committing of the crime, the criminal can only obtain his reward by a process where science is of no avail. He must go to a receiver: he must pass his dud fivers. And it is in the disposal of his goods, a thing over which the technique is much the same as it was last century, that he gets caught. That does not apply to murder.'

'Perhaps not. But since the time of Cain and Abel there is

one thing that has always applied to murder, and no science can alter that. Motive.'

'And suppose there is no motive.'

'Then the murderer is a madman,' said Drummond. 'Or someone of the Jack the Ripper type.'

'I will amend my remark. Supposing there is no motive that points to any particular individual.'

'I don't quite get you,' remarked Drummond.

Stedman hitched his chair a little nearer and lowered his voice.

'Let us take an academic case,' he said. 'Our friend over whom the precautions are being taken tonight. Now the reasons why anyone desires his removal are nothing whatever to do with his private life. There is no question of love, or jealousy, or personal hatred pointing at a specific being, and saying—"Thou art the man." The reasons are purely public and apply to his political views, which are intensely unpopular amongst thousands of people. That is why I say that if the Comte was murdered tonight, though the motive would be obvious, it wouldn't help the police to find the murderer.'

'That is true,' agreed Drummond. 'and provided the crime was committed with such skill that the criminal made a clear get-away and left no obvious clues behind him, doubtless he would never be discovered.'

'Which is what I was getting at in the first place,' said Stedman. 'Fifty years ago, with the precautions that have been taken tonight a get-away would have been impossible, because the methods of committing the crime were so crude. Short of a gang of men overpowering the police and shooting him, or someone poisoning his whisky, there was no method of doing the deed. Today that is not the case. And that is where science has helped the criminal more than the detective.'

'I wonder if the Yard would agree with you,' remarked Drummond with a smile.

'Somewhat improbable,' grinned Stedman. 'Though it doesn't alter the fact that it's the truth. I am firmly convinced that given time, brains and sufficiency of money it would be a comparatively simple matter to commit an undiscoverable murder.'

'A good many people have thought the same thing and found they were wrong,' said Drummond as they rose from the table.

'And quite as many have found they were right,' replied Stedman as they moved into the hall. 'However, let's hope there's no question of it's being put to the test tonight. I've promised to finish two more soldiers for Billy, and high art of that sort requires a steady hand.'

Certainly there had been no question of it when the house party reassembled about midnight prior to going to bed. The three statesmen had disappeared with their host into secret conclave; Stedman, refusing to join the others at slosh, had devoted himself to things military in a corner of the billiard-room. And now, as everyone helped himself to his own particular night-cap, he pointed with pardonable pride to the result of his labours.

Ranged in single file on a tray were the twelve gallant in-fantrymen and the Field Marshal on his prancing black horse. The command was small, Stedman admitted, for such an ex-alted officer, but any attempt to reduce him in rank had been firmly vetoed by Billy. And his actual position on parade was hardly according to the drill book. Instead of leading his army into action the cowardly old gentleman very nearly brought up the rear. Behind him strode a Greenjacket, a stout-hearted warrior leading an Army mule, and the sanitary squad in the shape of an R.A.M.C. orderly. The remainder of the force, led by the drum-major, stretched out in front, glistening in their scarlet tunics.

'Don't touch,' warned Stedman. They're still wet.'

'I don't envy the Highlander,' laughed his lordship. 'It seems to me that the off foreleg of the Field Marshal's charger is down his neck.'

'Specially arranged by Billy, sir,' said Stedman. 'The High-lander is the Field Marshal's own private guard.'

He put the tray on the window-sill, and glanced at Drummond.

'We compromised on the Black Watch,' he laughed. 'So honour is satisfied. Hullo! What has stung the Comte?'

The Frenchman was gesticulating freely by the fireplace, and Lord Surle was soothing him down.

'But, my dear fellow,' cried the Comte, 'it is absurd. I appreciate greatly your care for my safety, and the precautions of the good inspector. But to change my bedroom, because some madman has written a crazy note—is surely ridiculous. You will be asking that I look under the bed next, like a hopeful old lady. However, if you insist, I can only obey my so charming host. I will go, I think, now, if I may.'

'What's all the excitement?' whispered Stedman to Drummond.

'One of Inspector Andrews's precautions,' answered Drummond. 'Even the servants don't know. The Comte's bedroom has been changed, and Andrews himself is occupying the one he had originally. What on earth is the matter?' he added with a laugh. 'You seem quite distressed about it.'

'Don't be ridiculous,' said Stedman. 'Why should it distress me? Though I'm inclined to agree with the Comte as to its being most unnecessary.'

Drummond lit a cigarette, and his face was expressionless.

'Perhaps,' he agreed. 'Still, it's as well to be on the safe side.'

He turned away: why had Stedman registered any reaction at all on hearing the news? It had only been momentary—gone in a flash: but to a shrewd observer like Drummond it had stuck out a yard. And how could it possibly affect Stedman personally if the Comte slept in his own bedroom or the coal hole, unless . . .

Drummond sipped his drink thoughtfully; the conversation at dinner came back to him. Also Stedman's annoyance over the matter of the kilt. Could it be possible that they were two widely different manifestations of the same failing—conceit? The kilt —irritability because he had been proven wrong; the other, a sort of inverted pride in something planned, and which he could not resist bragging about even though his audience should be unaware of the fact.

''Old 'ard,' muttered Drummond to himself. 'You are not even trotting: you're galloping. You're accusing this bloke Stedman of being the nigger in the wood pile. And that's rot.'

'Then why,' came the reiterated question, 'should he care the snap of a finger which is old Dinard's bedroom? And he did. Of that there's not a shadow of doubt.'

He turned round to find Algy at his elbow.

'Coming to bed, old bird?' remarked that worthy. 'I thought of taking up one of the pikes out of the hall in case a general action occurs during the night. The only thing against it is that a man impaled on the end of a pike would be a dreadful sight at three in the morning. He wouldn't go with my yellow pyjamas at all well.'

He looked at Drummond curiously.

'What's stung you, Hugh? You seem devilish thoughtful.'

'I'm just wondering, Algy, if I'm being a complete half-wit, or if I'm not. By the way, Andrews did say, didn't he, that one of his minions was going to be on guard outside Dinard's door tonight?'

'He did and there he is. Further, there is one on sentry go in the corridor. I've just been up to fill my cigarette case and I saw 'em.'

'Good,' said Drummond. 'Then let's go to bed. I've probably got the mental jitters.'

It was half an hour later that the door of Algy's room opened. He had just smashed his tooth glass with his slipper, in an unsuccessful attempt to swat a mosquito, and was engaged in picking up the fragments when Drummond came in.

'Unless I'm much mistaken, Algy,' he remarked quietly, 'strange things will be abroad tonight.'

'What sort of things?'

'I haven't the faintest idea,' said Drummond. 'So the curtain goes up on a completely unknown play.'

'You annoying blighter,' cried Algy. 'Can't you be a bit more explicit?'

'I can't,' answered Drummond simply. 'I give you my word of honour I'm completely in the dark.'

And he still was the following morning, when by ones and twos the guests drifted in to breakfast. For nothing had happened in the night, except that, in common with most of the others, he had been bitten by a mosquito. Once in the distance he thought he had heard the sound of a motor being started and driven away; beyond that nothing had occurred. And with the coming of dawn he had slept.

Breakfast over he strolled out of doors followed by an openly derisive Algy. And outside the open window of the billiard-room, he paused and looked through at Billy arranging his army, now dry, in new formations, whilst fresh victims were being prepared for Stedman's art. Then, still in silence, he walked on with Algy beside him.

'What *did* you think was going to happen, old boy?' asked that worthy for the tenth time. 'Or what made you think that anything was going to happen?'

'The Cameron Highlanders,' said Drummond. 'Anyone sufficiently interested in toy soldiers to paint them ought to know the colour of their kilt. Hullo! What has Andrews got hold of?'

Coming towards them was the inspector with one of his men, holding in his hand what seemed to be a long thin twig.

'Good morning, Captain Drummond,' he cried cheerfully. 'What do you make of this?'

On closer inspection it proved to be a part of the top joint of a salmon rod, snapped off about three feet from the end. But the interesting thing was the small attachment. About an inch below the top of the rod was a small muslin box, fastened securely to the rod. The box was about two inches square, and the framework was made of wood with fabric stretched taut between. To one side was tied a piece of fine string which passed through the top ring of the rod in the fashion of an ordinary fishing line, and now hung trailing on the ground.

'As you can see,' said Andrews, 'when you pull that string you open the box. And unless you pull the string the box can't open because the end is held in position by that bit of elastic inside.'

'Where did you find it?' asked Drummond.

'Snapped off in the bush which is Jenkins's hiding-place by day. Moreover, it was not there yesterday, or he'd have seen it then.'

'Which means it was broken off last night. Any footprints?'

'None. But with the ground like a board one wouldn't expect any help in that direction.'

'What do *you* make of it, Andrews?' said Drummond.

'Since it obviously didn't get there by itself, there must have been someone prowling around last night carrying the rod this belongs to. In the darkness it got tangled up in the bush and snapped off, and whatever was inside here escaped. It was something, Captain Drummond, that he intended to poke up from outside through a window in the Castle and allow to escape into a room—the Comte de Dinard's room. "Guns are useless," don't forget. But when he broke his rod and the thing escaped, the whole plan failed.'

'Somehow or other I don't think I'd have left that in the bush even if it was broken,' said Drummond thoughtfully. 'That little muslin box is beautifully made and could be used again on another rod.'

'But he *did* leave it there.'

'Yes. But I wonder if it was on the way to the Castle. I wonder if by any chance he did just what you have suggested, then got alarmed or something and broke it on the way back, when the box was no longer of any use and he didn't mind losing it.'

'Ingenious, Captain Drummond, except for one point you overlook. You forget that so far as any outsider could know, I was occupying the Comte's room. And you may take it from me that nobody flapped boxes last night outside *my* window.'

'No: I hadn't overlooked it, old boy,' said Drummond quietly. 'Anyway, the great point is that the Comte's health, judging by his verbosity at breakfast, is quite unimpaired.'

The inspector looked at him curiously.

'You're not satisfied, sir?' he said.

'I'm not,' answered Drummond. 'Though I dare say I shall prove utterly wrong.'

'But what's stinging you?'

'The fact that a kilt of the Camerons is reddish in hue.'

The inspector looked at Algy: Algy looked at the inspector.

219

'He'll be better after he's had some beer, Andrews,' he said. 'Captain Drummond gets taken like this at times.'

That afternoon the party broke up, and a few days later the whole episode was beginning to fade from Drummond's mind. He had made a mistake: his suspicions had been fantastic. In any event the Comte de Dinard was still going strong in Paris, which was all that really mattered. No harm had come to him at Oxshott Castle: the worthy Andrews deserved full marks. And, so far as he knew, no harm had come to anyone else. So it came almost as a shock to him when, returning to dress for dinner one evening, he found the inspector waiting for him in his sitting-room.

'Have you a few minutes to spare, Captain Drummond?' he said gravely.

'Certainly, Andrews. As long as you like. I see,' he added, 'that something has happened.'

'Something so strange that I have come straight to you. I remember that you were not satisfied when you left the Castle, but at the time you would say nothing. Now, you must.'

'Go on,' said Drummond quietly.

'Have you ever heard of yellow fever?' asked Andrews.

'I have. A tropical disease,' answered Drummond surprised.

'And a very dangerous one. It is fatal more often than not. Do you know how it is carried?'

'I can't say that I do,' Drummond acknowledged.

'By mosquitoes.' Andrews paused. 'You may remember there were a good many mosquitoes at the Castle,' he continued.

'There were,' agreed Drummond.

'You may also remember that little muslin box?'

Drummond nodded.

'And our theory as to what it was for? To let out something —we didn't know what—into the Comte's bedroom.'

Once again Drummond nodded.

'We were right,' said the inspector. 'And what is more, you were right when you suggested that the rod had been broken *after* the owner had been to the Castle and not before.'

'I was, was I?'

'That muslin box, Captain Drummond, contained mosquitoes carrying germs of yellow fever. And the owner of the rod succeeded in reaching the Castle and liberating those mosquitoes. Only he set them free in the wrong room. This afternoon Mr Stedman died of yellow fever in the Hospital for Tropical Diseases.'

There was a long silence. Then Drummond rose and began pacing up and down the room.

'You may further remember,' continued Andrews, 'that you told me you hadn't overlooked the point when I alluded to the nocturnal visitor coming to my window. That now requires elucidation. Have you any idea as to why he went to Mr Stedman's? Or was it a fluke?'

'It wasn't a fluke,' said Drummond gravely. 'No: it wasn't a fluke. I sent him there.'

'*You* sent him there?' The inspector shot out of his chair as if he had been stung. 'What on earth do you mean?'

'You needn't think that I took him by the hand and led him there,' answered Drummond with a faint smile. 'Until this moment I didn't even know he'd been there. In fact I've never seen him or spoken to him. For all that, I sent him there. Listen Andrews, and I'll tell you.

'You remember the billiard-room, don't you, with its broad window-sill? Before we went to bed that night a tray of newly painted toy soldiers was placed on the sill. They had been painted by Stedman for the little boy, and we were all of us instructed not to touch them. They were arranged in single file—twelve infantrymen and one large man on a prancing horse. And one of the infantrymen was a Highlander in whom I was particularly interested, because of an argument on kilts that I had had with the artist. And my Highlander was placed so that he was just in front of the horseman.

'Then quite unexpectedly it was announced that the Comte de Dinard was going to change his room. He protested but complied, and everybody went to bed—everybody, that is, except me. I wasn't feeling sleepy, and I sat down in an alcove

221

in the room with a book. I was practically hidden, so that when Stedman returned he didn't see me. And he crossed to the window, remained there a second and then went out again.

'So after a moment or two I also went to the window, and there I noticed a very strange thing. My Highlander, in whom I was so interested, had changed places with the Field Marshal. Instead of having the horse's foot down his neck, he now had the tail in his eye. In other words the Field Marshal had moved one to the right. Why? Why was it necessary for Stedman to come down and move the horseman up one?'

'Good lord!' whispered Andrews. 'Good lord!'

'You see it, don't you?' said Drummond gravely. 'Stedman neither knew nor cared anything about soldiers, but hearing that little Billy did, he thought of a very original scheme for indicating the Comte's bedroom. Soldiers that had to be painted and so couldn't be moved: a tray placed on the window-sill so that any man looking in from the outside could see it and see where the Field Marshal was. Thirteen bedrooms there were on our floor: thirteen soldiers there were on the tray. And when the Comte moved into the next room . . .'

Drummond shrugged his shoulders.

'I wonder why Stedman wanted to have him murdered,' he went on thoughtfully. 'You'll probably find out some time, Andrews. If so, let me know.'

For a space there was silence whilst Andrews stared at him.

'But why should Stedman himself have fallen into it?' he asked at length. 'Stedman's bedroom was third from the other end.'

'I know. The Field Marshal made yet another move, you see. When I turned out the lights and went to bed, he had only two men in front of him. Have a drink.'

Select Bibliography

In his lifetime, Sapper published 15 volumes of short stories, as well as two massive omnibus volumes and three retitled collections of his war stories. The following is a checklist of his short story collections in the mystery, crime and adventure field:

The Man in Ratcatcher, Hodder & Stoughton, 1921
The Dinner Club, Hodder & Stoughton, 1923
Jim Maitland, Hodder & Stoughton, 1923
Out of the Blue, Hodder & Stoughton, 1925
Word of Honour, Hodder & Stoughton, 1926
The Saving Clause, Hodder & Stoughton, 1927
The Finger of Fate, Hodder & Stoughton, 1930
Ronald Standish, Hodder & Stoughton, 1933
When Carruthers Laughed, Hodder & Stoughton, 1934
Ask For Ronald Standish, Hodder & Stoughton, 1936

The stories in this present collection were originally published as follows:

The Sovereign Magazine
March 1920: 'The House by the Headland' (*The Man In Ratcatcher*)

Hutchinson's Magazine
December 1920: 'The Old Dining-Room' (*The Dinner Club*)
March 1924: 'Out of the Blue' (*Out of the Blue*)
March 1925: 'The Other Side of the Wall' (*Word of Honour*)
September 1925: 'Mrs Peter Skeffington's Revenge' (*Word of Honour*)

The Strand Magazine
December 1920: 'The Man with his Hand in his Pocket' (*The Man In Ratcatcher*)
February 1923: 'Mark Danver's Sin' (*Out of the Blue*)
March 1927: 'A Hopeless Case' (*The Finger of Fate*)
December 1928: 'The Hidden Witness' (*The Finger of Fate*)
February 1937: 'The Mystery Tour'

Select Bibliography

August 1937: 'Lonely Inn'
October 1937: 'The Oriental Mind'
November 1937: 'Wheels Within Wheels'
December 1937: 'Thirteen Lead Soldiers'

Acknowledgements

For help and information at one time or another I'd like to thank the following: Bob Adey, Derek Adley, J. Randolph Cox, A. J. Flavell (Assistant Librarian of the Bodleian Library), George Locke, Bill Lofts, Bob Sampson, and Joke Whitt.

J. A.